Lincoln Public Library

GALDÓS

DOÑA PERFECTA

TRANSLATION AND INTRODUCTION

BY HARRIET DE ONÍS

BARRON'S EDUCATIONAL SERIES, INC.

WOODBURY, NEW YORK

PEREZ GALDOS

March 1979

All inquiries should be addressed to
Barron's Educational Series, Inc.
113 Crossways Park Drive
Woodbury, New York 11797

PRINTED IN THE UNITED STATES OF AMERICA

8 9 10 11   M   9 8 7

BENITO PÉREZ GALDÓS
(1843-1920)

The dominant figure of Spanish literature in the nineteenth century is that of the novelist Benito Pérez Galdós.
Not since its Golden Age had Spain produced a writer
who possessed his gifts. Critics have been agreed that he
had no equal among his country's writers in scope, out-
put, and popularity during the period in which he lived.
To be sure, during his lifetime he shared this popularity
with others, for there were in Spain then, as elsewhere,
novelists of high order, Fernán Caballero, Pedro Antonio
de Alarcón, Pereda, Valera, Palacio Valdés, Emilia Pardo
Bazán, Leopoldo Alas, Blasco Ibáñez, to name only those
of first rank. But with the perspective lent by time, and
removed from the political and ideological conflicts of his
day, Galdós is now seen, not as a greatly endowed writer
among others, but in a class by himself. Discerning appraisal adjudges him the writer of his epoch whose work
gives the deepest, truest, most comprehensive vision of the
realities of his country, and its supreme literary artist, surpassed in his field only by Cervantes. As the English critic
Gerald Brenan says in *The Literature of the Spanish
People*: "He is a writer of first order, comparable to
Balzac, Dickens and Tolstoy, and it is only the strange
neglect in which nineteenth-century Spanish literature
has been held by the rest of Europe . . . that has failed
to give him the place that is due him as one of the great
European novelists." It is doubtful that any of those mentioned surpassed him in vitality, capacity for growth, understanding of the motives that drive the human heart,

humor, and that typically Spanish gift for creating characters that often seem more real than living beings.

The novel, which has been the major literary form of the past hundred and fifty years, is fundamentally a product of the nineteenth century. To be sure, in the sense that it tells a story, its ancestry can be sought in the fictional forms which preceded it, especially in Cervantes, the father of the form, and in the picaresque novel. Galdós, himself, makes this comment on the history of the novel. It first appeared, he says, in Spain whence it passed to England where its Spanish realism and dry wit were converted into English humor in the hands of Fielding, Thackeray and Dickens. It then passed to France. What it lost there in charm and grace it gained in analytic insight and scope, being applied to psychological states that do not easily fit into the picaresque form. Thence it returned to Spain as Naturalism. "Let us accept," he goes on, "this reform that the French have made in our own invention, restoring to it the humor they have taken from it and applying this in the narrative and descriptive parts in accordance with the tradition of Cervantes . . . For we must recognize that our native art of realism, with its happy blend of the serious and the comic, answers better to human truth than does the French sort."

Every epoch develops the artistic expression which best reflects its concerns, its hopes, its outlook on life. The nineteenth century was the age of the rise of the middle class, the bourgeoisie, which brought about profound changes in the entire social structure. As was natural, this new society was deeply interested in itself, and the writers of the time gave it back the reflection of its own image. The real hero of the nineteenth century novel was society rather than the individual, or, to be more exact, the individual against the background of his society. As Hazlitt put it, even before the major novels of the century had appeared: "We find there a close imitation of man and manners; we see the very web and texture of society as it really exists, and as we meet it when we come into the world. . . . We are brought acquainted with the motives and characters of mankind, imbibe our notions of virtue and vice from practical examples, and are taught a knowledge of the world through the airy medium of romance." It should also be pointed out that the practitioners of the novelist's craft could count on an ever-growing public. Education was one of the tenets of faith of the nineteenth century. Reading was no longer a prerogative of the privileged classes. Newspapers and journals were springing up everywhere which afforded a medium for the writer's work; the publication of books had become a profitable business; and writing to satisfy the public demand was a possible, and, at times, even a lucrative profession.

Benito Pérez Galdós was born in 1843 in the city of Las Palmas in the Canary Islands, which had been discovered and colonized by Spain shortly before the discovery of America. He was the youngest son of a middle-class family in comfortable circumstances. He received his early education in an English school in Las Palmas—the beauty of the landscape and the agreeable climate of the Canary Islands attracted many English visitors, some of whom became residents there—learning to speak English fluently, French, and to draw and paint. He was a shy, studious boy and an omnivorous reader. At the age of nineteen he went to Madrid to study law at the university there.

Although Galdós shared the liberal, democratic enthusiasm which prevailed at the university during those years (and which he has described so well in one of his greatest novels, Fortunata y Jacinta), and remained a liberal to the end of his long life, he never participated actively in politics. Nor did he pursue the legal profession for which he had prepared himself. His literary vocation manifested itself early. The goal he set himself was to explore, understand, and give expression to the prolonged cruel civil strife which from the beginning of the nineteenth century had rent Spain and blasted the hopes of several generations of Spaniards. The struggle was between the old and the new, the forces of tradition and those of change and progress. In varying degree this same struggle was going on throughout Europe; but in other countries, particularly England and France, these new and revolutionary ideas were indigenous, even forming a part of their tradition; whereas in Spain, except among small minorities, they were looked upon with suspicion and hostility as representing a threat to the nation's manner of being and very existence. For this reason, and because the Spanish character is not given to compromise, the struggle was so bitter and relentless there, and a real reconciliation between the two forces has not yet been achieved. It was not until 1870, with the restoration to the throne of Alfonso XII, "The Pacifier," as a constitutional monarch, that the civil wars of the nineteenth century came to an end. For fifty years Spain lived in peace. During this time it flourished and prospered; supporters of the most divergent views tolerated one another amicably, and it seemed that at last a *modus vivendi* for all Spaniards had been arrived at, thanks, in large measure, to the inspired statesmanship of Cánovas del Castillo. But, unfortunately, this proved to be only another episode in the tormented history of Spain. At the turn of the century manifestations of discontent began to make themselves felt, and the situation was aggravated by the loss of Spain's last remaining colonies, Cuba, Puerto Rico, the Philippines. The working classes and the supporters of new ideological trends became increasingly active, generating a similar activity in their opponents, and the growing unrest finally reached its climax in the fiercest civil war of all, that of 1936.

In 1870 Galdós published his first novel, *La fontana de oro*. It is a historical novel, but not in the manner of the Romantics, nor even of Walter Scott, who dealt with the past as a finished thing, a completed process. What Galdós was seeking out in the past was its relevance to the present. *La fontana de oro* treats of liberalism's first— and transient—triumph over the absolutism of Ferdinand VII in 1820. In his second novel, *El audaz* (1871) Galdós goes even farther back in his search, to the uprising of Aranjuez against the weak and corrupt government of Charles IV, which was the spark that set off the powder train which kept Spain ablaze for more than half a century, and one of whose consequences was the independence of Spanish America.

It was then that Galdós conceived his plan of the *Episodios nacionales*, that vast series of historical novels, numbering fifty in all, in which he portrayed Spain's immediate past in the manner referred to. Rather than isolated episodes, as might be assumed from the title, they are the closely knit picture of the nation during a period of its history. They begin with the Peninsular Wars (1808-1815), the moment when all Spain was united in a common cause against the French invaders. With the defeat of Napoleon's troops, and the restoration to the throne of the legitimate sovereign, Ferdinand VII, the irreconcilable forces of reaction and progress turned Spain into the theater of a civil war none the less unremitting for brief periods of truce during which the struggle went on in other fields than those of battle, until the establishment of the constitutional monarchy in 1870.

In part the *Episodios nacionales* are the careful reconstruction of the background against which these events were played out, and, at the same time, the personification of the forces and ideals that gave rise to these events, exemplified in fictional characters having a symbolic value. They are realistic in the sense that they relate the events of history as seen by a participant in them, never one of the important actors, but some insignificant character, which makes it possible for Galdós to present the social background, the relations between man and man, man and society, man and place with a feeling of immediacy. At the same time they are idealistic, not so much because they record the ideals of the heroes of the civil wars, liberals or reactionaries, but because Galdós superimposes on the multiplicity of facts an imaginative structure which unifies and interprets them, giving many of the personages and scenes a symbolic, even allegorical character. It is history coupled with imagination. As an English critic has written: "There is an abstract quality, however hidden or devious, which determines the real worth of any work . . . the one common factor implicit in all the arts of man resides in a certain juxtaposing of forms."

While Galdós was at work on the first of his five series of *Episodios nacionales,* published between 1873 and 1875, he also wrote four novels, *Doña Perfecta* (1876), *Gloria* (1877), *La familia de León Roch* (1878), and *Marianela* (1878). The first three, of which *Doña Perfecta* is the best and the best known, deal with the problem which lay at the root of the cleavage of Spain, which had basically motivated the series of civil wars, and given rise to "the two Spains": the religious problem. In them Galdós leaves the past behind to deal with an existing reality. (*Marianela,* whose setting is a small mining village, and whose heroine is an ugly little girl, is a brief, tender work in the romantic vein.)

In these novels Galdós was not carrying on anti-religious propaganda. Nothing could have been farther from his intention. It is clear from his treatment of certain of his characters in subsequent works that he had the utmost respect for those imbued with the faith, hope, and charity which are the essence of religion. What he analyzed in these works was the intransigence of those who believe that they alone possess the truth, and are implacable toward all who do not subscribe to their faith with their own fanatic fervor, those "who seem good and are not," as he says at the close of *Doña Perfecta*. It was in the name of such fanaticism that Socrates was sent to his death, Christ was crucified, thousands were killed in the religious wars, and in the annals of the martyrs their names are legion who suffered and died because they could not subscribe to "official" truth.

In *Doña Perfecta*, whose artistic value if often lost sight of and even denied because of the controversy it aroused, Galdós, although dealing with a reality, was not attempting to write a realistic novel. The setting and the personages are abstractions, symbols which represent, in synthesis, the drama of nineteenth-century Spain. Of the provincial city in which it takes place the author says "it could be in the north or the south—anywhere." The conflict hinges upon the war to the death between those who saw in every attempt to liberalize thought and customs, and bring Spain abreast of other modern nations, an attack on the Catholic religion, and those who, in their enthusiasm for progress and change overlooked all that was noble and worthy of respect in the past. Doña Perfecta—even the name is symbolic—, the heroine, more than a real person is the embodiment of tradition. By her lights and to those who shared her point of view, she was a model of virtue: devout, upright, a kind mother, sister, and neighbor. And, says Galdós, "we must admit that she had beauty." But she lacked the quality which it is clear throughout all his work that Galdos esteemed above all others: tolerance, which is another way of saying charity. When threatened or crossed in the thing that mattered most to her, her religious faith, her cruelty knew no bounds, and she did not hesitate to commit in the defense of that faith sins and crimes which it would have been the first to condemn. Doña Perfecta never doubted that she was right, and was prepared to carry her convictions to their ultimate consequences. Pepe Rey, the symbol of progress and enlightenment, is, though a good and well-meaning young man, obtuse in his self-assurance and his disdain for the customs and beliefs of his aunt and her circle. Out of this lack of understanding and mutual forbearance comes the tragedy that engulfs them all. *Gloria* deals with the tragedy that ensues as the result of the love of a Spanish girl for a Jew, whom the accident of shipwreck has brought to the shores of Spain. *La familia de León Roch* also deals with the religious problem, not in a symbolic setting but against the background of contemporary Madrid, and marks the transition to a new aspect of Galdós's creative activity, the realistic novel.

This phase, which covers the years from 1881 to 1889, in many ways represents the finest achievement of Galdós's art. He referred to this series as "contemporary" novels, but it might be more exact to call them "novels of Madrid." In fact, they could be regarded as a single novel, for the same characters appear and reappear, in some playing the leading, in others, a supporting role. They include *La desheredada, El amigo Manso, El Doctor Centeno, Tormento, La de Bringas, Miau,* and the four volume work which many consider his masterpiece, *Fortunata y Jacinta.* The life of Madrid is to be found in them, on every social level, and the characters have been drawn with such mastery, such penetration that at times it is hard for the reader to believe that he has not actually known them.

Certain critics, on the basis of these novels, have attempted to classify Galdós among the regional novelists, with Madrid as his province. But this is an error of judgment. The essence of the regional reality is its permanence; once it begins to change and adopt new ways it ceases to exist as such. In his presentation of the life and customs of Madrid, Galdós was not attempting to describe that which was outside the stream of social evolution and change; on the contrary, what he was doing was portraying the process of this evolution. These novels not only reflect the reality of the moment but could serve as the basis of a sociological study of the profound transformation Madrid underwent in the years that preceded and followed the Restoration of 1870.

But what gives these novels their incomparable artistic value is that in addition to being historic documents, they are human documents. All the characters live out their lives against the background of their moment in time and space. The tragic tension which characterizes every great novel is here the contrast between reality and the aspirations of these beings, what they seem in the eyes of the world and what they believe or dream they are. This disparity between their concept of reality and reality itself at times takes on pathological aspects. But their madness, like that of Don Quixote, instead of detracting from, heightens their human significance. In fact, they are descendants of the Knight of the Rueful Countenance, moved, like him, by noble and generous impulses, by errors that stem from over-optimism and confidence. And even though their lives, like his, are a series of failures, often tragic, their native goodness redeems them in our eyes from their mistakes and shortcomings.

This vision of life is peculiarly characteristic of the great works of Spanish art. The paintings of Velázquez and Goya, the novels of Cervantes and Galdós, are eloquent examples of it. To be able to convert the most ridiculous, abject specimens of mankind into beings who, through the power of understanding and love of their creators, can evoke our sympathy and admiration and sense of kinship is the hallmark of great art and great humanity. The Naturalistic novel, which was being so brilliantly cultivated in Europe at the time that Galdós was writing, and which regarded man as the hapless product of his environment and heredity, is pessimistic and disheartening. We cannot but feel a sense of rebellion and protest when, at the end of *Tess of the D'Urbervilles,* Hardy says: "The President of the Immortals, in Aeschylean phrase, had ended his sport with Tess." If all poor Tess, whose only fault was loving too much, had suffered was but sport for the "President of the Immortals," then life is meaningless. Contrast this with the end of *Miau;* the hero, a commonplace little man, harried beyond endurance by failure and frustration, all of the pettiest sort, in final desperation presses a revolver to his temple, muttering to himself: "I'll bet this won't work either." When the shot rings out, with his last breath he says in pleased amazement: "It worked!" To be able to elicit a laugh from the reader in such tragic circumstances is not only humor of the deepest kind, but is Miau's— and Galdós's—triumph over "foul circumstance," the affirmation of man's immortal value in the face of his own failure. For Galdós, like Dickens with whom he is so often compared, was a poet, not by virtue of any special use of language, but as the result of his visual sense and his awareness of the relationships below the outer level, enabling him to express states of consciousness common to all, but normally expressible only in poetry.

In 1889 Galdós, who with such fidelity and profound understanding had portrayed the lives of his "heroes" futilely beating their wings against the bars of life, began

to react against this realism. It had become apparent to
him that the data of consciousness alone were not enough
to illuminate the true nature of reality, and that there
were areas of human behavior that demanded a different
approach for their comprehension. His creation entered
upon a new phase, producing works which if not as
serene, harmonious and achieved as his "contemporary"
novels, explore problems which younger writers and
thinkers everywhere were posing to themselves. The work
which best represents this new manner is *Realidad*
(1889). Galdós had just finished the last of his novels
dealing with Madrid, *La incógnita* (1889), in which an
episode involving a small group of people is carefully
described in keeping with the methods of realism and
remains a mystery. By applying the psychological approach, in *Realidad,* to the same incident, and telling the
story from the inside, the enigma is cleared up. He employed a terse, dialogued form in this work, as in several
of his later novels, which foreshadowed his subsequent
dramas, for the theater had always keenly interested him,
and in his later years he wrote various plays, several of
which, like his dramatization of *Doña Perfecta,* and
Electra, which also deals with the religious problem, were
highly successful, perhaps more for controversial reasons
than for their intrinsic value.

The outstanding works of this period are *Ángel Guerra*
(1890) and the three volume series of *Torquemada*
(1889-1895). The first deals with the religious conver-
sion of the protagonist, and, as was pointed out before,
nobody could have been more discerning of and sympa-
thetic toward the manifestations of true religious feeling
than Galdós. But the work which achieves the perfect
fusion of his realistic and intuitive manners, and represents the peak of his aesthetic achievement, is *Torquemada.* Of the countless personages portrayed in his previ-

ous works, none is presented with the penetration, understanding and humor he brings to Torquemada. It was as though he had deliberately set himself a seemingly impossible task, for in Torquemada, who had appeared in various of his novels of Madrid, he chose a being apparently devoid of every human attribute except the most despicable. Yet by force of insight, by his God-like understanding of the motives that move the soul of this man—moneylender, usurer, utterly ruthless toward his fellowmen—Galdós succeeds in making us love this repulsive being, rejoicing over his triumphs and deploring his failures.

Galdós's vision of the totality of Spain, his ability to understand and harmonize in his work the most irreconcilable situations, his compassion, tolerance, and humor enabled him to create an entire world which we accept as true. As Wyndham Lewis has said: "The truth of the great novelists is a . . . meticulous fidelity to life." The test of the great novelist is his ability to say, and ours to accept: "Given the nature of man, then my situation, through the characters enacting it, can resolve itself only in this way." This is artistic truth, and few writers have possessed it to a greater degree than Galdós.

Harriet de Onís

I

VILLAHORRENDA! FIVE MINUTES!

When Number 65, the southbound way-train,[1] stopped at the small station between milestones 171 and 172 (the name of the line is unnecessary) almost all the second and third-class passengers stayed in their seats, sleeping or yawning, for the piercing cold of daybreak did not invite a stroll along the open platform. The solitary first-class passenger hurriedly alighted and, going up to the trainmen, asked them whether this was the Villahorrenda stop. (This name, like many others to appear later, is copyrighted by the author.)

"We are in Villahorrenda," replied the conductor, whose voice was drowned out by the cackling of the hens being loaded into the baggage car at that moment. "I forgot to call you, Señor de Rey. I think they're waiting for you here with saddle-horses."

"It's cold as blue blazes here!" said the traveller, wrapping his cloak around him. "Isn't there some place at this whistle-stop where I can rest and pull myself together before starting on a horseback ride through this freezing country?"

Before he had finished speaking, the conductor, called away by urgent official duties, walked off leaving our unknown traveller with his question unanswered. He saw another trainman coming toward him, holding in his right hand a lantern that traced a geometric pattern of waving light as it swayed in rhythm with his walk. The light fell upon the surface of the platform in zig-zag lines, like the drops from a sprinkling can.

---

[1] A way-train in Spain is usually a "mixed train," i.e., one that carries both passengers and freight, and stops at all the stations

"Is there an inn or any kind of sleeping accommodations at the Villahorrenda station?" the passenger asked the man with the lantern.

"There's nothing here," replied the latter, as he ran toward the baggagemen, showering them with such a stream of curses, oaths, blasphemies, and abusive language that even the hens, scandalized at such gross rudeness, clucked protestingly in their baskets.

"The best thing to do is to get out of here as soon as possible," said the gentleman to himself. "The conductor said the riding-horses were here."

As he was thinking this, he felt a light, respectful hand pull gently at his cape. Turning, he saw a dark mass of brown cloth wrapped about itself; through its main fold emerged the shrewd, nut-brown face of a Castilian peasant. He stared at the ungainly figure, which reminded him of a black poplar in a truck garden, and noted the keen eyes shining beneath the wide brim of an old velvet hat, the dark, strong hand grasping a greenwood staff, and the broad foot which, when it moved, set spurs to jingling.

"Are you Don José de Rey?" asked the man, touching his hat.

"Yes. And you must be Doña Perfecta's servant," answered the gentleman gaily, "come to meet me at this stop and take me to Orbajosa."

"The same. Whenever you're ready to start . . . The pony goes like the wind. I imagine Don José must be a good horseman. It's a family trait . . ."

"Which way do we go?" asked the traveller impatiently. "Let's go. Let's get out of here, señor . . . what's your name?"

"Pedro Lucas," replied the dark bundle of clothing, again touching his hat. "But they call me Uncle Licurgo. Where is the young gentleman's luggage?"

"I can see it down there under the clock. There are three pieces: two bags and a trunk of books for Don Cayetano. Here's the check."

A few minutes later, gentleman and servant turned their backs on the shack called a station and headed toward a trail which began there and lost itself in the barren hills nearby, where the miserable hamlet of Villahorrenda could be dimly seen. Three mounts would have to carry everything—the men and their baggage. A not ill-favored pony was for the gentleman. Uncle Licurgo would burden the back of a venerable nag, somewhat broken-down but sure-footed, and the mule, whose reins were in the hands of a young, light-footed and hot-blooded shepherd, was to carry the luggage.

The train pulled out, creeping along the tracks with the slow, leisurely pace of a local way-train, before the cavalcade started to move. The ever-more-distant rumble of the wheels sent forth deep tremors beneath the earth. As the train entered the tunnel at milestone 172, the whistle loosed a jet of steam and a loud screech echoed through the air. The tunnel, emitting a whitish breath from its black mouth, resounded like a trumpet, and at its strident voice hamlets, villages, cities, and provinces awakened. Here a cock crowed, farther along, another. Dawn was breaking.

II

A TRIP THROUGH
THE HEART OF SPAIN

When they had left the hovels of Villahorrenda behind them, the gentleman, who was young and very good-looking, said: "Tell me, Señor Solon . . ."[2]

"Licurgo, at your service . . ."

"Oh, yes, Señor Licurgo. I knew you were a wise law-maker of ancient times. Forgive the mistake. But let's get down to cases. Tell me: How is my aunt?"

"Beautiful as ever," answered the peasant, urging his mount ahead a few paces. "It seems the years don't pass for Señora Doña Perfecta. It's an old saying that God grants long life to the good, so that angel of the Lord ought to live a thousand years. If the blessings showered upon her in this world were feathers, the lady would have more than enough for wings to take her to heaven."

"And my cousin, Señorita Rosario?"

"God bless her and all her kind," said the villager. "What can I tell you about Doña Rosario except that she's the living image of her mother? You've got a treasure, Señor Don José, if what they say is true and you've come to marry her. A fine match, and the little girl won't have anything to complain of either. There's little to choose between you."

"And Don Cayetano?"

"Always buried in his books. He has a library bigger than the cathedral and he's still scouring the earth for

---

[2] *Solon.* A famous lawgiver of Athens. There is a jesting confusion here with Lycurgus—Licurgo—a noted Spartan lawgiver.

stones covered with some kind of devilish scrawls written by the Moors, they say."

"How soon will we get to Orbajosa?"

"By nine, God willing. The señora isn't going to be very happy to see her nephew—oh, no! And Señorita Rosarito, too. Yesterday she spent the day getting your room ready for you . . . Since they've never seen you, mother and daughter are dying a thousand deaths wondering what Señor Don José is going to be like, or not like. Now the time has come for the letters to stop and the chin-wagging to start. Cousin will meet cousin and all will be feasting and joy. Christ will come again and we'll all prosper, as they say."

"Since my aunt and cousin don't know me yet," said the gentleman with a smile, "it isn't wise to make too many plans."

"Very true. That's why they say it takes two to make a bargain," answered the peasant. "But faces don't lie . . . What a jewel you'll be getting! And what a fine lad for her!"

The young man did not hear the last words from Uncle Licurgo, for he had become preoccupied and somewhat meditative. They came to a bend in the road, and the peasant, turning the horses off to the side, said:

"Here we have to follow this path. The bridge is out and we can't ford the river except at El Cerrillo de los Lirios."

"The Hill of the Lilies," said the young man, emerging from his meditations. "How poetic names abound in these ugly places! Ever since I began to travel through this land, I've been struck by the frightful irony of the place names. An area known only for its wasteland and for the desolate sadness of the somber landscape is called Valle Ameno—Pleasant Valley. A clutter of adobe shacks sprawled miserably upon an arid plain, proclaiming its poverty in every possible way, has the impudence to call itself Villa Rica—Richtown! And there's a stony, dusty gulley where even the thistles have no juice, which is called, nevertheless, Val de Flores—Flowervale. Now what we see before us is called El Cerrillo de los Lirios. But where in Heaven's name are the lilies? All I can see are stones and parched grass. If you called that the Hill of Desolation, you'd be naming it correctly. Except for Villa-horrenda—Horribleville—which seems to have matched its name to the facts, everything here is ironical. Beautiful words, miserable, prosaic reality. In this country the blind would be happy, for it's paradise to the tongue and inferno to the eyes."

Either Señor Licurgo failed to comprehend young Rey's words or he paid no attention to them. When they had forded the river which ran muddy and roiled in its head-long rush, as though fleeing its own banks, the peasant stretched out his arm toward some land lying broad and bare to the left of them and said:

"There's Los Alamillos de Bustamante."

"My lands!" cried the young man jubilantly, his gaze sweeping the desolate fields lighted by the first rays of morning light. "This is the first time I've laid eyes on the inheritance my mother left me. She, poor dear, had such exaggerated ideas of this land, and she told me so many marvels about it, that as a child I thought it would be like going to heaven to come here. Fruit, flowers, big and small game, mountains, lakes, rivers, poetic brooks, pastoral slopes—there they all were at Los Alamillos de Bustamante, in this land of the blessed, the best, the most beautiful of all lands . . . What the devil! The people in this country live in their imagination. Perhaps if they had brought me here in my childhood, while I was still echoing the ideas and the enthusiasm of my poor mother, these barren hills, these dusty or flooded plains, these old peasants' huts, these broken-down irrigation wheels with buckets so leaky they could hardly water half a dozen cabbages, this miserable, hopeless desolation I'm seeing before me might have seemed charming to me, too."

"It's the best land in this region," said old Licurgo. "And there's nothing like it for chickpeas."

"Well, I'm glad of that, for ever since I inherited them, these precious lands haven't brought me in a penny."

The Spartan lawmaker scratched his ear and sighed.

"But I've been told," went on the young man, "that some of the neighboring landowners have sunk their plows in these great estates of mine and are nibbling them away little by little. There are no boundary lines nor landmarks here, nor any real ownership, Licurgo."

After a pause, during which the peasant seemed to busy his subtle spirit in searching reflections, he expressed himself thus:

"Uncle Pasolargo, whom we call the Philosopher because he's so wise, did sink his plowshare in Los Alamillos above the hermitage, and bite by bite he's chewed off six acres."

"What an incomparable school of philosophy," exclaimed the young man, laughing. "I'll bet he hasn't been the only—philosopher."

"Well," said the other, "every man to his own trade, and if the dovecote doesn't lack feed, it won't lack doves. . . . But you, Don José, can quote the saying that the eye of the owner fattens the cow, and now that you're here, you'll see about getting your farm back."

"It may not be that easy, Licurgo," replied the young man, just as they were entering a path bordered on either side by beautiful wheatfields, a delight to the eyes in their luxuriance and early maturity. "This field looks better cultivated. I see that all is not gloom and misery at Los Alamillos."

The peasant pulled a long face and affecting a measure of disdain for the fields just praised by the traveller, said in a most humble tone: "Señor, this is mine."

"Do forgive me," cried the young man quickly, "I was going to swing my sickle on your estates. Seemingly, philosophy is contagious here."

They descended abruptly into a gulley which formed the bed of a parched, sluggish brook, and beyond it, they entered a field full of stones and without the slightest sign of vegetation.

"This land is very poor," said the young man, turning his head to look at his guide and companion, who had lagged a little behind. "You'd have a hard time making any profit from it; it's all mud and sand."

Meek as Moses, Licurgo answered: "This . . . is yours."

"I can see that everything bad here is mine," affirmed the young man, laughing good-humoredly.

Talking thus, they returned to the highway. Now the morning sunlight, breaking gaily through all the windows and skylights of the Spanish horizon, bathed the fields in brilliant splendor. The immense, cloudless sky seemed to broaden and to recede from the earth in order to see it from higher up, and to delight in its contemplation. The desolate, treeless land, in some places the color of straw, in others chalky, and everywhere divided into black, yellow, brown or pale green triangles and quadrangles, recalled a beggar's cloak spread out in the sun. Christianity and Islam had fought epic battles over that miserable cloak.[3] Glorious lands, yes, but the quarrels of the past had ruined them.

"It seems to me that the sun will be very strong today,

---

[3] The allusion here is to the centuries of warfare between the Spaniards and the Moorish invaders of the Iberian peninsula which lasted from 711 until the conquest of Granada by Ferdinand and Isabella in 1492.

Licurgo," said the young man, partially loosening the cloak in which he was wrapped. "What a dismal road! As far as the eye can see, not a single tree. Everything here is reversed. Its ironies will never cease. Why, if there are neither small nor large poplars here, did they have to name it Los Alamillos?"

Uncle Licurgo made no reply to the question because he was listening with his whole being to certain distant noises which suddenly became audible. He halted his horse with an uneasy air, and scanned the road and the distant hills with a grave expression.

"What's the matter?" asked the traveller, pulling up, too.

"Are you armed, Don José?"

"A revolver . . . Ah, now I understand. Are there robbers about?"

"Maybe," answered the peasant with apprehension. "I thought I heard a shot."

"Well, let's see . . . Come on!" said the young man, spurring his mount. "They're nothing to be afraid of."

"Easy, Don José," cried the villager, stopping him. "Those people are worse than the devil himself. Only the other day they murdered two gentlemen on their way to catch a train . . . This is no time for joking. Gasparón El Fuerte, Pepito Chispillas, Meringue, and Ahorca-Suegras won't get a glimpse of my face as long as I'm alive. Let's take the path."

"Go ahead, Licurgo."

"After you, Don José," replied the peasant in stricken tones. "You don't understand what kind of people they are. They were the ones who robbed the church of Carmen of its ciborium, the Virgin's crown, and two candlesticks last month; they're the ones who held up the Madrid train two years ago."

Don José felt his boldness falter a little at hearing such deplorable reports.

"Do you see that big, high hill 'way off there? Well, the robbers hide there in some caves called the Estancia de los Caballeros."

"Gentlemen's Mansion?"

"Yes, sir. When the Civil Guards[4] aren't on the look-out, they come down the highway and steal whatever they can. Do you see a cross there beyond the bend in the road? It was erected to the memory of the mayor of Villahorrenda who was done to death by them during the elections."

"Yes, I see the cross."

"There's an old house there where they lie in wait for travellers. That place is called Las Delicias."

"The Delights!"

"If all those who've been robbed and killed as they came this way were to rise from the grave, they'd form an army."

As they were speaking, they heard closer shots which disturbed the stout hearts of the travellers, but not that of the young shepherd who, laughing boisterously, asked Licurgo's permission to forge ahead and watch the battle which had been joined so near by. Seeing the youth's determination, Don José was ashamed of having felt fear, or at least a measure of respect for the robbers, and spurring his pony, he cried:

"Then let's all go. Perhaps we can help the unlucky travellers who are in such straits, and also teach the "Gentlemen" to mind their p's and q's."

The peasant tried to convince the young man of the rashness of his intentions, as well as of the futility of his generous impulse, for the victims would already have

---

[4] The Civil Guard is a Spanish police force, operating mainly in rural areas, which is noted for its severity and incorruptibility.

been robbed and perhaps killed, and hence in no state to need help from anyone. The young man was deaf to this wise warning, and the villager was remonstrating in the strongest terms, when the presence of two or three carters, calmly coming down the road driving a wagon, put an end to the discussion. The danger could not have been great, since they were approaching so carelessly, singing gay songs. Indeed such was the case, for the shots, according to them, had not been fired by robbers, but by the Civil Guards, who wanted thus to prevent the escape of a gang of half a dozen pickpockets trussed together, whom they were escorting to the village jail.

"Now I know what it was," said Licurgo, pointing to a thin cloud of smoke appearing some distance away on the right. "They've been properly peppered by now. This happens every other day."

The young man did not understand.

"I assure you, Don José," added the Lacedemonian legislator emphatically, "it's a good deed well done; it wouldn't be worth while to try those rascals. The judge would cross examine them a little and then let them go. If one of them did go to jail after six years of lawsuits, he'd probably get away, or be pardoned, and then back to the Gentlemen's Mansion. The best thing to do with them is to shoot first and ask questions later. If they're on their way to jail and they come upon a suitable spot along the way, 'So, you were trying to get away, you dog!' Bang! Bang! That takes care of the preliminary hearing, the testimony, the evidence, and the sentence . . . All in one minute. It's a true saying that if the vixen is smart, her trapper is smarter."

"Let's move along faster, then, for the farther you go, the fewer the charms of this road," said Rey.

As they neared Las Delicias, they saw on the road a short distance ahead the Guards who only a few moments earlier had carried out the extraordinary sentence of which the reader knows. The shepherd boy was put out because they refused to let him go and view at close range the quivering bodies of the robbers, visible some distance away, lying in a gruesome heap. Then all continued on their way. But they had not gone twenty paces when they heard behind them a galloping horse coming so rapidly that it kept gaining on them every moment. Our traveller turned around and saw a man—a centaur rather, for more perfect harmony between horse and rider could not be imagined—who was of coarse and ruddy complexion, with large, burning eyes, a rough-hewn head and black mustache; he was middle-aged and generally brusque and challenging in appearance, his whole figure revealing signs of strength. He was riding a superb, well-fleshed horse like those on the Parthenon, saddled and bridled in the picturesque style of the region. On his crupper he carried a large leather pouch with the word MAIL in big letters on the lid.

"Hello! Good day, Señor Caballuco," said Licurgo, saluting the rider when he had drawn near. "What a head start we had on you! But you'll get there before us if you put yourself to it."

"Let's rest a while," answered Señor Caballuco, slowing his mount to the pace of our travellers and closely observing the foremost of the three, "since we have such good company."

"The gentleman," said Licurgo, smiling, "is Doña Perfecta's nephew."

"Ah . . . long life to you . . . my lord and master."

The two men greeted each other, Caballuco paying his respects with an air of hauteur and superiority which revealed at least an awareness of great importance and of his high standing in the community. When the proud horseman drew aside and stopped, talking for a moment

with the Civil Guards who had come along the road, the
traveller asked his guide:

"Who is this bird?"

"Who would he be? Caballuco."

"And who is Caballuco?"

"Come, come! . . . Haven't you heard the name?" said
the peasant, astonished at the utter ignorance of Doña
Perfecta's nephew. "He's a very brave man, a great horseman and the greatest expert on horses in all these lands
hereabouts. We like him very much in Orbajosa, because
he's . . . I'm telling the truth now . . . as good as the
blessing of God . . . Right here where you see him, he's
a political power, and the Governor of the province takes
off his hat to him."

"During the elections . . ."

"And the Government in Madrid writes him official
letters with many titles like 'Your Excellency' in the ad-
dress . . . He can heave the bar like a St. Christopher,[5]
and handles every kind of weapon as we handle our own
fingers. When he was Town Inspector, they could do
nothing with him, and every night at the city gates shots
were fired . . . He has men worth their weight in gold,
for there's nothing they can't turn a hand to . . . He
protects the poor and any outsider who dares to touch a
hair on the head of any son of Orbajosa will have him
to reckon with . . . Soldiers from Madrid almost never
come here; in the days when they used to come, blood
was shed constantly, because Caballuco would pick a fight
with them on one pretext or another. It seems he's poor
now, reduced to delivering the mail; but he's been lighting
a fire under the municipal government to restore the post
of Inspector and appoint him to it again. I don't know
how you haven't heard of him in Madrid, for he's the son

---

[5] The patron saint of travellers, a Christian martyr of the third
century, renowned for his size and strength.

of a famous Caballuco who was a guerrilla fighter, and that Caballuco, the father, was the son of another Caballuco, the grandfather, who was also a guerrilla in an earlier uprising . . . And since they're saying now that there's going to be another rebellion, now that everything's all twisted and topsy-turvy, we're afraid Caballuco will leave us, too, so he can round off in that way the deeds of his father and grandfather, who, to our glory, were born in this city."

Our traveller was surprised to see what kind of knight errantry still existed in the places he was visiting; but he had no opportunity to ask new questions, for the object of them joined the group, saying ill-humoredly:

"The Civil Guards killed three. I told them to watch their step. Tomorrow I'll have a talk with the Governor of the province . . ."

"Are you going to X—?"

"No, because the Governor is coming here, Señor Licurgo; they're going to station a couple of regiments in Orbajosa."

"Yes," said the traveller quickly, with a smile. "In Madrid I heard there was fear of an uprising by some small bands in this country . . . It's just as well to be forearmed."

"In Madrid they talk a lot of nonsense . . ." exclaimed the Centaur violently, accompanying his statement with a stream of tongue-blistering words. "They're all a bunch of rascals in Madrid . . . Why send us soldiers? To get more taxes and a couple of draft levies out of us? By God! If there isn't an uprising here, there ought to be. So you," he added, glancing slyly at the young man, "so you are Doña Perfecta's nephew?"

The impudent tone and the insolent stare of the arrogant fellow angered the young man.

"Yes, sir. Can I do anything for you?"

"I'm a friend of the señora and I love her as much as my own eyesight," said Caballuco. "Since you're going to Orbajosa, we'll be seeing each other."

And without another word he spurred his mount, which started off in a rush and disappeared in a cloud of dust.

After a half hour of travel, during which neither Don José nor Señor Licurgo showed himself very communicative, there appeared before their eyes an old village huddled on the slope of a hill; from it several dark towers stood out, along with the ruined hulk of a dilapidated castle at the top. A cluster of deformed, shapeless walls of earthen hovels, brown and dusty as the soil, formed its base, together with some fragments of battlemented walls in whose shelter a thousand humble cottages reared their miserable adobe fronts like wan and hungry faces begging alms of the passerby. A niggardly stream girdled the village like a tin belt, refreshing in its passage some orchards which provided the only green trees to gladden the view. People went in and out on horseback or on foot, and their movement, though slight, gave some appearance of vitality to that great mass of dwellings whose architectural aspect was more one of ruin and death than of progress and life. The innumerable and repulsive beggars who dragged themselves along on either side of the road, begging pennies of the traveller, presented a pitiable spectacle. No creatures could be more in keeping with nor more appropriate to the fissures of that sepulchre wherein a city lay not only entombed but crumbling into dust. When our travellers approached, bells, ringing in discord, indicated with their expressive sound that the mummy still had a soul.

The name of the place was Orbajosa, a city which figures not in Coptic or Chaldean geography, but in that of Spain, with its 7324 inhabitants, its Town Hall, its episcopal see, court house, seminary, stud farm, secondary school, and other official prerogatives.

"The bell is ringing for high mass in the cathedral," said Uncle Licurgo. "We're here earlier than I expected."

"The look of this country of yours," said the young man as he scanned the view stretching before him, "could hardly be more unpleasant. The historic city of Orbajosa (it has already been said the place names are imaginary) whose name is undoubtedly a corruption of *urbs augusta*,[6] looks like a big dunghill."

"That's because only the poor outskirts can be seen from here," the guide declared with displeasure. "When you enter Real Street and Condestable Street you'll see buildings as beautiful as the cathedral."

"I don't want to speak ill of Orbajosa before getting to know it," said the young man. "What I've said isn't an. indication of contempt either; however miserable and humble, or beautiful and proud it may be, this city will always be very dear to me, not only as my mother's home town, but also because people whom I already love without knowing them live here. Now let's enter the august city."

They were now climbing a road leading to the outlying streets, and were passing alongside the walls of the orchards.

"Do you see that big house at the end of this large orchard, inside this adobe wall we're passing now?" asked Uncle Licurgo, pointing to the thick, whitewashed wall belonging to the only dwelling with an appearance of comfortable and pleasant livability.

"Yes . . . is that my aunt's house?"

"Exactly. What we can see is the back of the house. The front faces on Condestable Street. It has five iron balconies like five castles. This fine orchard behind the

_____
[6] Latin for "majestic city."

wall is the señora's, and if you raise yourself in your stirrups, you'll see it all from here."

"So we're home already," said the young man. "Can't we enter this way?"

"There is a little gate, but the señora had it walled up."

The young man stood up in his stirrups, and stretching his neck as far as he could, he stared over the top of the wall.

"I can see the whole orchard," he pointed out. "Beneath those trees there, is a woman, a girl . . . a young lady."

"That's Señorita Rosario," declared Licurgo.

Immediately he raised himself in his stirrups to look, too.

"Hey, Señorita Rosario," he called, making meaningful gestures with his right hand. "We're here . . . I'm bringing your cousin."

"She's seen us," said the young man, stretching his neck to its fullest extent. "But unless I'm mistaken, there's a clergyman with her, a priest."

"That's her confessor," replied the peasant, casually.

"My cousin has seen us . . . she's left the priest, and she's starting to run to the house . . . She's pretty . . ."

"Like the sun."

"She's blushing like a rose. Let's go, let's go, Señor Licurgo."

III

PEPE REY

Before we go any further, it would be best to tell who Pepe Rey was and what business had brought him to Orbajosa.

When Brigadier General Rey died in 1841, his two

children, Juan and Perfecta, had just been married, the
latter to the richest landowner in Orbajosa, the former
to a young girl from the same city. Perfecta's husband
was D. Manuel María José de Polentinos, and Juan's
wife was María Polentinos; but despite the same surname,
their relationship was distant and difficult to make out.
Juan Rey was a distinguished attorney, graduated from
Seville, where he practiced law for thirty years with as
much renown as profit. By 1845 he was a widower with
a son old enough to get into mischief; the boy used to
amuse himself by building earthen viaducts, mounds, res-
ervoirs, dams and ditches in the patio of the house, then
turning on the water and running it among those fragile
works. The father let him do it. "You'll be an engineer,"
he used to say.

Perfecta and Juan stopped seeing each other after both
were married, for she went to live in Madrid with the
wealthy Polentinos, whose property matched his extrava-
gance. Gambling and women so captivated the heart of
Manuel María José that if death had not carried him off
before he could squander it, he would have dissipated
his entire fortune. The days of that provincial tycoon
suddenly came to an end in the course of a night's orgy.
He had already been voraciously bled by the leeches of
the Court and the insatiable vampire of gambling. His
only heiress was a little girl a few months old. With the
death of Perfecta's husband, the family alarms came to
a halt; but then began a prodigious struggle. The house
of Polentinos was ruined; the estates in danger of seizure
by the moneylenders; total disorder, enormous debts,
lamentable administration in Orbajosa; discredit and ruin
in Madrid.

Perfecta appealed to her brother, who hastened to the
aid of the poor widow and demonstrated such diligence
and skill that within a short time the greater part of the

dangers had been removed. He began by requiring his sister to reside in Orbajosa, administering her vast lands herself, while he faced the formidable pressures of the creditors in Madrid. Little by little he began to lift the enormous burden of debts from the house, for the good Don Juan Rey, with the greatest talent in the world for such matters, argued with the court, drew up contracts with the principal creditors, and established regular payments, so that thanks to his able negotiations, the rich patrimony of Polentinos was kept afloat to lend splendor and glory to the illustrious family for many long years to come.

Perfecta's gratitude was so keen that in writing to her brother from Orbajosa, where she had determined to live until her daughter was grown, she said to him, among other endearments: "You've been more than a brother to me, and more than her own father to my daughter. How can she and I repay you for your great benefactions? Ah, dear brother, I shall teach my daughter to bless you from the moment she can talk and speak your name. My gratitude will last as long as I live. Your unworthy sister regrets she can find no opportunity to demonstrate to you how much she loves you, and to recompense you in some appropriate manner for the greatness of your soul and the immense goodness of your heart."

When her mother wrote this, Rosarito was two years old. Pepe Rey, enrolled in a school in Seville, was drawing lines on paper, busily proving that "the sum of the interior angles of a polygon equals as many times two right angles as the sides minus two." These tiresome commonplaces kept him very busy. Years passed, and then more years. The boy grew and continued to draw lines. Finally, he drew one called the Tarragona-Mont Blanch line. His first real toy was the 120-meter bridge over the Francolí River.

Doña Perfecta went on living in Orbajosa. As her brother remained in Seville, years went by without their seeing each other. A letter every three months, punctually written and answered, kept those hearts in communion with a warmth neither time nor distance could chill. In 1870, when Don Juan Rey, satisfied that he had discharged with credit his mission to society, retired to live in his beautiful house in Puerto Real, Pepe, after having been at work for a few years on projects for several important construction companies, set out upon a study trip to Germany and England. His father's fortune (as large as any accruing from an honest law-office can be in Spain) made it possible for him to escape the need for paid employment for brief periods. A man of high ideals and an immense love for science, he found his purest enjoyment in the observation and study of the wonders by which the genius of his century has contributed to the culture, physical well-being, and moral perfection of man.

Upon his return from the trip, his father announced that he had an important project to present. Before Pepe could conclude that it would concern a bridge, a dock, or at least draining marshes, Don Juan enlightened him, expressing his idea in these terms:

"It is March now, and Perfecta's quarterly letter has arrived on schedule. Read it, son, and if you agree with what my sister, that pious and exemplary woman, has to say, you'll bring me the greatest happiness I could wish for my old age. But if you don't care for the proposal, don't hesitate to refuse it, even though your refusal will sadden me, for there won't be a shadow of pressure on my part. If this were to come about through the intervention of a stern father, it would be unworthy of us both. You're free to accept it or not, and if there's even the slightest resistance of your free will, arising from the law of the heart or for any other reason, I should not want you to go against your wishes on my account."

After glancing through the letter, Pepe laid it on the table and said calmly:

"My aunt wants me to marry Rosario."

"She answers by accepting my idea with joy," said the father, greatly moved. "For it was my idea . . . yes, a long time ago, a long time ago it came to me . . . but until I knew what my sister thought I didn't want to say anything to you. Perfecta is delighted with my plan, as you see. She says she had thought of the same thing but had not dared to suggest it to me, because you are . . . You see what she says: 'You are a young man of exceptional merit, and my daughter a young village girl, brought up with no worldly attractions, nor brilliance . . .' She says so herself. My poor sister! How good she is! . . . I see you're not angry; I see this scheme of mine doesn't seem to you absurd, even though it's a little like the officious arrangements of old-fashioned parents who married off their children without consulting them, bringing about foolish, premature marriages more often than not . . . God grant that this one may be, or at least promise to be, one of the happiest. You don't know my niece, it's true. But you and I have heard about her virtue, her discretion, her modesty, and her noble simplicity. To top it off, she's even pretty . . . In my opinion," he added gaily, "you'd better be on your way to tread the ground of this secluded cathedral city, this *Urbs augusta*. There, in the presence of my sister and her charming Rosarito, you can make up your mind whether she'll be something more than my niece."

Pepe picked up the letter again and read it carefully. His face expressed neither pleasure nor displeasure. He seemed to be examining a plan for the junction of two railroads.

"Surely," Don Juan was saying, "life must pass with the serenity and sweetness of an idyl in remote Orbajosa, where, I may say in passing, you have estates you can now explore. What patriarchal customs! What nobility in such simplicity! What rustic, Virgilian peace! If you were a classicist instead of a mathematician, you'd be reciting the *ergo tua rura manebunt*[7] as you entered. What an admirable place to dedicate yourself to the contemplation of the soul and to good works! Everything is goodness and honor there. The lies and hypocrisy of our great cities are unknown. Good inclinations, now drowned in the hurly-burly of modern life, are reborn there. Dormant faith awakens and a strong, indefinable impulse arises in the heart, like impatient youth crying out from the depths of its soul, 'I want to live.' "

A few days after this conversation, Pepe left Puerto Real. Some months earlier he had rejected a Government commission to examine the bed of the River Nahara in the valley of Orbajosa for mining possibilities. But the plans arising from the above conversation led him to say: "It's just as well to make use of my time. God knows how long this courtship will last and what kind of boredom it will bring with it." He went to Madrid, sought the commission to explore the bed of the Nahara and was given it without any difficulty, even though he did not belong officially to the Bureau of Mines. Then he set forth, and after changing trains twice, was carried by way-train No. 65, as we have seen, to the loving arms of Uncle Licurgo.

Our excellent young man was approaching the age of thirty-four. He was well-knit, a veritable Hercules, with a rare perfection of form, and so arrogant that if he had worn a military uniform, he would have cut a most war-

---

[7] Virgil, *Eclogue I*, ". . . therefore your fields shall remain yours."

like figure. His hair and his beard were fair, but his face, far from showing the phlegmatic imperturbability of the Anglo-Saxons, was so full of life that his eyes looked black, although they were not. His person might have served as a model of manly beauty, and if he were a statue, his sculptor might have engraved on its base the words: *Intelligence, Strength*. He bore this inscription, although not in visible letters, in the brightness of his gaze, the strong attraction of his personality, and the warm response his winning manner invited.

He was not one of the most talkative of men; only those whose ideas are unsure and whose standards are unstable tend to be verbose. His deep moral sense made that outstanding young man sparing of words in the arguments upon various subjects which constantly engaged the young men of his day. Yet in polite conversation, he could display a witty and discreet eloquence, the result of his good sense and his careful and exact appraisal of the things of this world. He refused to tolerate fallacies and ambiguities, as well as those quirks of thought with which some intellectuals addicted to Gongorism[8] amused themselves. Pepe Rey sometimes used to employ the weapon of ridicule to uphold reality, and not always with moderation. In the eyes of many people who admired him, this was almost a defect, for he seemed somewhat disrespectful toward many of the common phenomena of the world which are accepted by all. At the risk of lowering his prestige, it must be said that Rey failed to comprehend the soft tolerance of this easygoing century, which has invented strange veils of language and deed to cover up what might appear disagreeable to the public eye.

---

[8] Gongorism, an elaborate literary style which employs involved concepts and erudite allusions. The name comes from the Spanish poet, Luis de Góngora y Argote (1561-1627), who initiated it.

This is an exact description of the man whom Uncle
Licurgo introduced to Orbajosa at the very moment when
the Cathedral bell was ringing for high mass, whatever
slanderous tongues may say about him. It was then that
both men, peering over the wall, beheld the girl and her
confessor, and saw the swift flight of the former toward
the house. They spurred their horses toward Real Street,
where many of the idle paused to start at the traveller as
a strange guest, an intruder in the patriarchal city. Turning to the right, in the direction of the Cathedral whose
massive structure dominated the entire town, they entered Condestable Street, where the horses' hoofs re-
echoed in a strident clatter along its narrow stony length
and alarmed the neighbors, who appeared at windows and
balconies to satisfy their curiosity. The venetian blinds
opened with their characteristic rattle, and various faces,
almost all women's, peeped out above and below. By the
time Pepe Rey arrived at the ornate threshold of the
Polentinos house, he had been the subject of numerous
and varied comments about his person.

IV

THE ARRIVAL OF THE COUSIN

When Rosario took abrupt leave of him, the Father Confessor looked toward the wall, and upon seeing the heads of Uncle Licurgo and his travelling companion, said to himself.

"So, here's the prodigy."

For a moment he was thoughtful, holding his cloak with both hands crossed over his stomach, his gaze on the ground, his gold-rimmed spectacles softly sliding toward the end of his nose, his lower lip protuberant and moist, and his salt-and-pepper eyebrows contracted in a slight frown. He was a good, pious man of more than sixty years, far from ignorant, irreproachable in his ecclesiastical work, affable in mien, refined and well-bred, a great giver of advice and admonition to men and women. For many years he had been a teacher of Latin and rhetoric in the *Instituto*. This noble profession had provided him with a huge store of quotations from Horace, and of flowery metaphors which he employed neatly and wittily. No more need be added concerning this personage, except that when he heard the trot of the horses hastening toward Condestable Street, he arranged his cloak, straightened his hat, somewhat askew on his venerable head, and, turning toward the house, he murmured:

"Let's go and see that prodigy."

Meanwhile, Pepe had dismounted and was being received at the door in Doña Perfecta's loving arms, her face bathed in tears. She could express her affection only in short, stumbling words:

"Pepe . . . How you've grown! . . . and a beard . . .

It seems only yesterday when I was holding you on my knee . . . You're a man now, a grown man . . . How the years fly! . . . Heavens! And here's my daughter, Rosario."

As she was speaking, they entered the lower drawing-room, generally used for visitors, and Doña Perfecta presented her daughter.

Rosarito was a girl of a delicate and fragile appearance which bespoke a tendency toward what the Portuguese call *saudade*.* Her fine, pure face had that soft, pearly pallor most novelists bestow upon their heroines. Without this sentimental polish, it would seem that no Enriqueta or Julia can be interesting. Rosario's expression was so sweet and modest that the perfections she lacked were not missed. That is not to say that she was ugly; yet, truly, it would have been an exaggeration to call her beautiful in the strict sense of the word. The real beauty of Doña Perfecta's daughter lay in a type of translucency, not borrowed from pearl, alabaster, marble, or other materials employed in description of the human face; a type of translucency, I mean, through which all the depths of her soul could be plainly seen; depths not bottomless and forbidding like those of the sea, but like those of a clear and gentle river. But the material to make a complete person was missing. She lacked channels; she lacked banks. The great stream of her spirit overflowed, threatening to eat away the banks that confined it. At her cousin's greeting, she blushed crimson and was barely able to murmur a few commonplaces.

"You must be faint with hunger," said Doña Perfecta to her nephew. "I'll give you breakfast immediately."

"With your permission," replied the traveller, "I'd like to wash off the dust of the road."

"That's a good idea. Rosario, take your cousin to the

---

* An untranslatable word referring to tender and happy recollections accompanied by thoughts of regret and a vague yearning.

room we've made ready for him. Hurry, nephew. I'm going to order your breakfast."

Rosario led her cousin to a beautiful room on the ground floor. The moment he set foot in it, Pepe recognized the diligent and loving hand of a woman in all the details of the house. Everything was arranged with great taste, and the neatness and freshness of everything invited rest in such a charming nest. The guest noticed minute details which made him laugh.

"Here's your bell," said Rosarito picking up the cord whose tassel hung over the head of the bed. "You've only to stretch out your hand. The writing desk is placed so you'll have the light over your left shoulder . . . Look: you can throw your waste paper in this basket . . . Do you smoke?"

"I have that vice," replied Pepe Rey.

"Then you can put out your cigarettes here," she said, touching a sand-filled gilded brass fixture with her toe. "Nothing looks worse than to see a floor covered with cigarette stubs . . . Here is the wash basin. You've a wardrobe and chest for your clothes. I think the watch-case is in a poor place here, so you can put it next to your bed . . . If the light bothers you, you've only to draw the curtains by pulling the cord . . . See? . . . Zip . . ."

The engineer was charmed.

Rosarito opened a window.

"Look," she said, "This window opens on the garden. The afternoon sun comes in here. We hung the canary's cage here; it sings like mad. If it bothers you, we'll take it away."

She opened another window on the opposite side of the room.

"This other window," she added, "faces on the street. Look, you can see the Cathedral from here. It's very beautiful and full of treasures. Many English people

come to see it. Don't open both windows at once, because
the draughts are very strong."

"Dear cousin," said Pepe, his heart flooded with an
inexplicable pleasure, "in everything before my eyes, I
see the hand of an angel. It can only be yours. What a
beautiful room this is! It seems to me I've lived in it all
my life. It's an invitation to peace."

Rosario made no answer to these affectionate words,
and went out, smiling.

"Don't be long," she said from the doorway. "The
dining-room is down here, too . . . in the middle of this
hallway."

Uncle Licurgo came in with the luggage. Pepe re-
warded him with a generosity the peasant was unused
to, and he, after giving humble thanks, raised his hand to
his head, like one neither taking off nor putting on a
hat, and in an embarrassed tone, and chewing his words
like one who speaks yet does not speak, he managed to
express himself thus:

"When would be the best time to speak to Señor Don
José about a . . . a little matter?"

"A little matter? Why right now," answered Pepe,
opening his trunk.

"This is not a good time," said the peasant. "Señor Don
José ought to rest; we've got plenty of time. There's more
time than food as they say, and one day comes after
another . . . Rest, Señor Don José . . . When you want
to ride . . . the nag isn't bad . . . And so, good day, Señor
Don José. May you live a thousand years . . . Ah! I forgot," he added, coming back into the room, after a few
moments' absence, "if you have any message for the justice of the peace . . . I'm going to talk to him about our
little matter now . . ."

"Give him my regards," said Pepe gaily, not knowing of
any better way to get rid of the Spartan legislator.

"God keep you, Señor Don José."

"Good-bye."

The engineer had not yet unpacked his clothing when for the third time the shrewd little eyes and crafty face of Uncle Licurgo appeared in the doorway.

"Pardon me, Señor Don José," he said, showing his white teeth in an affected smile. "But . . . I wanted to tell you that if you'd like this matter to be settled by friendly arbitrators . . . Although, as the saying goes, if you ask advice about your own affairs, some will say black and others white . . ."

"Look, man . . . will you get out of here?"

"I'm only telling you because I hate the law. I want nothing to do with the law. The less of it the better. So . . . good-bye, Señor Don José. God preserve you to help the poor."

"Good-bye, man, good-bye."

Pepe turned the key in the lock and said to himself:

"The people in this village seem to be very fond of litigation."

V

WILL DISSENSION ARISE?

Soon afterward, Pepe presented himself in the dining-room.

"If you eat a big breakfast," said Doña Perfecta in fond tones, "you'll spoil your dinner. We dine here at one. You won't like the customs of the country."

"I'm charmed, Aunt."

"Then say which you'd prefer, a big breakfast now, or something light to tide you over till dinner time?"

"I'll take something light so as to have the pleasure of dining with you; and I wouldn't be having anything at this hour if I could have found something to eat in Villahorrenda."

"Of course I needn't tell you you're not to stand on ceremony. Order what you wish here as if you were in your own home."

"Thank you, Aunt."

"How very much you look like your father!" added the lady as she watched the young man eating with real delight. "It's as though I were looking at my dear brother Juan. He used to sit as you are sitting, and he ate as you eat. In the matter of looks, especially, you're as like as two peas in a pod."

Pepe started on his scanty breakfast. The expressions, as well as the attitudes and glances of his aunt and cousin, filled him with such confidence that he could fancy himself in his own home.

"Do you know what Rosario said to me this morning?" asked Doña Perfecta, her eyes fixed on her nephew. "Well, she told me that you, a man reared in the manners and style of the Court and in foreign ways, wouldn't be able to stand this rustic simplicity of ours, this lack of formality, because everything here is plain and simple."

"What a mistake!" answered Pepe, looking at his cousin. "No one hates more than I do the falseness and farce of what's known as high society. Believe me, for a long time I've wanted to take a complete bath in Nature, as someone has said; to live far from the hurly-burly, in the solitude and peace of the country. I long for the tranquillity of a life without struggle or anxiety, neither envied nor envious, as the poet said.[9] First my studies, then my work have kept me from the rest I need and

---

[9] The reference is to Fray Luis de León (1528-1591), who was one of Spain's greatest poets.

which body and soul require. But, dear Aunt and dear Cousin, since setting foot in this house, I've felt all around me the atmosphere of peace I've longed for. You needn't talk to me, then, about high or low society, wide or narrow worlds, for I'd willingly exchange them all for this corner."

As he was speaking, the panes of the door leading from the dining-room to the garden were darkened by a large, black bulk. The lenses of spectacles, struck by sunlight, flashed a fleeting ray. The latch creaked, the door opened, and the Father Confessor gravely entered the room. He greeted them and bowed, taking off his hat and nearly touching the floor with its brim.

"This is the Father Confessor of our holy Cathedral," said Doña Perfecta. "A person we greatly esteem and with whom I hope you'll be friends. Sit down, Señor Don Inocencio."

Pepe shook hands with the venerable clergyman and both sat down.

"Pepe, if you're in the habit of smoking after a meal, please do so," said Doña Perfecta, graciously. "And you, too, Father."

The good Don Inocencio immediately drew forth from beneath his cassock a big leather pouch, scarred with the unmistakable signs of long use. He opened it, taking out two cigarettes, one of which he offered to our friend. Rosario drew a match from a little cardboard box, which the Spaniards ironically call a *coach*, and soon engineer and priest were blowing smoke at each other.

"And how does our beloved city of Orbajosa seem to Señor Don José?" asked the clergyman, tightly closing his left eye as he habitually did while smoking.

"I haven't yet had time to form an idea of this town," said Pepe. "But from the little I've seen, it seems to me that Orbajosa could do with half a dozen fortunes to spend on it, a couple of intelligent minds to direct its renovation, and a few thousand willing hands. Between the entrance to the town and the door of this house, I saw more than a hundred beggars. Most of them are healthy, even robust men. They're a pitiful army, and the sight of them is depressing."

"That's what charity is for," stated Don Inocencio. "Moreover, Orbajosa is not a poverty-stricken town. You know they raise the best garlic in Spain here. And we have more than twenty wealthy families among us."

"It's true," remarked Doña Perfecta "that the last few years have been wretched, owing to the drought; but even so the granaries are not empty, and lately thousands of strings of garlic have been marketed."

"During the many years I've lived in Orbajosa," said the priest, frowning, "I've seen innumerable people come here from the Court, some drawn by the political struggle, others to visit some abandoned site, or to see the Cathedral's antiquities. All of them have come talking about English ploughs, threshing-machines, water-power, banks, and I don't know what new-fangled things. The burden of their song is that everything is very bad and needs improving. They can go to the devil. We're very well off here without visitors from Madrid, much better off without having to listen to constant chatter about our poverty and the bigness and the wonders of other places. The madman knows more in his own house than the wise man in that of another. Isn't that so, Don José? Of course, you mustn't think for a moment that I'm referring to you. By no means! That would never do. I'm aware that we have with us one of the most outstanding young men of modern Spain, a man who would have the capacity to transform our arid wastes into rich fields . . . It won't bother me if you sing me the old song about English ploughs, and fruit-growing, and forestry . . . Not at all.

Men of such great, such very great talents, may be forgiven the scorn they display toward our lowliness. It's
all right, my friend. It's all right, Señor Don José. You
can do anything, even to telling us that we're little better
than savages."

This philippic, ending on a note of marked irony, and
all of it extremely impertinent, did not sit well with the
young man. But he refrained from showing the slightest
displeasure and went on with the conversation, trying as
best he could to avoid topics that might offend the priest's
touchy local pride. The latter got up when Doña Perfecta
began talking to her nephew on family matters, and took
a few turns around the room.

This room was light and spacious, and covered with
an old-fashioned paper whose flowers and branches, although faded, retained their original design, thanks to the
cleanliness reigning throughout the house. The big clock
with a decorated dial, its motionless weights and swinging
pendulum hanging down in the open from its works and
constantly ticking "No, no," occupied the most prominent
place among the solid furnishings of the dining-room. The
adornment of the walls was completed by a series of
French engravings depicting the deeds of the Conqueror
of Mexico, with wordy captions which mentioned a *Ferdinand Cortez* and a *Donna Marine*,[10] names as unlikely
as the figures portrayed by the ignorant artist. Between
the two glass doors which led to the garden, there was
a brass fixture which needs no description beyond saying
that it served as a perch for a parrot which balanced itself there with the seriousness and circumspection typical
of these creatures which observe everything. The hard,
ironical faces of parrots, their green plumage, red caps,

---

[10] French spelling of Hernán Cortés, the conqueror of Mexico,
and Doña Marina, the Indian woman who was his interpreter
and the mother of one of his sons.

yellow boots, and finally the hoarse, mocking words they
prate, give them a strange, disturbing air, half-serious,
half-ridiculous. They have something of the indefinable
stiffness of diplomats. At times they seem to be buffoons;
always they resemble certain conceited people who,
through their efforts to appear superior, turn into caricatures.

The Father Confessor was very fond of the parrot. On
leaving the señora and Rosario to chat with the traveller,
he went up to it, and indulgently letting it bite his index
finger, he said:

"Rascal, knave, why don't you talk? You wouldn't
amount to much if you weren't a chatterbox. The world
of men and birds is full of chatterboxes."

With his own venerable hand, he picked some chickpeas out of the little cup nearby and give them to it to
eat. The creature began to call the maid, demanding
chocolate; its words distracted the two ladies and the
gentleman from a conversation which must not have been
very important.

VI

WHEREIN IT APPEARS
THAT DISHARMONY MAY EMERGE
WHERE LEAST EXPECTED

Suddenly Señor Don Cayetano Polentinos appeared.
Doña Perfecta's brother-in-law entered with arms opened
wide, crying:

"Come here, Don José, my dear friend."

They embraced cordially. Don Cayetano and Pepe knew each other because the distinguished savant and bibliophile used to take trips to Madrid whenever an auction of the estate of some book collector was announced. Don Cayetano was tall and thin, in his middle years, although continual study or ill-health had greatly aged him. He expressed himself with an elaborate perfection which greatly became him, and he was friendly and affectionate, sometimes to the point of exaggeration. What can be said of his vast learning but that it was a marvel? In Madrid, his name was spoken with respect, and had Don Cayetano lived in the capital, he could not have escaped membership in every present and future academy. But he enjoyed his quiet isolation, and the place held by vanity in the soul of others was occupied in his by his bibliomaniacal passion, his love for solitary study without aim or incentive other than books and study for their own sake.

He had collected in Orbajosa one of the richest libraries to be found in all Spain. He spent long hours of the day and night with this, compiling, classifying, taking notes and selecting various and precious data, or perhaps carrying out some unheard-of or undreamed-of work, worthy of such a great mind. His habits were those of a patriarch. He ate little, drank less, and his only dissipations consisted of an afternoon snack at Los Alamillos on red-letter days, and daily walks to a place called Mundogrande, where Roman medals, architrave stones, strange plinths of unknown architecture and perhaps an amphora or some Roman night-lamp of inestimable value were frequently dug out of the mud of twenty centuries.

Don Cayetano and Doña Perfecta lived in such harmony that the peace of Paradise could scarce equal it. They never quarreled. True, he never became involved in any of the household matters, nor she in his library, other than to have it swept and cleaned every Saturday, always respecting with a religious admiration the books and papers in use upon the table and various other places.

After the questions and answers appropriate to the occasion, Don Cayetano said to Pepe:

"I've already looked at the box. I'm so sorry you couldn't bring me the edition of 1527. I shall have to go to Madrid myself . . . Will you be here long? The longer the better, dear Pepe. I'm so glad to have you here! Between us we can arrange part of my library and make an index of the works on Moorish horsemanship. I don't often find a man of your talents . . . You shall see my library . . . You can have your fill of reading . . . Anything you wish . . . You'll see wonders, true wonders, invaluable treasures, rarities that only I possess, only I . . . But, after all, it seems to me it's time for dinner now. Isn't that so, José? Isn't that so, Perfecta? Isn't that so, Rosarito? Isn't that so, Don Inocencio? . . . Today you're twice a confessor: I say that because you're going to help us do penance."

The priest bowed, and smiling, he graciously indicated his acceptance. The meal was pleasant, and in all the dishes one could observe the disproportionate abundance of village dinners, achieved at the cost of variety. There was enough to surfeit twice the number of people gathered there. The conversation turned upon numerous subjects.

"You must visit our Cathedral as soon as you can," said the priest. "There are few to equal it, Señor Don José! . . . But surely, after seeing so many marvels abroad, you'll find nothing unusual in our old church . . . We, the poor yokels of Orbajosa, consider it divine. Master López de Berganza, its prebendary in the sixteenth century, called it *pulchra augustina*[11] . . . However, to a man

---

[11] Latin for "majestically beautiful."

of such sophistication as you, it may have no merit. Any market built of iron would seem more beautiful."

The ironic remarks of the wily clergyman were increasingly displeasing to Pepe Rey; but, determined to contain and hide his anger, he answered only in vague commonplaces. Doña Perfecta quickly picked up the priest's remarks and gaily expressed herself thus:

"Take care, Pepito. I warn you that if you speak ill of our holy church, you'll spoil our friendship. You know a great deal and you're an eminent man, able to understand everything; but if you should conclude that our great structure is not the eighth wonder of the world, keep your knowledge to yourself and leave us in our ignorance."

"Far from thinking that the building lacks beauty," answered Pepe, "it seemed to me that what little I've seen of the exterior has an imposing beauty. So, Aunt, there's nothing to be afraid of; I'm not learned, nor anything like it."

"Now, now," said the priest holding out his hand and resting his jaws from chewing the short while he was talking, "stop it. Don't come here making yourself out to be modest, Señor Don José, for we know your worth very well; we know the great fame you enjoy and the important role you play wherever you go. We don't meet men like you every day. But now that I've extolled your merits . . ."

He paused to resume eating, and as soon as his tongue was free again, went on:

"Now that I've extolled your merits, allow me to express another opinion with the frankness that is part of my character. Yes, Señor Don José, yes, Señor Don Cayetano; yes, my lady and my child; science, as it's studied and taught today by the moderns spells the death of feeling and of pleasant illusions. The life of the spirit falters;

everything comes down to fixed rules, and even the sublime enchantments of Nature are dimmed. Science de-
stroys the wonders of the arts as well as faith in the
soul. Science says that everything is a lie; it seeks to put
everything into figures and lines, not only *maria ac
terras*[12] where we exist, but also *coelumque profundum*[12]
where God dwells . . . The noble reveries of the soul, its
mystical rapture, the very inspiration of the poets—all lies.
The heart is a sponge, the brain a breeding place for
maggots."

Everyone burst out laughing, while he swallowed his
wine.

"Come, do you deny it, Señor Don José?" added the
priest. "That science as it is taught and disseminated
today is moving straight toward converting the world and
humankind into a great machine?"

"That depends," said Don Cayetano. "Everything has
its pro and con."

"Have some more salad, Father," said Doña Perfecta.
"It has plenty of mustard, the way you like it."

Pepe Rey disliked to take part in futile arguments. He
was not a pedant, nor one to display his learning, especially before women or in intimate gatherings. But the
aggressive, nagging verbosity of the priest needed a cor-
rective, he thought. In administering it, it seemed to him
that it would be useless to expound ideas that might flat-
ter the priest by agreeing with him. He decided to state
opinions which would most annoy and embarrass the
mordant Father Confessor.

"You want to make fun of me," he said to himself,
"Well, we'll see what a bad time I can give you."

Aloud, he said:

"What the Father Confessor has said in a joking way

---

[12] From Virgil's Aeneid, I, 58. "The seas and lands . . . and
lofty heaven."

is true. But it isn't our fault that with hammer blows science is constantly destroying false idols, superstitions, sophistry, the thousand lies from the past, some of them beautiful, others ridiculous, for in the vineyard of the Lord there is everything. The world of illusion, which we might call a second world, is coming down with a crash. Mysticism in religion, routine in science, mannerism in art, all are falling as the pagan gods fell, amid laughter. Farewell, silly dreams. Man is awakening and his eyes see clearly. Vain sentimentality, mysticism, fever, hallucinations, delirium are all disappearing, and what was sick before is now whole and in full enjoyment of the true appraisal of things. Fantasy, that terrible madness which was mistress in the house, is now the servant . . . Look about you, Father, and you'll see the admirable whole of the reality that has replaced the fable. The sky is not a vault; the stars aren't little lanterns; the moon is not a capricious huntress, but a mass of opaque stone; the sun is no vagrant, glittering coachman, but a fixed ball of flame. The Syrtes are not nymphs but two sunken reefs; the sirens are seals; and in the human hierarchy, Mercury is the banker Manzanedo; Mars is an old, thin-bearded man, Count von Moltke; Nestor possibly a gentleman in a frock coat named M. Thiers; Orpheus is Verdi; Vulcan is Krupp; Apollo any poet. Would you like to hear more? Well, Jupiter, a god who ought to be jailed if he still existed, doesn't dispatch the lightning, but lightning strikes when electricity releases it. There is no Parnassus, no Olympus, no River Styx, no Elysian fields except those in Paris. There are no more descents into Inferno other than those of geology, and the geologist, upon returning, tells us there are no damned souls in the center of the earth. The only ascents into heaven are those of astronomy, and, returning, it assures us it hasn't seen the six or seven planetary heavens which Dante tells about, as do the mystics and dreamers of the Middle Ages. There is nothing but stars and distances, orbits, vastnesses of space, nothing more. No longer are there false computations of the earth's age, for paleontology and prehistory have counted the teeth of this cadaver on which we live and verified its true age. Fable, call it paganism or Christian idealism, no longer exists, and imagination is dead. Every possible miracle can be boiled down to what I do in my laboratory whenever I wish to, with a Bunsen burner, a wire conductor, and a magnetic needle. There are no miracles of the loaves and fishes other than those wrought by industry with moulds and machinery, and that of printing which imitates Nature by running off millions of copies from a single set of type. In short, dear Father, orders have been issued to cease and desist from all the absurdities, falsehoods, illusions, dreams, sentimentalities, and preoccupations which obfuscate man's understanding. Let us rejoice that it has come to pass."

At the conclusion of his speech, a little smile was playing about the lips of the priest, and his eyes had taken on a strange animation. Don Cayetano was busying himself with shaping pellets of bread, now into rhomboids, now into prisms. But Doña Perfecta was pale, and was staring into the priest's eyes with watchful intensity. Rosarito was looking at her cousin in stupefaction. He leaned toward her and said slyly in a low voice:

"Pay no attention to me, little cousin. I'm talking all this nonsense to annoy the priest."

VII

THE MISUNDERSTANDING
GROWS

"Perhaps," Doña Perfecta declared with a slight air of vanity, "you think that Don Inocencio is going to keep still and not answer each and every one of your points."

"Oh, no!" cried the priest, raising his eyebrows. "I'm not going to match my poor wits against a champion like this, so valiant and so well-armed. Señor Don José knows everything, that is, he has the whole arsenal of the exact sciences at his disposal. I know full well that the doctrine he's expounding is false, but I have neither the talent nor the eloquence to combat it. I'd use the weapons of sentiment; I'd use theological arguments, drawn from Revelation, from the faith, from the Divine Word; but, alas, Señor Don José, an eminent scholar, would laugh at theology, at the faith, Revelation, the holy prophets, the Gospel . . . A poor, ignorant clergyman, a wretch who knows neither mathematics nor that German philosophy where they talk about ego and non-ego;[13] a poor dominie knowing nothing but the science of God and something of the Latin poets, can't break a lance with these brave champions."

Pepe Rey burst into frank laughter.

"I see," he said, "that Señor Don Inocencio has taken my nonsense seriously . . . Come, Father, let's call a truce and make that the end of it. I'm sure my actual ideas and yours aren't so far apart. You're a pious and educated

---

[13] The reference is to the theories of the German philosopher, Johann Gottlieb Fichte (1762-1814).

man. I'm the ignoramus here. Forgive me, everyone, for
trying to play a joke. I'm like that."

"Thanks," answered the priest, visibly annoyed. "Is that
the way you're trying to get out of it? I know very well—
we all know very well—that the ideas you've upheld are
your own. It couldn't be otherwise. You're a man of this
century. It can't be denied that your intelligence is prodigious, in every way prodigious. I must naively confess
that while you were talking, even as I was inwardly deploring such great error, I couldn't help admiring the
loftiness of your expression, the enormous eloquence, the
surprising line of reasoning, the strength of your arguments . . . Señora Doña Perfecta, what a head this young
nephew of yours has! When they took me to the Ateneo[14]
while I was in Madrid, I must admit I was absorbed by
the astonishing ingenuity given to atheists and Protestants
by God."

"Señor Don Inocencio," said Doña Perfecta, her eyes
moving from her nephew to her friend, "I think you've
gone beyond the limits of charity in judging this boy . . .
Don't be angry, Pepe, and don't pay any attention to
what I say, for I'm not a scholar, a philosopher, or a theo-
logian. But it seems to me that Don Inocencio has just
proved his great modesty and Christian charity in refusing
to crush you, as he could have done if he'd wanted to . . ."

"Señora, please," murmured the priest.

"That's the way he is," added the lady, "always under-
rating himself . . . And he knows more than the seven
doctors of the Church . . . Ah, Señor Don Inocencio,
how well your name suits you! But don't come to me
with your misplaced humility. My nephew makes no
pretenses . . . He knows what he's been taught, and that's
all . . . If he's learned the wrong things, what could be

---

[14] An intellectual center established in Madrid in 1835 for the
discussion of progressive ideas, frowned upon in reactionary circles.

better than for you to show him the way and lead him out of the hell of his errors?"

"Indeed I'd like nothing better than to be led by the Father Confessor," murmured Pepe, realizing that he had got himself into a maze all unawares.

"I'm a poor priest who knows nothing but ancient learning," answered Don Inocencio. "I recognize the immense, worldly, scientific worth of Señor Don José, and I prostrate myself and hold my tongue before such a brilliant oracle."

So saying, the priest crossed both hands on his breast and bowed his head. Pepe Rey was somewhat disturbed by the turn his aunt had given to a silly argument begun in fun where he had played a part merely to enliven the conversation. He decided it would be wise to put a stop to such dangerous discourse, and with that in mind he directed a question to Don Cayetano as the latter, rousing himself from the lethargy which afflicted him after dessert, passed the diners the indispensable toothpicks, stuck into a porcelain peacock with its tail spread.

"Yesterday I found a hand grasping the handle of an amphora on which there are various hieratic symbols. I'll show it to you," said Don Cayetano, pleased to introduce a theme to his liking.

"I presume Señor de Rey is very expert in archaeology, too," said the implacable priest, pursuing his victim even into his most hidden refuge.

"Of course," said Doña Perfecta. "What don't these smart youngsters know today? They have all the sciences at their fingertips. The universities and academies teach them everything in the twinkling of an eye, and then hand them diplomas."

"Oh, that's not fair," replied the priest, observing the pained expression on the engineer's face.

"My aunt is right," agreed Pepe. "Today we learn a

little of everything and leave school with only the rudi-
ments of various subjects."

"I was saying," went on the priest, "that you must be
a great archaeologist."

"I don't know a thing about that science," replied the
young man. "Ruins are ruins, and I've never liked to get
dirty in them."

Don Cayetano made a very expressive face.

"I'm not condemning archaeology," added Doña Perfecta's nephew quickly, sadly becoming aware that he
was offending someone with every word he spoke. "I
know very well that history is made from dust. Such
studies are both valuable and useful."

"You," remarked the Confessor, delving into his third
molar with a toothpick, "must be more inclined to the
study of argumentation. I've just had a wonderful idea.
Señor Don José, you should have been a lawyer."

"The law is a profession I detest," answered Pepe Rey.
"I know some very respectable lawyers, my father among
them, who is the best of men. But despite such a good
example, I could never in my life have practiced a profession which consists in taking either the pro or the con
of every dispute. I know of no error, no preoccupation,
no greater blindness than the zeal in many families to
encourage the best of our youth toward law. Spain's worst
and most terrible plague is the mob of young men trained
in law, whose very existence depends upon a multitude
of law-suits. Disputes multiply in proportion to the sup-
ply of lawyers. Even so, a great many of them are idle,
and since an attorney can't turn a hand to the plow nor
sit down to the loom, the result is that brilliant troupe
of loafers, full of pretensions, who are always jockeying
for office, disturbing the body politic, working up public
opinion, and fomenting revolution. They must eat some-
how. It would be worse if law-suits were plentiful."

"Pepe, for Heaven's sake, mind what you say," said Doña Perfecta in a tone of marked severity. "But do forgive him, Señor Don Inocencio . . . for he doesn't know you have a young nephew who's a prodigy as a lawyer, although only recently graduated from the University."

"I'm talking in general terms," declared Pepe firmly. "Being, as I am, the son of a famous lawyer, I can't be unaware that some people practice this worthy profession with true distinction."

"But my nephew is still a child," said the priest, affecting humility. "I couldn't find it in my heart to say he's a prodigy of learning, like Señor de Rey. Perhaps in time . . . His nature is not brilliant or subtle. Of course, Jacintito's ideas are sound, his judgment healthy; what he knows, he knows by heart. He's a stranger to sophistries and hollow words . . ."

Pepe Rey was growing more and more uneasy. The realization that, without wishing to be, he was at odds with the ideas of his aunt's friends, embarrassed him. He resolved to keep quiet for fear he and Don Inocencio might end by throwing the dishes at each other's heads. Happily the Cathedral bell extricated him from his painful position by calling the canons to the important work of the choir. The old man got up and took leave of everyone, treating Pepe in such a flattering and friendly manner that they might have been united by a long and intimate friendship. After offering to do anything he could for him, the priest promised to introduce him to his nephew so the latter could take him around to see the town. Finally, with many affectionate words, he deigned to favor Pepe with a pat on the shoulder as he left. Nevertheless, even as he was gladly accepting those outward signs of concord, Pepe Rey felt the atmosphere clear at the priest's departure from the house.

VIII
WITH ALL SPEED

Shortly afterward, the scene changed. Don Cayetano, stretched out in an armchair in the dining-room resting from his lofty tasks, had fallen into a gentle slumber. Doña Perfecta was going about the house performing her usual tasks. Rosarito, sitting near one of the windows opening on the garden, was looking at her cousin, speaking to him with the silent eloquence of the eyes:

"Sit down here next to me, Cousin, and tell me all you have to tell me."

Mathematician though he was, Pepe understood.

"How we must have bored my dear little cousin with our arguments," he said. "God knows I didn't want to pontificate like that, but it's the canon's fault . . . You know that priest strikes me as a bit odd."

"He's a fine person!" cried Rosarito, showing how pleased she was to be able to give her cousin all the data and the information he might need.

"Oh, yes, an excellent person. Of course!"

"You'll see as you keep meeting him . . ."

"That he's priceless. After all, it's enough that he's a friend of your mother and you to make him a friend of mine, too," declared the young man. "Does he come here often?"

"Every single day. What a good and kindly man he is! He's very fond of me!"

"Well, now I'm beginning to like the gentleman."

"He comes in the evening, too, to play cards," added the girl, "because several people come early every night—the judge of the lower court, the district attorney, the dean, the bishop's secretary, the mayor, the tax collector, Don Inocencio's nephew . . ."

"Ah, Jacintito, the lawyer."

"The same. He's a poor lad, as good as gold. His uncle adores him. Ever since he came from the University with his doctor's hood . . . for he's a doctor with a couple of degrees, and *summa cum laude*, too . . . What do you think of that? Well, ever since he came, his uncle has brought him here often. Mother also likes him very much . . . He's a very serious young man. He leaves early with his uncle. He never goes to the Casino at night; he doesn't gamble or dissipate, and he works in the office of Don Lorenzo Ruiz, the best lawyer in Orbajosa. They say Jacinto will make a fine trial lawyer."

"His uncle didn't exaggerate when he praised him," said Pepe. "I'm sorry I said such stupid things about lawyers . . . Wasn't I a little rude, Cousin?"

"No such thing! I think you were quite right."

"But, honestly, wasn't I a little . . ."

"Not at all, not at all."

"What a load you've taken off my mind! I don't know how it happened, but actually I found myself constantly and painfully at odds with that venerable priest. I'm truly sorry."

"What I think," said Rosarito, gazing affectionately into his eyes, "is that you don't belong among us."

"What does that mean?"

"I don't know how I can explain myself, Cousin. I mean it isn't easy for you to get used to the conversations and ideas of the people in Orbajosa. I imagine so . . . it's just a supposition."

"Oh, no! I think you're mistaken."

"You come from outside, from another world where people are very bright, very well-educated, where they have fine manners and a clever way of speaking, a style

. . . perhaps I'm not expressing myself well. I mean you're used to living in a select society. You know a great deal . . . You won't find what you need here. There are no learned people here, and no great refinements. Everything is simple, Pepe. I imagine you'll be bored; you'll be very bored, and finally you'll have to go away."

The sadness normal to Rosarito's expression became so marked that Pepe Rey felt deeply stirred.

"You're wrong, my dear cousin. I'm not bringing with me the ideas you suggest, nor are my character and mind out of harmony with those of the people here. But let's suppose for the moment that they were."

"Let's suppose . . ."

"In that case, I'm sure that between you and me, between us two, dear Rosario, perfect agreement will be established. I can't be mistaken about that. My heart tells me I'm not deceiving myself."

Rosarito blushed. But overcoming her blushes with smiles and glances directed here and there, she said:

"Don't keep talking nonsense. If you're saying that because I'll think everything you think is all right, you're correct."

"Rosario," cried the young man, "from the moment I saw you, my heart has been filled with a great joy . . . at the same time I've felt sad because I didn't come to Orbajosa sooner."

"That I'm certainly not going to believe," she said, pretending gaiety in order partly to conceal her feelings. "So soon? . . . Don't go on with your big words . . . Look here, Pepe, I'm a village girl. The things I say are ordinary. I don't know French. I don't dress in fashion. I can hardly play the piano. I . . ."

"Oh, Rosario!" cried the young man warmly, "I wouldn't have believed you were perfect. Now I know you are."

Suddenly the mother came in. Rosarito, who was not obliged to answer her cousin's last words, realized, however, the need to say something, and looking at her mother, she remarked:

"Oh, I forgot to feed the parrot."

"Don't bother about that now. Why are you both sitting here? Take your cousin for a walk through the garden."

The señora was smiling with a motherly air, and pointing out to her nephew the leafy grove of trees visible through the glass.

"Let's go out there," said Pepe, rising.

Like a bird set free, Rosarito flew to the window.

"Pepe, who knows so much and must understand trees," declared Doña Perfecta, "can show you how to make grafts. Let's see what he thinks of those little pear trees that are going to be transplanted."

"Come on, come on," said Rosarito from outdoors.

She called to her cousin impatiently. They both disappeared through the foliage. Doña Perfecta watched them as they moved farther away, then took care of the parrot. As she was filling his feed-cups, she said in a low voice with a pensive air:

"How indifferent he is! He didn't even give the poor little bird a pat."

Thinking she might be heard by her brother-in-law, she added aloud:

"Cayetano, what do you think of our nephew? . . . Cayetano!"

A stifled groan indicated that the antiquarian was coming back to an awareness of this miserable world.

"Cayetano . . ."

"All right, all right," murmured the savant in a drowsy voice. "Like everyone else, that young man will be sure to hold the erroneous opinion that the statues at Mundogrande date from the first Phoenician invasion.[15] I'll convince him . . ."

"But, Cayetano . . ."

"But, Perfecta . . . Bah! Are you going to claim that I've been asleep again?"

"No, sir. Why should I claim anything so foolish! . . . But why don't you tell me what you think of that youngster?"

Don Cayetano hid a yawn behind the palm of his hand before embarking upon a long conversation with his sister-in-law. Those who have passed on to us the information necessary for writing this story have skipped this dialogue, doubtless because it was too secret. As for what the engineer and Rosarito talked about in the garden that afternoon, obviously it was unworthy of mention.

On the afternoon of the following day, however, some things happened which cannot be passed over in silence, for they were of the utmost gravity. At a late hour of the afternoon, the two cousins found themselves together, having traversed various parts of the garden, hanging on each other's words, and having no thought or feeling but to look at and listen to each other.

"Pepe," Rosario was saying, "everything you've told me is a fantasy, one of those stories you clever men know so well how to spin. You think because I'm a country girl I believe everything you say."

"If you knew me as well as I think I know you, you'd realize that I never say anything I don't feel. But let's lay aside those silly subtleties and lovers' quibbling which serve no purpose but to falsify emotions. I will never speak any but true words to you. Are you perchance some young lady I met out walking or at a reception, with whom I intend to flirt for a while? No. You're my cousin.

---

[15] Presumably the eleventh century B.C. when the Phoenicians great seamen and traders, are thought to have first reached Spain.

You're more than that, Rosario . . . Let's get things straight, once and for all. Fancy language aside, I came here to marry you."

Rosario felt her face burn and her heart seemed too big for her chest.

"Listen, dear cousin," added the young man. "I swear I'd be far from here by now if I hadn't liked you. And even though politeness and good taste would have forced me to make an effort, I wouldn't have been able to hide my disenchantment. That's the way I am."

"But, cousin, you've barely got here," said Rosarito laconically, with a forced laugh.

"I've just arrived, and already I know all I need to know. I know I love you; that you're the woman my heart has long promised me, telling me night and day . . . 'she's coming now; she's near; you're warm, you're warm.' "

This phrase served Rosario as a pretext for releasing the laughter playing around her lips. Her heart, in its happiness, was soaring through an atmosphere of joy.

"You insist you're a nobody," went on Pepe, "and you're wonderful. You have the marvelous quality of being able constantly to project the lovely light of your spirit over everything around you. Since I first saw you, first looked at you, I've felt the sensitivity and purity of your heart. Seeing you, I see a heavenly being on earth through God's oversight; you're an angel and I love you madly."

As he said this, he looked as if he had just accomplished a dangerous mission. Rosarito suddenly felt so overcome that the slight energy of her body failed to match her mind's excitement. Feeling weak, she sank down on a stone which served as a bench in that pleasant place. Pepe bent over her. He noticed that her eyes were closed, her forehead resting on her hand. In a moment, Doña Perfecta Polentinos' daughter gave her cousin a tender look from tear-filled eyes, followed by these words:

"I loved you even before I knew you."

Placing her hands in those of the young man, she rose, and they disappeared among the leafy branches of an avenue of oleanders. Dusk was falling and soft shadows were spreading over the lower part of the garden, while the last rays of the sun crowned the tops of the trees in splendor. The noisy republic of the birds had set up a busy chattering in the upper branches. It was the hour when, after flitting through the joyous immensity of the sky, they were making ready for bed. Now they argued among themselves over the branches chosen as bedrooms. At times their twittering sounded like recrimination and dispute, at times like play and repartee. With their voluble chirping, the little rascals were flinging insults at one another, pecking at each other, and flapping their wings like orators waving their arms and trying to make credible the lies they utter. But words of love, appropriate to the peaceful hour and the beautiful setting, could also be heard. An expert ear might have been able to make out the following:

"I loved you even before I knew you. If you hadn't come, I'd have died of grief, I think. Mother used to give me all your father's letters to read, and as he praised you so highly in them, I used to think: 'This will be my husband.' For a long time your father failed to mention that you and I might marry, which seemed to me a serious oversight. I didn't know what to think of such negligence . . . Every time he mentioned you, Uncle Cayetano used to say: 'There aren't many like him in this world. The woman who catches him can consider herself lucky.' . . . Finally your father said what he couldn't help saying . . . No, he couldn't help saying it; I'd been waiting for it all that time . . ."

Soon after these words, the same voice added with alarm:

"Someone is coming, behind us."

Emerging from the oleanders, Pepe saw two people approaching, and, fingering the leaves of a tender shrub growing nearby, he said aloud to his companion:

"It's not advisable to do the first pruning on a young tree like this until it is completely rooted. Newly planted trees lack the vigor to withstand such an operation. You know that roots can't form without the help of the leaves; so if you take off the leaves . . ."

"Ah, Señor Don José," exclaimed the Father Confessor with open laughter, as he approached the young people and bowed. "Are you giving lessons in horticulture? *Insere nunc, Meliboee, piros, pone ordine vites,*[16] as the great singer of work in the fields has said. 'Graft your pear trees, dear Meliboeus, cultivate your vines . . .' And how is your health, Señor Don José?"

The engineer and the canon shook hands. Then the latter turned and beckoning to a young fellow coming along behind him he said, smiling:

"I have the pleasure to present to you my dear Jacintillo . . . a scamp . . . a rattlebrain, Señor Don José."

IX

DISSONANCE GROWS
AND THREATENS TO
BECOME DISCORD

A fresh and blushing face emerged from the black cassock. Jacintito greeted our young man, not without self-consciousness.

---

[16] Virgil's *Eclogues*, I, 73.

He was one of those precocious youngsters sent forth
into the harsh struggles of the world by the University
before their time, with the notion that because they are
graduates, they are men. Jacintito had a delicate, plump
face, with cheeks as pink as a girl's. He was short, almost
small, with a chubby body and no more than the fore-
runner of a beard, a light fuzz. He was hardly more than
twenty years old. From childhood, he had been educated
under the guidance of his excellent and learned uncle,
and as the twig was not bent, he grew up straight. A
severe morality had kept him always on the right path,
and he had seldom faltered in the completion of his
scholastic duties. At the conclusion of his astonishingly
successful university career (in none of his classes had
he won anything but most outstanding marks) he went
to work. Now, with his diligence and talent for the law,
he promised to keep fresh and green in court the laurels
of the lecture-room.

Sometimes he was a mischievous little boy, sometimes
a man of formal manners. Indeed, indeed, if Jacintito had
not liked the girls a little, or more than a little, his uncle
would have considered him perfect. He did not fail to
lecture the boy in and out of season, thus hastening to
clip his venturesome wings; but even this worldly turn of
the young man's mind could not cool the love our good
canon felt for this charming offspring his dear niece,
María Remedios had brought forth. He indulged the little
lawyer in everything. Even the good priest's fixed and
routine habits always yielded in any matter having to
do with his precocious pupil. That rigorous method, fixed
as a planetary system, usually went off balance whenever
Jacintito was ill or had to take a trip. So much for the
celibacy of priests! If the Council of Trent forbade them
to have children, God, not the devil, gives them nephews
so they may experience the sweet cares of parenthood.

If the qualities of that industrious youth were examined impartially, his merits could not be ignored. In general, his character was inclined to be honorable; high-minded acts awakened a frank admiration in his soul. As for his intellectual gifts and social savoir-faire, he had all of them he needed to become in time one of those notable men who abound in Spain. He could be what we are often pleased to call, exaggeratedly, "a distinguished citizen" or "an eminent public figure," types so abundant they are scarcely given their just due. At that tender age when a university degree acts to merge boyhood and manhood, few youths, especially if pampered by their teachers, are free of that annoying pedantry which, if it brings them great prestige in the eyes of their mothers, is laughable among sensible, grown men. Jacintito was guilty of this fault, excusable not only because of his tender years, but also because his good uncle encouraged his childish vanity with ill-advised applause.

The four having met, they continued their walk. Jacinto kept quiet. The canon, returning to the interrupted theme of the *piros* to be grafted and the *vites* to be trimmed, said:

"I feel sure Don José is a famous agronomist."

"Not at all; I don't know a thing about it," replied the young man, noting with great displeasure that mania for endowing him with a knowledge of all the sciences.

"Oh, yes. A great agronomist," went on the Confessor. "But don't give me any new-fangled theories about agronomy. To me, Señor de Rey, that entire science is condensed in what I call *The Country Bible,* the *Georgics* of the immortal Latin poet. From that great sentence, *Nec vero terrae ferre omnes omnia possunt,* that is, not all land is good for all trees, it is wholly admirable, Señor Don José, even to the minute treatise on the bees, where

the poet explains all about these clever little insects, and
defines the drone as:

ille horridus alter

desidia latamque trahens inglorius alvum

a horrid, lazy figure, dragging his heavy, ignoble belly,
Señor Don José."

"It's a good thing you've translated it for me," said
Pepe, "for I know very little Latin."

"Ah, these modern men. How can they enjoy studying
those old-fashioned things?" continued the priest with
irony. "Nobody has written in Latin except weaklings
like Virgil, Cicero,[17] and Livy.[18] However, I'm on the
other side, as my nephew, to whom I taught the sublime
language, will bear witness. That rascal knows more than
I do. Unfortunately, he's forgetting it for modern reading,
and some fine day he'll find himself an ignoramus without suspecting it. For my nephew, Señor Don José, has
taken to entertaining himself with new books and extravagant theories. Everything in heaven and earth is
Flammarion's[19] astronomy, and if you please, the stars are
filled with people. Come, I think you two are going to
be great friends. Jacinto, ask this gentleman to teach you
the wonders of mathematics, to instruct you concerning
the German philosophers, and then you'll be a man."

The good priest was laughing at his own sallies,
whereas Jacinto, pleased at seeing the conversation led
into a field so much to his taste, begged Pepe Rey's pardon, and suddenly fired this question at him:

"Tell me, Señor Don José, what do you think of Dar-
winism?"

---

[17] Marcus Tullius Cicero, Roman orator and writer of the first
century B.C.

[18] Titus Livius Patavinus, Roman historian of the first century
B.C.

[19] Camille Flammarion (1842-1925), French astronomer and
author of works on science that were highly popular in his day.

The engineer smiled at such out-of-place pedantry, and was tempted to lead the youth farther along the path of infantile vanity. But thinking it more prudent not to encourage either nephew or uncle, he replied, simply:

"I have no opinion on Darwin's theories for I scarcely know them. My professional work doesn't permit me to devote myself to studying them."

"Now, now," said the canon, laughing. "Everything boils down to our descent from monkeys . . . If that could be said only about some people I know, it would be true."

"The theory of natural selection," added Jacinto emphatically, "seems to have many followers in Germany."

"I don't doubt it," said the priest, "if this theory is true, they can't be sorry in Germany as far as Bismarck[20] is concerned."

Doña Perfecta and Don Cayetano met the four of them face to face.

"What a beautiful evening," said the lady. "How is it going, nephew? Are you very bored?"

"Not at all," replied the young man.

"Don't deny it. Cayetano and I were just talking about that. You're bored and you're trying hard to conceal it. Few young people these days have the self-abnegation, like Jacinto, to spend their youth in a village where there's no Royal Theatre, no variety shows, no dancing, no philosophy, no Ateneo, no trashy papers, no meetings, nor any other pastimes and diversions."

"I'm very well off here," answered Pepe. "Just now I was saying to Rosario that this town and this house are so pleasing to me I'd like to live and die here."

---

[20] Otto von Bismarck (1815-1898), eminent Prussian statesman who brought about the unification of Germany. His attempts to bring the Catholic Church under the state made his name anathema to Catholics.

Rosario blushed brightly, and the others were silent. They all sat down in a summer house, Jacinto hastening to place himself on the girl's left.

"Look, nephew, I must warn you about something," said Doña Perfecta, with that smiling expression of goodness which emanated from her spirit, like the perfume of a flower. "But you mustn't think I'm scolding, or giving you lessons. You're not a child, and you'll grasp my ideas immediately."

"Scold me, dear Aunt, for I'm sure I shall deserve it," answered Pepe, who was beginning to get used to the virtues of his father's sister.

"No, this is only a warning. These gentlemen will see I'm right."

Rosarito was listening with all her heart.

"Well," continued the señora, "it's only that when you visit our beautiful Cathedral again, try to show a little more devotion."

"But what have I done?"

"I'm not surprised that you yourself don't know your own mistake," said the señora with seeming good-nature. "Accustomed as you are to going into athenaeums, clubs, academies, and meetings without the slightest ceremony, it's natural that you should think you can enter in the same way a church where His Divine Majesty dwells."

"But, forgive me, señora," said Pepe soberly. "I went into the Cathedral with the greatest decorum."

"I'm not scolding you, boy, I'm not scolding. Don't take it like that or I'll have to keep still. Gentlemen, forgive my nephew. A little carelessness, a little heedlessness is not to be wondered at . . . How many years is it since you set foot in a consecrated place?"

"Señora, I swear . . . After all, my religious opinions are whatever they are; but I'm not in the habit of behaving incorrectly inside a church."

"I assure you . . . Come, if you're going to be offended, I won't say another word . . . I assure you that many people noticed it this morning. The González ladies, Doña Robustiana, Serafinita, even . . . I must tell you you even attracted the attention of the Bishop himself . . . His Grace complained to me about it this afternoon in my cousin's house. He told me it was only because they said you're my nephew that he didn't order you put out into the street."

Rosario was anxiously watching her cousin's face, trying to divine his answers before they were given.

"They undoubtedly have me confused with someone else."

"No . . . no . . . It was you . . . But don't be offended, for we're among friends and intimates. It was you. I myself saw you."

"You!"

"Precisely . . . Do you deny that you went around examining the paintings, and passed through a group of the faithful hearing mass? . . . I vow you distracted me so much with your comings and goings, that . . . Well . . . You mustn't do it again. Then you went into St. Gregory's chapel. They were elevating the Host on the main altar, and you didn't even turn around or give any demonstration of respect. Then you crossed the church from one side to the other, went up to the tomb of the Governor, put your hands on the altar, passed through another group of worshippers and attracted their attention. All the girls looked at you, and you seemed satisfied at having so completely disturbed the devotion and piety of those good people."

"My heavens! What abominations!" cried Pepe, half-angry, half-smiling. "I'm a monster, and I never even suspected it."

"No. I know very well that you're a good boy," said

Doña Perfecta, glancing at the affected and unchanging severity of the canon's face, which looked like a cardboard mask. "But, son, it's one thing to think a thing, and another to show it like that with a kind of irreverence. There's a line which a prudent and well-bred man should never cross. I know that your ideas are . . . don't be angry; if you get angry, I'll keep still . . . I say it's one thing to have ideas concerning religion and another to display them . . . I shan't let myself upbraid you for believing that God has not created us in his image and likeness, but that we're descended from monkeys; nor for denying the existence of the soul and maintaining that the soul is a drug like one of those paper-wrapped doses of magnesia or rhubarb which are sold in the drugstore . . ."

"Señora, for Heaven's sake!" exclaimed Pepe with vexation. "I see I have a very bad reputation in Orbajosa."

The others kept silent.

"Well, as I was saying, I'm not going to upbraid you for those notions . . . Furthermore, I have no right to. If I tried to argue with you, you'd refute me a thousand times with your uncommon intelligence . . . no, nothing of the sort. What I do say is that these poor, wretched inhabitants of Orbajosa are good, devout Christians, even if not one of them knows German philosophy. Therefore, you must not scorn their beliefs publicly."

"Dear Aunt," said the engineer gravely, "I have not scorned anyone's beliefs, nor do I hold the ideas you attribute to me. Perhaps I was a little disrespectful in church. I'm somewhat absent-minded, and my thoughts and attention were fixed on the architectural work. Frankly, I didn't notice . . . But that was no reason for the Bishop to think of throwing me out in the street, nor for you to suppose me capable of attributing the functions of the soul to a paper-wrapped dose from the drugstore. I can forgive that as a joke, but only as a joke . . ."

Pepe Rey was so worked up that despite his prudence and moderation he could not hide his excitement.

"Come, I see I've made you angry," said Doña Perfecta, lowering her eyes and folding her hands. "So be it! If I'd known you'd take it this way, I wouldn't have said anything. Pepe, I beg you to forgive me."

Hearing this and seeing his good aunt's submissive attitude, Pepe felt ashamed of the harshness of his words, and tried to calm himself. The venerable Confessor, smiling with his habitual benevolence, extricated him from his embarrassing situation.

"Señora Doña Perfecta, you must be tolerant toward artists . . . Oh, I've known a good many. These gentlemen forget everything else whenever they see before them a statue, a rusty suit of armor, a mouldering picture, or an old wall. Señor Don José is an artist. He was visiting our Cathedral as the English visit it. They'd gladly cart it off to their museums to the last flagstone . . . What if the worshippers were praying; if the Sacred Host was being elevated; if the moment of utmost piety and devotion had come; all right—what does all that matter to an artist? True enough I don't know the value of art if it's separated from the sentiments it expresses . . . but, after all, it's the custom today to adore the form, not the idea . . . God save me from getting into an argument on this subject with Señor Don José who knows so much he could instantly confound my mind which contains only faith, by arguing with the neat subtlety of the moderns."

"You people's insistence upon considering me the wisest man on earth embarrasses me a great deal," said Pepe, again speaking in a harsh tone. "Take me for a fool, for I'd prefer the name of idiot to that of owning the wisdom of Satan which you attribute to me."

Rosarito burst out laughing, and Jacinto decided the opportune moment had come to display his erudition.

"Pantheism[21] or Panentheism are condemned by the Church, as well as the doctrines of Schopenhauer and the modern Hartmann."[22]

"Ladies and gentlemen," said the canon gravely, "those who make such a fervent cult of art, even if considering form only, are worthy of the greatest respect. It's better to be an artist and delight in beauty, even if represented only by nude nymphs, than to be indifferent and skeptical about everything. A mind consecrated to the contemplation of beauty can't be all bad. *Est Deus in nobis*[23] . . . *Deus,* you understand. Go on admiring the wonders of our church, then, Señor Don José, and for my part, I'll forgive you your irreverence willingly, with all due respect to the opinion of the Prelate."

"Thank you, Señor Don Inocencio," said Pepe, feeling a prickling, rebellious sense of hostility toward the shrewd canon, a desire to annoy which he was unable to dominate. "Apart from that, none of you need believe that the artistic beauties with which you think the church abounds were absorbing my attention. Except for the imposing architecture of a part of the structure and the three sepulchers in the chapels in the apse, plus some carvings in the choir, I can see none of those beauties anywhere. My mind was preoccupied with observing the deplorable decadence of religious art, and the countless artistic monstrosities which fill the Cathedral caused me no astonishment, only anger."

---

[21] The doctrine that the universe in its totality is God.

[22] The pessimistic philosophy of the German Arthur Schopenhauer (1788-1860) taught that only the cessation of desire could solve the problems arising from the universal impulse of the will to live. Eduard von Hartmann (1842-1906), a follower of Schopenhauer and Hegel, took the position that thought and reason are the ultimate reality, and life futile.

[23] "God is in us". From the Roman poet Ovid's *Ars Amatoria.*

The stupefaction of the others was complete.

"I can't stand those varnished, red images, so like the dolls that overgrown girls play with, if God will forgive me the comparison. What can I say about the theatrical costumes in which they're garbed? I saw Saint Joseph in a cloak the look of which I shouldn't care to describe out of respect for the Great Patriarch and the Church which worships him. Images in the most deplorable artistic taste were stacked on the altars, and the quantity of crowns, palm branches, stars, moons and other decorations of metal or gilt paper added up to an ironmongery offensive to religious feeling and depressing to the soul. Far from being exalted by religious contemplation, one is downcast and distracted by a sense of the comic. Great works of art, lending sensitive form to ideas, dogmas, faith, mystical exaltation, play a noble part. Caricatures and perversions of taste, the grotesque work with which a poorly comprehended piety fills the churches, also achieve their object; but it is a very unfortunate one. They encourage superstition, chill enthusiasm, repel the worshipper's eyes from the altars, and also repel the souls which lack a deep and secure faith."

"The doctrine of the iconoclasts," said Jacintito, "also seem to be very widespread in Germany."

"I'm not an iconoclast, though I'd prefer the abolition of all images to this buffoonery I'm talking about," went on the young man. "Seeing this, it's fair enough to maintain that religion ought to regain the majestic simplicity of ancient times. But no. It's not necessary to relinquish the aid that all the arts, beginning with poetry and ending with music, lend to the relationship between man and God. Keep the arts, display all possible pomp in religious ceremonies. I'm on the side of pomp."

"Just an artist, an artist, an artist," cried the canon, shaking his head with an expression of regret. "Good

paintings, good statues, fine music . . . A feast for the
senses. And let the soul go to the Devil."

"And apropos of music," said Pepe Rey, failing to observe the deplorable effect his words were having upon
mother and daughter, "You can imagine how my mind
was prepared for religious contemplation during my visit
to the Cathedral, when right at the start, at the moment
of the Offertory in high mass, the organist played a passage from *La Traviata*."[24]

"Señor de Rey is right," said the little lawyer emphatically. "The other day the organist played the drinking
song and the waltz from the same opera, and later a
rondeau from *La Gran Duquesa*."[25]

"But what really clipped the wings of my heart," continued the engineer implacably, "was seeing an image of
the Virgin which, judging by the number of people before her and the number of candles lighted to her, must
be highly venerated. They'd dressed her in a puffed-out
gown of velvet embroidered with gold, in such a curious
style that it outdid the most extravagant modes of today.
Her face was lost from sight in a thicket of pleated lace
ruffles, and her crown, half a yard high, was a clumsy
catafalque erected on her head. The panties of the Infant
Jesus were of the same material and with the same em-
broidery . . . I won't go on, for the description of how
the Mother and Son were got up might lead me to say
something irreverent. I'll say no more, except that I
couldn't help laughing, and I gazed a while at the pro-
faned image, thinking, 'Blessed Mother, what they have
done to you!' "

As he finished speaking, Pepe looked at his hearers,
and although the evening shadows made it impossible to

---

[24] A well-known opera by Guiseppe Verdi (1813-1901).
[25] A light opera by Jacques Offenbach (1819-1880).

see their faces clearly, he fancied there were signs of bitter consternation on some of them.

"Well, Señor Don José," exclaimed the canon quickly, laughing with an expression of triumph. "That image which appears so ridiculous to your philosophy and your Pantheism is Our Lady of Perpetual Help, the patroness and intercessor of Orbajosa, whose inhabitants venerate her so greatly they'd be capable of dragging anyone who spoke ill of her through the streets. Our chronicles and history, my dear sir, are full of the miracles she has performed, and even today we see constant, irrefutable proof of her protection. You must also know that your aunt, Doña Perfecta, is lady-in-waiting to the Most Blessed Virgin of Perpetual Help, and that the dress which seems to you so grotesque . . . well . . . I say that dress, so grotesque to your impious eyes, came from this house, and the Infant's costume is the combined work of the clever needle and the true piety of your cousin, Rosarito, who is listening to us."

Pepe Rey was utterly disconcerted. At the same moment Doña Perfecta rose brusquely and without a word went toward the house, followed by the Confessor. The others stood up. The stunned young man was preparing to beg his cousin's forgiveness for his irreverence, when he noticed that Rosarito was crying. Fixing on her cousin a look of sweet and kindly reproach, she cried:

"What ideas you have!"

Doña Perfecta's voice, calling in an agitated tone, was heard: "Rosario! Rosario!"

The girl ran toward the house.

X

OPEN DISCORD

Pepe Rey felt bewildered and confused, furious with the others and with himself, as he tried to ascertain the reason for that quarrel between his ideas and those of his aunt and her friends which had broken out against his will. He remained seated on the bench of the summerhouse for a while, thoughtful and sad, foreseeing trouble, his chin sunk on his chest, his brow furrowed, hands folded. He thought he was alone.

Suddenly he heard the chorus of a comic opera song gaily whistled between the teeth. Looking up, he saw Don Jacinto in the opposite corner of the summerhouse.

"Ah, Señor de Rey," said the youth abruptly, "the religious sensibilities of the overwhelming majority of a nation can't be wounded with impunity . . . If you doubt it, think what happened during the first French Revolution . . ."

Pepe's irritation increased at hearing the buzzing of that insect. However, he felt in his heart no hatred for the young pedant. He was bothersome, as flies are bothersome; nothing more. Rey felt the annoyance aroused by all meddlesome people, and he answered as though shooing away a blue-bottle:

"What has the French Revolution to do with the Virgin Mary's dress?"

He got up to go toward the house, but had taken no more than four steps when he again heard the buzz of the mosquito, saying:

"Señor de Rey, I must talk to you about a matter very much to your interest, and which might cause you some trouble . . ."

"A matter?" asked the young man, turning back. "Let's see what it is."

"Perhaps you've already suspected it," said the youth, going up to Pepe and smiling with an expression like that of a businessman about to deal with some serious project. "I want to talk to you about the suit."

"What suit? . . . You, my friend, like a good lawyer, are dreaming about litigation and seeing red tape in front of your eyes."

"What? . . . Haven't you been notified about your suit?" asked the boy in astonishment.

"About my suit! . . . It so happens I have not and never have had a lawsuit."

"Well, if you haven't been notified, I'm glad I warned you so you can be on your guard . . . Yes, sir, you'll be engaged in a lawsuit."

"With whom?"

"With Uncle Licurgo and others whose land adjoins the estate called Los Alamillos."

Pepe Rey was astonished.

"Yes, sir," added the little lawyer. "Señor Licurgo and I had a long conference today. Since I'm such a good friend of this family, I didn't want to fail to warn you, so that if it suits you, you can soon straighten it all out."

"But what have I to straighten out? What does that scoundrel want with me?"

"It seems that some waters which originate on your estate have changed course and are falling on some of the said Licurgo's tile-works and on someone else's mill, causing considerable damage. My client—for he's taken it into his head that I must get him out of this bad situation— my client, I say, claims you must restore the water to its old channel to avoid further damage, and must indemnify the injured parties who have suffered through the negligence of the upstream landowner."

"So I'm the upstream landowner! . . . If I get involved in a suit, it will be the first fruit the famous Alamillos has yielded me in all my life. It was mine and now, as I understand it, it's everybody's, for that same Licurgo as well as other peasants in the region have been filching chunks of my land little by little, year after year, and it will cost me a great deal to reestablish the boundaries of my property."

"That's another question."

"It is not another question. The fact of the matter is," said the engineer, unable to contain his anger, "that I'm the one who should be suing this trash. Undoubtedly they've undertaken to annoy and discourage me to the point where I'll abandon everything and leave them in possession of what they've stolen. We shall see whether or not there are lawyers and judges to uphold the clumsy maneuvers of these village pettifoggers who make their money in lawsuits and are the termites of other people's property. I thank you, young sir, for having warned me against the base plans of those rustics, who are worse than Cacus.[26] I may tell you that the very roof-tiles and the mill upon which Licurgo bases his claims, are mine . . ."

"A search of the deed to the property should be made in order to determine if possession may not constitute title in this matter," said Jacintito.

"What do you mean possession! Those rascals are not going to make a fool of me. I presume the Department of Justice in the city of Orbajosa is honest and upright . . ."

"Oh, it's all of that!" cried the little scholar in a tone of admiration. "The Judge is an excellent man. He comes here every night . . . But it's strange you've had no noti-

---

[26] A mythological Roman robber giant.

fication of Señor Licurgo's claims. Hasn't the Arbitration
Tribunal summoned you yet?"

"No."

"Tomorrow it will . . . In short, I'm very sorry that
Señor Licurgo's pressure has denied me the pleasure and
the honor of defending you; but since it must be—Licurgo
has set his heart on having me to get him out of his diffi-
culties—I shall study the matter with the greatest delibera-
tion. These petty real estate cases are the bane of juris-
prudence."

Pepe entered the dining-room in a state of complete
demoralization. He saw Doña Perfecta talking with the
Confessor, and Rosarito sitting alone, her eyes on the
door. Doubtless she was waiting for her cousin.

"Come here, you rascal," said the señora, smiling with
forced spontaneity. "You've insulted us, you great atheist;
but we shall forgive you. I know that my daughter and
I are country folk, incapable of soaring into the realms
of mathematics, where you dwell; but after all . . . it's
still possible that some day you'll get down on your knees
to us, begging us to teach you Christian doctrine."

Pepe answered with vague words and the conventional
phrases of regret.

"For my part," said Don Inocencio, putting on an expression of modesty and sweetness, "if I've said anything
that might offend Señor Don José in the course of these
vain arguments, I beg his pardon. We're all friends here."

"Thank you. It's not worth mentioning."

"In spite of everything," stated Doña Perfecta, smiling
more naturally now, "I'll always feel the same toward my
dear nephew, in spite of his extravagant and anti-religious
ideas . . . What do you think I'm going to do tonight?
Why, I'm going to get those stubborn ideas that Uncle
Licurgo is pestering you with right out of his head. I've
ordered him to come, and he's waiting for me in the hall.

Don't worry, I'll fix him; even though I know he's not entirely in the wrong . . ."

"Thank you, Aunt," replied the young man, feeling himself swept by a wave of the generosity that rose so easily in his heart.

Pepe Rey glanced toward his cousin, intending to join her; but various artful questions by the canon kept him at Doña Perfecta's side. Rosario was downcast, listening with a melancholy indifference to the words of the little lawyer, who, installing himself beside her, embarked upon a flood of nauseating opinions, interspersed with ill-timed jokes and other fatuities in the worst taste.

"It's your fault," said Doña Perfecta to her nephew, as she saw him stare at the ill-matched pair Rosario and Jacinto made. "You've hurt poor Rosario's feelings. You must do your best to make your peace with her. The poor little thing is so good! . . ."

"Oh, yes, so good!" added the canon, "I don't doubt she'll forgive her cousin."

"I think Rosario has already forgiven me," declared Rey.

"Of course. Resentment doesn't last long in angelic hearts," said Don Inocencio mellifluously. "I have some influence over the child, and I'll try to dispel from her generous soul any prejudice against you. A few words from me . . ."

Pepe Rey felt a cloud darken his thoughts, and said meaningfully, "Perhaps it won't be necessary."

"I'm not going to speak to her now," said the priest, "because she's entranced with Jacintillo's nonsense . . . Little imps! There's no stopping them when they once begin."

The judge of the lower court soon made his appearance, together with the mayor's wife and the dean of the Cathedral. They all greeted the engineer, showing in words and manner that in meeting him they were satisfying their keen curiosity. The judge was a clever, youngish man, one of those who appear every day in the incubator of eminent figures, aspiring, still newly-hatched, to the highest posts in administration and politics. He gave himself no little importance, and in speaking of himself and his recently acquired robes, he seemed angered that he had not been made Chief Justice of the Supreme Court right away. The State had placed the extremely delicate and difficult decisions of human justice in those inexpert hands, that brain blown up with wind, that absurd presumption. His manners were those of the perfect courtier, revealing a scrupulous attention to everything that had to do with him. The constant putting on and taking off of his gold-rimmed glasses was an ugly mannerism rather than a habit. And in his conversation he frequently indicated his desire to be transferred immediately to Madrid, there to lend his irreplaceable services to the Department of Justice.

The mayor's wife was a good-natured lady whose only weakness was to imagine that she was in very close touch with the Court. She asked Pepe Rey many questions about fashions, mentioning several well-known establishments where she had had a tippet or a skirt made for her on her last trip which went back to the war between Spain and Morocco, and she also named a dozen duchesses and marchionesses, speaking of them with the familiarity of an old schoolmate. She said the Countess of M. (famous for her salons) was a friend of hers, and that in '60 she had visited her, and the Countess had invited her to her box in the Royal Theatre where she had seen Muley-Abbas[27] in Moorish costume, accompanied by his

---

[27] A Moorish prince who visited Madrid shortly after the war between Spain and Morocco (1859-1860).

Oriental entourage. The mayor's wife talked thirteen to the dozen, as the saying goes, and was not short of wit.

The Dean was a man of advanced age, red-faced and corpulent, plethoric and apoplectic. He seemed to burst out in his skin, so fat and paunchy was he. A product of the dissolution of the monasteries,[28] he could talk of nothing but religious subjects, and displayed, from the beginning, the greatest scorn for Pepe Rey. The young man, inept at adapting himself to a society so little to his taste, showed up in an increasingly poor light. His character was not at all malleable—firm and inflexible, rather— and he rejected the duplicities and compromises of speech which simulate harmony where there is none. In the course of the tiresome evening, his gravity was unchanging as he was forced to endure the oratory of the mayor's wife, who, although not the fabled hundred-tongued Rumor, was privileged to wear out the human ear. If Pepe Rey tried to approach his cousin during the brief respite this lady gave her listeners, the Confessor clamped onto him, like a mollusk to a rock, and drawing him aside with a mysterious air, proposed a trip to Mundogrande with Don Cayetano, or a fishing trip to the clear waters of the Nahara.

At last it came to an end, as everything must in the natural course of events. The Dean retired, leaving the house less crowded; then soon all that was left of the mayor's lady was an echo like the humming in the ears which follows the passing of a storm. The judge also deprived the gathering of his presence, and finally Don Inocencio gave his nephew the signal to depart.

"Come, come, boy, it's late. Let's go," he said, smiling. "You've made poor Rosarito's head swim! Hasn't he, child? Come on, you rascal, straight home."

---

[28] In 1837 nearly all communities of religious orders were suppressed in Spain. Many of the excloistered monks became priests.

"It's time for bed," said Doña Perfecta.

"Time for work," replied the little lawyer.

"No matter how often I tell him to finish his business during the day, he pays no attention."

"There's so much work . . . so much!"

"No. It's that devilish work you've taken on yourself instead . . . He won't want me to say it, Señor Don José, but he's set himself to writing a treatise on *The Influence of Woman in Christian Society,* plus *A Glance at the Catholic Movement in* . . . I don't know where. What do you know about glances or influences? . . . These youngsters of today have nerve enough for anything. Ugh! What kids! . . . Let's go home. Good night, Doña Perfecta . . . good night, Señor Don José . . . Rosarito . . ."

"I'll wait for Don Cayetano to give me his *Augusto Nicolas.*"[29]

"Always carrying around books! . . . Sometimes you look like an overburdened donkey when you come into the house. All right, we'll wait."

"Señor Don Jacinto," said Pepe Rey, "would not write frivolously and he's making a good start at turning out treasures of erudition."

"But that child is going to make himself mentally sick, Señor Don Inocencio," objected Doña Perfecta. "Take care, for goodness' sake. I'd set a limit to his reading."

"Since we're waiting," stated the little pedant in a tone of blatant vanity, "I'll take the third volume of the *Concilios,*[30] too. Don't you think I should, Uncle?"

"Why, yes. Don't let that out of your hands. How could you do without it?"

Luckily, Señor Don Cayetano (who generally spent his

---

29 Probably refers to Jean-Jacques Auguste Nicolas (1807-1888), French lawyer and writer, who was an ardent defender of the Catholic faith.

30 *The History of the Church Councils.*

evenings in the house of Don Lorenzo Ruiz) soon arrived, and uncle and nephew departed, with the books
under their arms.

Rey read in the downcast face of his cousin a pressing
desire to talk to him. As Don Cayetano and Doña Perfecta drew aside to discuss a domestic matter, he went to
the girl.

"You've offended Mother," said Rosario.

Her features showed a kind of terror.

"True enough," answered the young man. "I've offended your mother and I've offended you."

"No, not me. It had already occurred to me that the
Infant Jesus oughtn't to wear panties."

"But I hope you'll both forgive me. Your mother has
been so good to me lately . . ."

Doña Perfecta's voice suddenly filled the dining-room
with such strident tones that her nephew shuddered as
though a cry of alarm had been heard. The voice cried
imperiously:

"Rosario, go to bed!"

The girl, disturbed and dismayed, made several turns
around the room, as though looking for something. As she
passed by her cousin, she said these vague words in a
low voice:

"Mother is angry . . ."

"But . . ."

"She's angry . . . be on your guard, be on your guard."

Then she left. She was followed by Doña Perfecta, for
whom Uncle Licurgo was waiting. The voices of the
señora and the villager could be heard for a time mingled
in a private discussion. Pepe Rey stayed with Don Cayetano, who picked up a lamp and said:

"Good night, Pepe. You needn't think I'm going to
sleep; I'm going to work . . . Why are you so pensive?
What's the matter? . . . Well, to work. I'm taking notes

for a study on the genealogy of Orbajosa . . . I've uncovered data and facts of the greatest value. There can
be no question about that. During all the periods in
our history, the Orbajosans have been distinguished for
their high-mindedness, their nobility, their courage, their
intelligence. The Conquest of Mexico, the Wars of the
Emperor,[31] of Philip II[32] against the heretics all bear witness . . . But, are you ill? What's the matter with you? . . .
Well, eminent theologians, brave soldiers, Conquistadors,
saints, bishops, poets, politicians, all sorts of illustrious
men have flourished in this humble land of the garlic . . .
No, in all Christendom there's no village more illustrious
than ours. All Spanish history is filled with her virtues
and her glories, with some left over . . . Come, I see that
you are sleepy. Good night . . . Indeed, I wouldn't exchange the glory of being a son of this noble earth for
all the gold in the world. *Augusta,* the ancients called her,
now I call her Most August, for now, as then, high-
mindedness, generosity, courage, nobility, constitute the
patrimony she confers . . . So good night, dear Pepe . . .
it seems to me you're not well. Didn't your supper agree
with you? . . . Alonso González de Bustamante[33] was
right in his *Floresta amena* when he said that the inhabitants of Orbajosa alone would suffice to lend grandeur
and honor to a kingdom. Don't you think so?"

"Oh, yes, sir, without a doubt," replied Pepe Rey
brusquely, making for his room.

---

[31] Charles V (1500-1558), King of Spain and Emperor of the
Holy Roman Empire.
[32] Philip II (1527-1598), son of Charles V, who waged war
against the Protestants in the Low Countries, which at the time
belonged to Spain.
[33] A fictitious author invented by Galdós.

XI

THE DISCORD GROWS

During the following days, Pepe Rey made the acquaintance of several people in the village and visited the Casino, becoming friendly with a few of those who spent their time in the rooms of that organization.

But the youth of Orbajosa did not spend all their time there as malicious gossip might imply. In the afternoons, they could be seen on the corner by the Cathedral and in the small plaza formed by the junction of Condestable and Tripería Streets. A group of gentlemen, romantically wrapped in their capes, stood as if on guard to watch the people pass by. If the weather was fair, those leading lights of *urbsaugustine* culture, always in their indispensable capes, turned to the promenade called Las Descalzas, composed of two files of consumptive elms and some faded broom. There the brilliant constellation stared at So and So's and Such and Such's girls, also out for a walk, and the afternoon passed as usual. At nightfall, the Casino filled up again, and while one wing of the membership directed its keen intelligence to the delights of card-playing, another read newspapers, and the rest, gathered in the coffee-room, discussed various subjects, such as politics, horses, bullfights, or perhaps local gossip. The debates all boiled down to the superiority of Orbajosa and its inhabitants over all the other towns and peoples in the world.

The cream of those outstanding figures in that illustrious city were in part rich landowners, in part poverty-stricken men, but all of them devoid of lofty ambitions. They possessed the imperturbable serenity of the beggar who craves nothing as long as he has a crumb to appease his hunger and bright sunlight to keep him warm. The Orbajosans of the Casino were distinguished mainly for their deep hostility to everything from the outside. And whenever a distinguished stranger showed himself in their majestic corridors, they believed he had come to cast doubt on the superiority of the land of the garlic, or to dispute enviously the incontrovertible preeminence which Nature had granted her.

When Pepe Rey appeared, he was received with some suspicion. As witty people abounded in the Casino they had made all sorts of jokes about the new member within fifteen minutes of his arrival. When he answered the repeated queries of the members by saying that he had come to Orbajosa commissioned to explore the coal-bearing bed of the Nahara and to lay out a road, they all agreed that Señor Don José was a fatuous idiot, trying to make himself important by inventing coal deposits and railroads. Someone added:

"But he's come to the wrong place. These smart fellows think we're all fools here and that they can take us in with their big words . . . He came here to marry Doña Perfecta's daughter. All his talk about coal-bearing beds is just an act."

"Only this morning," declared a bankrupt businessman, "at the Domínguez's, they told me this gentleman hasn't a red cent and that he came here so his aunt would support him while he tries to land Rosarito."

"It looks to me as if he isn't any kind of engineer, or anything like one," added an olive-grower who had mortgaged his farms to twice their value. "But we'll see . . . These hungry fellows from Madrid get a kick out of fooling the poor provincials. They think, my friend, that we go around in breech-clouts here . . ."

"Everyone knows he's hungry."

"Half in joke and half in earnest, he told us last night we're lazy barbarians."

"That we live like nomads, taking the sun."

"That we're living in our imagination."

"That's it. We live in our imagination."

"And this city is exactly like the ones in Morocco."

"That kind of talk wears out my patience. Where would he have seen (unless it was in Paris) a street like the Adelantado, with a front of seven houses all in line, all magnificent, from Doña Perfecta's to Nicolasito Hernández's . . . ? These scoundrels think no one has ever seen anything, or ever been in Paris . . ."

"He also said with a great deal of delicacy, that Orbajosa is a beggars' town, and he made it quite clear that we're living here in the utmost squalor and we don't even know it."

"Lord help us! There'd have been a scandal in the Casino if he'd said that to me," cried the tax collector. "Why didn't they tell him how many *arrobas* of olive oil Orbajosa produced last year? Doesn't that fool know that Orbajosa provides all Spain and even all Europe with bread in good years? Of course, we've had I don't know how many years of poor crops. But that's not the rule. What about the garlic harvest? I'll bet that gentleman doesn't know that Orbajosan garlic left the judges at the London Exposition pop-eyed."

These and other remarks could be heard in the rooms of the Casino during those days. Despite such chatter, common enough in small towns—the smaller they are, the prouder—Rey did make some sincere friends in the learned organization, for not all were scandalmongers, nor was there a lack of people with good sense. But the engineer had the misfortune, if misfortune it could be called, to make known his impressions with unusual frankness, and this made him enemies.

The days kept on passing. Added to the natural displeasure which the social customs of the episcopal city
aroused in him, a deep sadness began to develop in his
spirit, one of the principal causes of which was the
nuisance of the lawsuits descending on him like a swarm
of savage bees. Uncle Licurgo was not alone. A host of
other neighbors were suing him for damages or petition-
ing for an accounting of lands administered by his grandfather. Also they presented him with some sort of crop-
sharing contract which his mother had had executed and
which had apparently not been fulfilled. Likewise they
demanded his recognition of a mortgage on the lands of
Los Alamillos, drawn by his uncle in an irregular form.
His property had become a dunghill for lawsuits, breeding them like maggots. He had resolved to give up ownership of his farms; but meanwhile his dignity would not
let him yield to the sly tricks of his shrewd neighbors.
As the Town Magistrates had also brought a claim
against him for an alleged confusion of his farm with
adjoining property belonging to the Town, the unfortunate young man found himself in the position of
having to clear up doubts which arose at every turn
regarding his rights. His honor was at stake, and he had
no choice but to engage in litigation or die.

Doña Perfecta, in her magnanimity, had promised to
help him out of such sordid entanglements by a friendly
compromise. But day followed day, and the good offices
of that exemplary lady brought no results whatsoever.
The lawsuits multiplied with the frightening speed of
a violent illness. Every day, the young man spent long
hours in court making statements, answering questions
and more questions. When he returned home, tired and
cross, he was soon confronted with the sharp, grotesque
mask of the notary, who brought him a daily lot of

stamped papers covered with appalling legal language for
his further study of the question.

Clearly Rey was not the man to suffer such annoyances if he could avoid them by absence. His mother's
noble city began to appear in his imagination as a horrid
beast which had fastened its ferocious claws in him and
was drinking his blood. In his opinion, flight would free
him of the beast; but a deep interest, the interest of the
heart, kept him there, chaining him to the rock of his
martyrdom with strong bonds. Nevertheless, he began
to feel so out of place, to consider himself so foreign, so
to speak, in that dismal city of lawsuits, of outworn
customs, of envy and malice, that he was planning to
quit it post haste, yet at the same time he clung to the
purpose which had brought him there. One morning,
finding the occasion propitious, he announced his plan
to Doña Perfecta:

"My dear nephew," replied the lady with her usual
sweetness, "don't be rash. Come, you're like a fire. Your
father was the same. What a man! You're a firebrand . . .
I've told you I'll call you my son with the greatest pleasure. Even if you lacked the good qualities and talent
which distinguish you (except for a few little defects,
which are there, too); even if you weren't a fine young
man, the fact that this match was suggested by your
father, to whom my daughter and I owe so much would
be enough to make me accept you. Rosario will not object either, since I wish it. What's wanting, then?
Nothing. Only a little time. No one marries in the haste
you want. It might give rise to unfavorable judgments
of my daughter's honor . . . You think only of machinery,
so you want to drive everything by steam. Wait, boy,
wait . . . What's the hurry? This hatred you've taken
against our poor Orbajosa is a passing whim. It's obvious you can live only among counts and marquises,

amid orators and diplomats . . . You want to marry and take my daughter away from me forever!" she added, squeezing out a tear. "Since that's how it is, you inconsiderate young man, at least have the goodness to postpone for a while that marriage you want so much . . . Such impatience! Such a great love! I wouldn't have believed a poor village girl like my daughter could inspire such a volcanic passion."

His aunt's arguments failed to sway Pepe Rey; but he did not want to annoy her. He resolved, therefore, to wait as long as he could. A new reason for irritation was soon added to those already embittering his life. He had been in Orbajosa two weeks, and during that time he had not had a letter from his father. This he could not attribute to the carelessness of the Orbajosa Post Office because the official in charge of this service was a friend and protégé of Doña Perfecta. Every day she cautioned him to take great care that letters addressed to her nephew might not go astray. Furthermore, the mail carrier, named Cristóbal Ramos, nicknamed Caballuco, a personage we have already met, used to come to the house where Doña Perfecta would warn and reprimand him in terms as energetic as the following:

"You furnish fine mail service! How is it that my nephew hasn't received a single letter since he's been in Orbajosa? . . . What's the world coming to when the mail delivery is entrusted to such a thickhead! I'll speak to the Governor of the province and tell him to be careful what kind of people he puts in office."

Caballuco, shrugging his shoulders, stared at Rey with an expression of complete indifference. One day he arrived with a letter in his hand.

"Thank heaven!" said Doña Perfecta to her nephew. "Letters from your father. Aren't you glad, man? My brother's laziness about writing gave us a fine scare . . .

What does he say? He's well, no doubt," she added, seeing Pepe Rey open the envelope with feverish impatience.

The engineer turned pale as he skimmed the first lines.

"Heavens, Pepe . . . What's the matter?" cried the señora, getting to her feet in alarm. "Is your father ill?"

"This letter is not from my father," replied Pepe, his face showing complete consternation.

"Then what is it?"

"An order from the Ministry of Public Works relieving me of the commission that was entrusted to me . . ."

"What! . . . Is it possible?"

"A dismissal pure and simple, in terms quite unflattering to me."

"I've never seen such knavery!" cried the señora, coming out of her wonderment.

"What humiliation!" murmured the young man. "It's the first time in my life I've ever been so affronted."

"But this Government is unforgivable! To slight you! Do you want me to write to Madrid? I have some good contacts there and I can see to it that the Government will rectify that stupid mistake and give you satisfaction."

"Thank you, señora, I don't want any recommendations," replied the young man with displeasure.

"One sees such injustices, such outrages! . . . To dismiss such a capable young man just like that, an outstanding scientist! . . . I can hardly contain my anger."

"I shall find out," said Pepe with the greatest energy, "who is busying himself with doing me harm . . ."

"That Minister . . . But what can you expect of these base politicians?"

"There's someone here who has set out to make me die of despair," declared the young man, visibly agitated. "This isn't the work of the Minister; this and similar reverses which I'm experiencing here are the result of a

plan of revenge, of some underhanded calculation, of
some irreconcilable enmity, and this plan, this calculation, this enmity are here in Orbajosa. Never doubt that,
dear Aunt."

"You're out of your mind," replied Doña Perfecta with
an emotion very like compassion. "You have enemies in
Orbajosa? Someone who wants to revenge himself on
you? Come, Pepe, you've lost your mind. Your brains
have been addled by reading those big books which say
we had monkeys and parrots for ancestors."

As she spoke the last sentence, she smiled sweetly,
and, taking an itimate and affectionate tone of admonition, she added:

"My son, we people of Orbajosa may be crude rustics
without any education, refinement or good manners; but
no one, no one, but no one has more loyalty or good
faith."

"Don't think," said Rey, "that I'm accusing the people
in this house. But I maintain that a fierce and implacable
enemy of mine is in this city."

"I'd like you to show me this traitor out of a melo-
drama," answered the señora, again smiling. "I suppose
you won't accuse Licurgo or the others who are suing,
for the poor things are only defending their rights. And
incidentally, they aren't without justice in the present
case. Besides, Uncle Licurgo likes you very much. He's
said so. He's taken a fancy to you from the moment he
met you, and the poor old man is very fond of you . . ."

"Oh, yes! . . . Very fond, indeed," murmured Pepe.

"Don't be an idiot," continued the señora, putting a
hand on his shoulder and gazing straight at him. "Don't
think nonsense, and be sure that if you have an enemy,
he's in Madrid, that center of corruption, of envy and
rivalries, not in this peaceful, quiet corner where everything is all good will and harmony . . . No doubt it's

someone envious of your ability . . . I'll tell you one
thing, and that is, if you want to go there and find out
the cause of this insult and to demand explanations of
the Government, don't let us stand in your way."

Pepe Rey fixed his eyes on his aunt's face as though
he would like to scrutinize it to the very depths of
her soul.

"I say if you want to go, don't let us stand in your
way," repeated the señora with admirable calm, her expression a mixture of openness with the utmost honesty.

"No, señora. I'm not thinking of going there."

"Better not, that's my opinion, too. You're more tran-
quil here, in spite of the suspicion that's tormenting you.
Poor Pepe! Your intelligence, your unusual intelligence,
is the cause of your misfortune. We poor rustics in
Orbajosa are happy in our ignorance. I'm sorry you're
not content. But is it my fault that you're bored and
worried for no reason? Don't I treat you like a son?
Haven't I received you like the hope of my house? Can
I do anything more for you? If, in spite of that, you
don't like us, if you're so indifferent to us, if you make
fun of our faith, if you scorn our friends, is it because
we don't treat you well?"

Doña Perfecta's eyes grew moist.

"Dear Aunt," said Rey, feeling his anger dissipate.
"I've made some mistakes, too, since I've been a guest
in this house."

"Don't be silly . . . What mistakes! Among members
of the same family, all things are forgiven."

"But where is Rosario?" asked the young man, rising
to his feet. "Am I not to see her today, either?"

"She's better. Do you know, she didn't want to come
down?"

"I'll go up."

"No, dear. That girl is so stubborn . . . ! Today she's

taken it into her head not to go out of her room. She's locked herself in it."

"How strange!"

"She'll get over it. Of course she'll get over it. Probably we'll get those melancholy ideas out of her head tonight. We'll arrange a party to amuse her. Why don't you go to Señor Don Inocencio's house and ask him to come here tonight and bring Jacintillo?"

"Jacintillo?"

"Yes. Whenever Rosario has these attacks of melancholia, that lad is the only one who can amuse her . . ."

"But I'll go up . . ."

"No, dear."

"I see the rules of etiquette are not lacking in this house!"

"You're making fun of us. Do as I tell you."

"But I want to see her."

"No. How little you know the girl!"

"I think I know her very well . . . All right, I won't . . . But that solitude is terrible."

"Here comes the notary."

"A thousand curses on him!"

"And it seems the attorney is here, too . . . a fine person."

"Let him go hang, too."

"Business interests, when they're your own, serve to divert the mind. Someone else is coming . . . It seems to me it's the agricultural expert. They'll keep you busy a while."

"A hellish while."

"Well, well! Unless I'm mistaken, Uncle Licurgo and Uncle Pasolargo have just arrived. Perhaps they've come to propose a compromise."

"I'll throw myself in the pond first!"

"How ungrateful you are! And they all like you so

much! . . . Well, to make sure everyone is present, here's the constable, too. He must have come to summons you."

"To crucify me."

All the personages named were coming into the drawing-room.

"Good-bye, Pepe. Have a good time," said Doña Perfecta.

"I wish the earth would swallow me up!" exclaimed the young man in desperation.

"Señor Don José . . ."

"My dear Señor Don José . . ."

"Señor Don José, my friend . . ."

"My dear friend, Señor Don José . . ."

At the sound of these honeyed greetings, Pepe Rey heaved a sigh and gave up. He yielded himself body and soul to his executioners, who were brandishing ominous stamped documents, while the victim, raising his eyes to heaven, said to himself with Christian humility:

"My God, my God, why hast thou forsaken me?"[34]

XII

THIS WAS TROY

What Pepe Rey needed desperately was love, friendship, a healthy atmosphere to give him moral sustenance, light for his soul, sympathy, an easy exchange of ideas and feelings. Lacking them, the shadows enveloping his spirit deepened, and his inner gloom made his behavior toward others disagreeable and bitter. On the day following the scenes described in the preceding chapter,

---

[34] Among the last words of Christ on the cross.

he felt especially mortified by the now overlong and
mysterious confinement of his cousin, apparently due to
a minor indisposition at first, and later to whims and
nervousness difficult to explain.

Rey wondered at behavior so contrary to the idea he
had formed of Rosarito. Four days had gone by without
his seeing her, certainly not because he lacked the desire
to be at her side. Such a situation began to seem humiliating and ridiculous unless he remedied it by boldly
taking the initiative.

"Am I not to see my cousin today, either?" he asked
his aunt ill-humoredly when they had finished dinner.

"No, not today. Heaven knows I'm sorry! . . . I've
given her a good talking-to today. This afternoon we
shall see . . ."

The suspicion that his sweet cousin was the helpless
victim of this unreasonable seclusion rather than the
stubborn agent, acting on her own initiative and voli-
tion, induced him to control himself and wait. Except for
this suspicion, he would have left that very day. He had
no doubt whatever that he was loved by Rosario; but
it was evident that some unknown influence was at work
with the object of separating them. It seemed to him that
it behooved an honorable man to find out from whom
that malign force was emanating and to checkmate it
with all his will.

"I hope that Rosario's stubbornness will not last much
longer," he said to Doña Perfecta, hiding his true feelings.

That day he had a letter from his father complaining
that he had had no word from Orbajosa, a circumstance
which increased the engineer's disquiet and further confused him. Finally, after wandering alone for some time
through the garden of the house, he set forth and went
to the Casino, entering it like a man in despair throwing
himself into the sea.

In the main room he met several people, talking and arguing. One group was discussing with subtle logic some difficult problems of the bullring; another was holding forth on which, among the breeds of Orbajosa and Villahorrenda, were the best donkeys. Completely disgusted, Pepe Rey abandoned those debates and went into the periodical room where he leafed through several magazines without finding any pleasure in his reading. Then, wandering from room to room, he stopped in the game room without knowing how he came there. For nearly two hours he was in the grip of that awful yellow devil whose glittering gold eyes bring torment and fascination. But even the emotions of gambling could not dispel the gloom in his soul, and the boredom which had earlier impelled him toward the green table also drew him away from it. Fleeing the noise, he found himself in a space intended for an assembly room, where at the moment there was not a living soul. He seated himself aimlessly by the window, staring out into the street.

This was very narrow, with more angles and corners than houses, completely overshadowed by the formidable Cathedral which reared its mouldering black wall at one end. Pepe Rey looked all around him, above and below, observing the placid silence of the grave: not a footstep, not a voice, not a glance. Suddenly strange noises came to his ears, like the whispering of feminine lips, and then the rustling of curtains being drawn, words, and finally the soft humming of a song, the bark of a little lap dog, and other indications of social life which seemed odd in such a spot. Looking closer, Pepe Rey saw that the sounds came from a huge balcony with venetian blinds which reared its massive form across from the window. He had not finished his observation when a member of the Club appeared suddenly at his side, and laughing, accosted him thus:

"Ah! Señor Don Pepe, you rascal! Did you shut your-self up in here to make eyes at the girls?"

The speaker was Don Juan Tafetán, an amiable man and one of the few who had shown real admiration and a cordial friendliness toward Pepe Rey. With his scarlet face, his mustache dyed black, his lively little eyes, his diminutive height, his hair carefully combed to hide his baldness, Don Juan Tafetán presented an appearance hardly comparable to that of Antinous, the handsome page of the Emperor Hadrian. But he was very pleasant; he was witty, and had a happy gift for relating amusing adventures. He laughed a good deal, and when he did so, his face was covered with grotesque wrinkles from forehead to chin. Despite these qualities and the applause which might have stimulated his tendency toward sting-ing ridicule, he was not a scandalmonger. Everyone liked him, and Pepe Rey had spent some agreeable moments with him. Poor Tafetán, formerly employed in the civil administration of the provincial capital, was now living modestly on his salary in the Social Welfare Department, and he eked out his livelihood by jauntily playing the clarinet in parades, on solemn occasions in the Cathedral, and in the theatre whenever some troupe of destitute actors came to that part of the country with the worthless notion of playing in Orbajosa.

But the strangest thing about Don Juan Tafetán was his fondness for pretty girls. Before he used to hide his baldness with six pomaded hairs, before he used to dye his mustache, in the days when he walked straight and tall under the slight weight of his years, he himself had been a formidable Don Juan.[35] To hear him tell of his conquests was enough to make you laugh yourself sick,

---

[35] The hero of Tirso de Molina's drama *El burlador de Sevilla*. The name has become synonymous with libertine.

for there are Don Juans and Don Juans, and he was one
of the most original.

"What girls? I don't see any girls anywhere," replied
Pepe Rey.

"Go on, make yourself out to be an anchorite."

One of the blinds on the balcony opened, disclosing a
young, charming, and smiling face. At once it disappeared like a light put out by the wind.

"Now I see."

"Don't you know them?"

"No, upon my word."

"They're the Troyas, the Troya girls. Well, you've
missed something good . . . Three very pretty girls,
daughters of a Colonel on the General Staff who died
in the streets of Madrid in '54."[36]

The blind opened again and two faces appeared.

"They're making fun of us," said Tafetán, giving the
girls a friendly wave.

"Do you know them?"

"Of course I know them. The poor things are penniless.
I don't know how they live. When Don Francisco Troya
died a subscription was taken up to support them, but
it didn't last long."

"Poor girls! I suppose they're hardly models of
decorum."

"Why not? I don't believe what they say about them
in the town."

The blind moved again.

"Good afternoon, girls," cried Don Juan Tafetán,
addressing the three who now showed themselves in an
artistic group. "This gentleman says that good things
shouldn't hide themselves and that you ought to open
the blind."

---

[36] In July of 1854 the people of Madrid revolted against a
corrupt and reactionary government, and several days of bloody
street fighting ensued.

But the blind closed, and a merry chorus of laughter spread an unusual gaiety through the sad street. It was as though a flock of birds had passed by.

"Shall we go over there?" asked Tafetán suddenly.

His eyes shone and a mischievous smile played around his purple lips.

"What kind of people are they?"

"Go on, Señor de Rey . . . The poor little things are decent people. Bah! They must live on air like chameleons. Tell me, can anyone be a sinner who doesn't eat? These unfortunates are virtuous enough. And if they did sin, they would atone for it by the strict fast they keep."

"Let's go, then."

A moment later, Don Juan Tafetán and Pepe Rey entered the living-room. The young man felt depressed by the air of poverty which made immense efforts to hide itself. The three girls were very pretty, especially the two younger ones—pale, with black eyes and slender figures. If they had been dressed well and well-shod, they would have looked like the daughters of a duchess, worthy of a royal marriage.

All three were quite abashed when the visitors arrived; but soon their gay, frivolous natures emerged. They were living in poverty, like birds which sing as well through the bars of a cage as in the abundance of the forest. They spent their days sewing, thus indicating at least an honest background; but in Orbajosa no one in their social class would have anything to do with them. To a certain degree, they were ostracized, déclassé, proscribed, all of which formed a basis for gossip. But it must be said, out of respect for the truth, that the bad name of the Troyas lay for the most part in their reputation as gossips, tattlers, pranksters, and no respecters of persons. They sent anonymous letters to important people; they

nicknamed everyone in Orbajosa from the bishop down
to the last good-for-nothing; they threw pebbles at
passersby; they hissed from behind the iron grill, then
laughed at the confusion and fright of those in the street;
they knew all the doings of the neighborhood through
constant use of the dormer windows and openings in the
upper part of the house. They sang at night on the balcony. They dressed in masquerade costume to get into
the houses of the best people at Carnival time, along
with other pranks and liberties common to small towns.
But for whatever reason, the fact is that the Troya trio
carried that stigma which once affixed by suspicious
neighbors would accompany them implacably even beyond the grave.

"Is this the gentleman who's come to open up gold
mines, they say?" asked one.

"And to tear down the Cathedral to build a shoe
factory out of the stones?" added another.

"And to take away Orbajosa's garlic harvest to plant
cotton or cinnamon trees?"

Pepe could not help laughing at such nonsense.

"The only reason he came was to make a collection of
pretty girls and carry them off to Madrid," said Tafetán.

"Oh! I'd be glad to go!" cried one.

"I'll take all three, all three," declared Pepe. "But tell
me something: why were you laughing at me when I
was in the window of the Casino?"

His words were the signal for renewed laughter.

"These girls are silly," said the eldest.

"It was because we said you deserve something better
than Doña Perfecta's daughter."

"It was because she said you were wasting your time
on Rosario because she doesn't love anyone but church
people."

"What's the matter with you! I never said such a

thing! You said this gentleman is a Lutheran atheist, and that he goes into the Cathedral smoking and with his hat on."

"Well, I didn't make it up," said the youngest. "Suspiritos told me so yesterday."

"And who is this Suspiritos who talks such nonsense about me?"

"Suspiritos is—Suspiritos."

"My children," said Tafetán with a smiling face. "Here comes the orange vendor. Call him so I can buy oranges for you."

One of the three called the vendor.

The conversation started by the girls had displeased Pepe Rey, destroying his feeling of contentment among that gay and talkative company. However, he could not help laughing when he saw Don Juan Tafetán take down a small guitar and strum it with the grace and skill of his youth.

"They tell me you sing marvelously," said Rey.

"Let Don Juan Tafetán sing."

"I don't sing."

"Nor I," said the second girl, offering the engineer some segments of the orange which she had just peeled.

"María Juana," said the eldest Troya, "don't neglect your sewing. It's late and the cassock has to be finished tonight."

"No work today. To the devil with needles," cried Tafetán, and immediately he began a song.

"People are stopping in the street," said the second Troya, going over to the balcony. "Don Juan Tafetán's shouts can be heard in the plaza . . . Juana! Juana!"

"What?"

"Suspiritos is going down the street."

The youngest flew to the balcony.

"Throw an orange peel at her."

Pepe Rey looked out, too. He saw a lady passing by in the street, and with expert aim, the youngest of the Troyas hit her on her knot of hair with a piece of orange peel. They closed the blind precipitately and the three choked down their laughter in order not to be heard in the street.

"No work today," cried one, kicking over the sewing basket.

"That's the same as saying, 'no eating tomorrow,'" said the eldest, picking up the materials.

Pepe Rey instinctively put his hand in his pocket. He would gladly have given them some money. The sight of those unlucky orphans, condemned by the world for their frivolity, saddened him. If the only sin of the Troyas, if the only pleasure with which they compensated for their solitude, their poverty, and their ostracism, lay in throwing orange peels at some passerby, he could easily excuse them for it. Perhaps the austere customs of the wretched town in which they lived had kept them from vice; but the unfortunate girls lacked decorum and good breeding—the first and most obvious sign of modesty—and it might be guessed that they had thrown something more than peels out of the window. Pepe Rey felt a profound pity for them. He noticed their wretched clothes, made over, trimmed, and mended in a thousand ways to make them look new. He noticed their worn-out shoes . . . and again he put his hand into his pocket.

"Perhaps vice may reign here," he said to himself, "but their faces, the furniture, everything indicates to me that these girls are the unhappy remnants of an honorable family. If the poor creatures were as bad as they say they are, they would not be living so poorly and they would not be working. There are rich men in Orbajosa!"

The three girls approached him one after the other. They went from the balcony to him, from him to the balcony, carrying on a lightly malicious conversation, which it must be admitted indicated a kind of innocence in the midst of so much frivolity and unconventionality.

"Señor Don José, what a good lady Doña Perfecta is!"

"She's the only person in Orbajosa who isn't nicknamed, the only one in Orbajosa who isn't spoken ill of."

"Everyone respects her."

"Everyone loves her."

The young man answered these phrases with praise of his aunt. But still the wish stayed with him to take money out of his purse and say: "María Juana, buy yourself some shoes. Pepa, take this and buy yourself a dress. Florentina, take this so you can all eat for a week . . ." He was on the point of carrying out his thought. At a moment when the three had run to the balcony to see who was going by, Don Juan Tafetán came over to him and said in a low voice:

"How cute they are! Aren't they? . . . Poor creatures! It seems impossible they can be so gay when . . . you can be sure they haven't eaten today."

"Don Juan, Don Juan," cried Pepilla. "Here comes your friend, Nicolasito Hernández, Easter Candle, with his three-cornered hat. He's praying to himself, for the souls of those he's sent to their graves with his usury, no doubt."

"I'll bet you won't call him by his nickname!"

"We will, too."

"Juana, close the blinds. Let's let him get by and when he's at the corner, I'll call Candle, Easter Candle! . . ."

Don Juan Tafetán ran to the balcony.

"Come on, Don José, so you can watch this fellow!"

Pepe Rey took advantage of the moment when the three girls and Don Juan were making merry on the balcony, calling Nicolasito Hernández by the nickname which made him so furious, and cautiously approaching one of the work-baskets in the room, he put in it the gold coin left over from gambling.

Then he ran to the balcony, at the very moment when the two younger girls shouted amid madcap laughter: "Easter Candle! Easter Candle!"

XIII

CASUS BELLI[37]

After this prank, the girls launched into a long conversation with the men concerning the happenings and the people in the city. The engineer, fearing that his gift might be discovered in his presence, wanted to leave, to the great disappointment of the Troyas. One of them, who had left the room, came back saying:

"Suspiritos is outdoors now hanging up clothes."

"Don José ought to see her," said another.

"She's a beautiful woman. And now she's doing her hair in the style of Madrid. Come on."

They led the men to the dining-room of the house (a seldom used place) which opened onto a terrace where there were some flowers in pots and various articles of abandoned and broken furniture. From there they could see into the deep patio of a neighboring house with a gallery full of green vines and potted flowers beautifully cared for. Everything there indicated the dwelling of modest, neat, and industrious people.

Going to the edge of the flat roof, the Troya girls stared at the neighboring house, and, imposing silence

---

[37] Latin for "A cause for war."

on the men, they retreated to the part of the terrace where they could not look down, and were in no danger of being seen.

"Now she's going out of the pantry with a dish of peas," said María Juana, stretching her neck a little in order to see.

"Bing!" exclaimed another, tossing a pebble.

The sound of the projectile striking the panes of the glassed-in porch was heard, followed by an angry voice which cried:

"Now they've broken another pane, those—"

The three of them, hidden in a corner of the terrace, next to the two gentlemen, choked down their laughter.

"Señora Suspiritos is very angry," said Rey. "Why do you call her that?"

"Because when she talks she sighs with every word, even though she wants for nothing; she's a great complainer."

There was a moment of silence in the house below. Pepita Troya watched cautiously.

"Here she comes again," she murmured in a low voice, demanding silence. "María, give me an orange. Let's see . . . bing! . . . there it goes."

"You missed. It fell on the ground."

"Let's see . . . if I can . . . Let's wait until she goes out of the pantry again."

"Now! She's going out now. Get ready, Florentina."

"One, two, three! Bang!"

A cry of pain was heard below, a curse, an exclamation in a male voice, for it was a man whom she had hit. Pepe clearly made out these words:

"The deuce! They've knocked a hole in my head, those . . . Jacinto! Jacinto! What kind of a neighborhood is this?"

"Jesus, Mary, and Joseph, what have I done!" ex-

claimed Florentina, full of consternation. "I hit Señor
Don Inocencio on the head."

"The Father Confessor?" asked Pepe.

"Yes."

"Does he live in that house?"

"Where else would he live?"

"And that lady of the sighs . . . ?"

"She's his niece, his housekeeper, or whatever. We
tease her because she's very tiresome. But we're not in
the habit of playing jokes on the Confessor."

While these words were being spoken very rapidly,
Pepe Rey saw a window open in the bombarded house,
facing the terrace, and very close to him. He saw a
smiling face, a face he knew, a face which astounded
him and filled him with chagrin. He turned pale and
shaken. It was Jacintito who had opened the window of
his study, interrupting his serious work and showing
himself with a pen behind his ear. His modest, fresh,
rosy countenance gave him the look of the breaking dawn.

"Good afternoon, Señor Don José," he said gaily.

The voice from below shouted again: "Jacinto,
Jacinto!"

"I'm coming. I was speaking to a friend . . ."

"Let's go, let's go," cried Florentina fearfully. "The
Father Confessor is going up to Don Nominavite's room
and he'll bless us out."

"Yes, let's go. Close the dining-room door."

They left the terrace in a troupe.

"You should have foreseen that Jacinto would see
you from his temple of wisdom," said Tafetán.

"Don Nominavite is our friend," replied one of them.
"From his temple of learning he whispers lots of endearments and he throws us kisses, too."

"Jacinto?" asked the engineer. "What kind of nickname have you given him?"

"Don Nominavite . . ."[38]

The three burst out laughing.

"We call him that because he's very wise."

"No, because when we were little, he was little, too; . . . we used to go out on the terrace to play then, and we'd hear him studying his lessons aloud."

"Yes, he used to be singing all day long."

"Declining, girl. That's it. He used to go on like this: Nominavite, *rosa*; Genivite, Davite, Acusavite."

"I suppose I must have my nickname, too," said Pepe Rey.

"Let María Juana tell him," answered Florentina, hiding herself.

"I? . . . You tell him, Pepa."

"You have no name yet, Don José."

"But I shall have. I promise I'll find it out before I'm confirmed,"[39] stated the youth, getting ready to leave.

"But must you go?"

"Yes. You've wasted enough time. To work, girls. This business of throwing stones at the neighbors and the passersby is no proper occupation for such pretty and deserving young girls . . . so long, then . . ."

And without waiting for more protests nor paying attention to the girls' civilities, he rushed out of the house, leaving Don Juan Tafetán there alone.

The scene he had witnessed; the indignity to the canon; the inopportune appearance of the little scholar, increased the confusion, apprehension, and dark forebodings churning in the mind of the poor engineer. With all his heart he regretted having entered the Troyas' house, and he roamed the streets of the town resolved

---

38 The girls' mispronunciation of "Nominative". See *genivito* for "Genitive", *davito* for "Dative", etc.

39 This refers to the practice in the Catholic Church of taking a name at confirmation.

to employ his time better as long as his hypochondria stayed with him.

He visited the market, Tripería Street, where the main stores were; noticed the various manifestations of industry and commerce in the great Orbajosa, and as he found nothing there but new sources of boredom, he strolled toward the promenade of the Descalzas, but saw nothing there but some stray dogs, for owing to the nagging wind which was blowing, both ladies and gentlemen had stayed at home. He went to the drugstore, where several ruminant progressives met to talk. They would chew on a subject for ever and ever; but he was bored there, too. At last he passed by the Cathedral where he heard the organ and the fine voices of the choir. He went in and knelt before the main altar, recalling the warnings his aunt had given him regarding his demeanor inside the church. Then he visited a chapel, and was preparing to enter another, when an acolyte, or beadle (whose task it was to chase dogs out of the church) approached him and in very rude manner and with unseemly language, spoke to him:

"His Grace says for you to beat it out to the street."

The engineer felt the blood rush to his head. Without a word, he obeyed. Driven by superior force or his own boredom from everywhere, he had no recourse but to go to his aunt's house where there awaited him:

1. Uncle Licurgo to notify him of a second suit. 2. Don Cayetano to read him a new excerpt from his speech on the genealogy of Orbajosa. 3. Caballuco, on an undisclosed matter. 4. Doña Perfecta, with her benevolent smile, for a purpose which shall appear in the next chapter.

XIV

DISCORD GROWS APACE

A new attempt to see his cousin Rosario having failed at the end of the afternoon, Pepe Rey secluded himself in his room to write letters, but could not rid his mind of a fixed idea.

"Tonight or tomorrow," he said, "this must end one way or another."

When he went down to supper, Doña Perfecta came over to him in the dining-room, saying without any preliminaries:

"Dear Pepe, don't worry; I'll calm down Señor Don Inocencio . . . I know all about it. María Remedios, who just left here, told me the whole story."

The lady's face radiated satisfaction, like that of an artist proud of his work.

"What?"

"I'll forgive you, dear. You probably had a few drinks in the Casino, didn't you? This is what comes of keeping bad company. Don Juan Tafetán! The Troya girls! That's shocking, terrible. Have you thought it over well?"

"I have thought it all over, señora," replied Pepe, determined not to get into any arguments with his aunt.

"I'll take good care not to write your father about what you've done."

"Write him whatever you please."

"Come, you'll defend yourself by giving the lie to it?"

"I'll give the lie to nothing."

"Then you must confess that you were in those girls' house . . ."

"I was."

"And that you gave them a gold piece, for, according to what María Remedios tells me, Florentina went down to the Estramaduran's store this afternoon to change a half *onza*. They couldn't have earned it with their sewing. You were in the house today, so—"

"Then I gave it to them. Precisely."

"You don't deny it?"

"Why should I deny it? I think I can do whatever suits me with my money."

"But surely you'll claim you didn't throw stones at the Father Confessor."

"I do not throw stones."

"I mean that in your presence they . . ."

"That is another matter."

"And they insulted poor María Remedios."

"I don't deny that either."

"Then how do you justify your conduct? Pepe . . . For Heaven's sake. You don't say a word. You're not sorry. You don't protest. You don't—"

"Not at all. Absolutely not at all, señora."

"You don't even try to make amends to me."

"I haven't offended you . . ."

"Why, the only thing left for you to do is to take that stick and beat me."

"I don't beat people."

"What a lack of respect! What . . . Aren't you eating supper?"

"I'll eat supper."

There came a pause that lasted more than a quarter of an hour. Don Cayetano, Doña Perfecta, and Pepe Rey ate in silence. This was interrupted when Don Inocencio entered the dining-room.

"How sorry I was, my dear Señor Don José! . . . Believe me I was truly sorry," he said, holding out his hand to the young man and staring at him with a sorrowful mien.

The engineer was at a loss to reply, so great was his confusion.

"I'm referring to the happenings of this afternoon."

"Oh! . . . yes."

"To your expulsion from the hallowed precincts of the Cathedral."

"The Bishop," said Pepe Rey, "should think twice before throwing a Christian out of the church."

"True enough. I don't know who has put it into His Grace's head that you're a very low-living man. I don't know who told him that you brag everywhere about your atheism, that you make fun of sacred things and persons, and that you're even planning to tear down the Cathedral to build a huge tar-factory out of its stones. I've tried to tell him otherwise. But His Grace is rather stubborn."

"Thank you for your kindness."

"The Father Confessor has no reason to show you such consideration. They almost laid him out this afternoon."

"Nonsense! . . . What of it?" said the priest, laughing. "Does anyone here pay attention to mischievousness? . . . I'll bet María Remedios was here with her story. I forbade her to, I strictly forbade her to. The thing is of no importance in itself, is it, Señor de Rey?"

"Not if you don't think so . . ."

"That's what I think. Childish pranks . . . Whatever the moderns say, youth is inclined to viciousness and to vicious acts. Señor Don José, although a greatly gifted person, could not be perfect. What is so unusual about those charming girls seducing him and then, after getting money out of him, making him their accomplice in their shameless and criminal assaults on the neighbors? My dear friend, I'm not offended by the painful part I played in this afternoon's games," he added, lifting a hand to the injured spot, "nor shall I embarrass you at all by harking back to such a disagreeable incident. I was truly pained to learn that María Remedios had come here to tell everything . . . My niece is quite a gossip . . . ! I'll bet she told you about the gold coin, too, and your frolics with the girls on the terrace, and the running and the pinching, and Don Tafetán's capers . . . Bah! Such things should be kept quiet."

Pepe Rey did not know which embarrassed him the more, his aunt's severity or the condescending hypocrisy of the canon.

"Why shouldn't they be known?" demanded the señora. "He doesn't seem to be ashamed of his conduct. Let everyone know about it. Only from my dear daughter must it be kept secret, for outbursts of anger are to be avoided in her present nervous state."

"Come, come, señora. It's not so serious as all that," continued the Father Confessor. "In my opinion, it's best not to talk any more about the matter, and when the one who was struck by the stone can say that, everyone else should consider himself satisfied . . . That blow was no joke, Señor Don José, for I thought they had laid my head open and my brains were falling out."

"I'm so sorry about that incident! . . ." stammered Pepe Rey. "It truly grieves me, even though I wasn't taking any part . . ."

"Your visit to those Troya women will be the talk of the town," said the canon. "We're not in Madrid, sir. We're not in that sinkhole of corruption and scandal here . . ."

"There you can visit the vilest places without anyone's knowing about it," declared Doña Perfecta.

"Here we watch one another carefully," Don Inocencio

went on. "We take notice of everything the neighbors do. With such a system of vigilance, the public morality is kept at a high level . . . Believe me, my friend, believe me, and I don't say this to embarrass you: you're the first gentleman in your position who, in broad daylight . . . the first. Yes, sir . . . *Troiae qui primus ab oris.*"[40]

He burst out laughing, slapping the engineer on the back as a token of friendship and benevolence.

"How grateful I am," said the young man, hiding his anger beneath words he considered an appropriate answer to the covert irony of his interlocutors, "to see such generosity and tolerance, when, for my criminal conduct, I deserve . . ."

"Why not? Can a person of our own blood, who bears our name, be treated like just anyone? You're my nephew, you're the son of the best and most saintly of men, my dear brother Juan, and that is enough. Yesterday afternoon the Bishop's secretary was here to tell me that His Grace is very displeased that I have you in my house."

"He went that far?" murmured the canon.

"That far. I replied that with all the respect which the Bishop merits from me, and for all that I love and revere him, my nephew is my nephew and I cannot throw him out of my house."

"This is a new oddity I find in this country," said Pepe Rey, pale with anger. "Seemingly, the Bishop rules other people's households here."

"He is a pious man. He is so fond of me that he imagines . . . he imagines that you're going to communicate your atheism to us, your heedlessness, your strange ideas . . . I've told him repeatedly that at heart, you're good."

---

40 "Who first came from the shores of Troy." From the opening lines of Virgil's *Aeneid.*

"Some concession must be made to unusual talent," declared Don Inocencio.

"This morning when I was in the Cirujedas' house, heavens! You can't imagine what a state my head was in . . . You'd come to tear down the Cathedral. You were sent by the English Protestants to preach heresy in Spain. You spent the entire night gambling in the Casino. You were drunk when you left . . . 'But, ladies,' I said to them, 'Do you think I'd send my nephew to the hotel?' Furthermore, they're wrong about your drinking, and I didn't know until today that you gambled."

Pepe Rey was in that state of mind where even the most prudent man feels raging within him a fire and a blind and brutal force urging him to strangle, strike, break heads, and crush bones. But Doña Perfecta was a lady, and his aunt besides; Don Inocencio was an old man and a priest. Moreover, violent acts are in bad taste and not proper for well-bred Christians. There remained only the recourse of giving vent to his suppressed fury through words, correctly phrased and not unworthy of him. But even this final recourse seemed premature to him; in his judgment, he must not speak them until the moment he left that house and Orbajosa for good. Conquering his furious impulse, he remained silent.

Jacinto arrived as supper was ending.

"Good evening, Señor Don José," he said, holding out his hand to the young man. "You and your friends wouldn't let me work this afternoon. I couldn't write a single line. And I had a lot to do . . ."

"I'm so sorry, Jacinto. But according to what they told me, you sometimes accompany them in their games and frolics."

"I!" exclaimed the youth, blushing violently. "Nonsense! You know Tafetán never speaks a word of truth . . . But is it true, Señor de Rey, that you're going away?"

"Is that what they're saying?"

"Yes. I heard it at the Casino and in Don Lorenzo Ruiz's house."

Rey stared for a time at the fresh features of Don Nominavite, then said:

"Well, it's not true. My aunt is very pleased with me, she despises the slanders the Orbajosans are spreading about me . . . And she will not order me out of her house even though the Bishop insists upon it."

"Order you out! . . . Never. What would your father say?"

"But in spite of your goodness, dear Aunt, in spite of the cordial friendship of the canon, perhaps I shall decide to leave."

"To leave!"

"You'll leave!"

A peculiar light shone in Doña Perfecta's eyes. The canon could not hide his joy, in spite of being a man well versed in dissimulation.

"Yes. Perhaps this very night."

"But how hasty you are, dear! . . . Why don't you wait at least until tomorrow morning? . . . Let's see . . . Juan, go and call Uncle Licurgo to get the saddle-horses ready . . . I suppose you'll want some lunch . . . Nicolasa! . . . that piece of veal that's on the sideboard . . . Librada, the gentleman's clothes . . ."

"No. I can't believe that you've made up your mind so suddenly," said Don Cayetano, thinking himself obliged to take some part in the discussion.

"But you'll come back . . . won't you?" asked the canon.

"What time does the train leave in the morning?" asked Doña Perfecta, her eyes alight with the feverish impatience in her overjoyed heart.

"Yes, I'm going away this very night."

"But, man, there's no moon."

In the soul of Doña Perfecta, in the soul of the
Father Confessor, in the young soul of the little scholar,
these words "this very night" echoed like a celestial
harmony.

"Of course you'll come back, dear Pepe . . . I wrote
your father, your excellent father, today—" said Doña
Perfecta, with all the facial symptoms of one about to
shed a tear.

"I'd like to trouble you with some orders," remarked
the savant.

"This will give me a chance to order the missing
volume from the work of the Abbé Gaume,"[41] declared
the little lawyer.

"Goodness me, Pepe, what whims and impulses you
have," murmured the señora, smiling, her eyes fixed on
the dining-room door. "But I forgot to tell you that
Caballuco is waiting. He wants to speak to you."

XV

IT GROWS UNTIL WAR
IS DECLARED

Everyone looked toward the door, where the imposing
figure of the Centaur appeared—serious, frowning, embarrassed at his own efforts to greet them with friendliness, handsomely savage, but twisted up by the violent
effort he was making to smile politely, to walk softly,
and to hold his herculean arms in a proper posture.

[41] The Abbé Jean-Joseph Gaume (1802-1879), a French writer
of works on religion.

"Come in, Señor Ramos," said Pepe Rey.

"No, no," objected Doña Perfecta. "What he has to say to you is all nonsense."

"Let him say it."

"I can't permit such ridiculous matters to be aired in my house . . ."

"What do you want with me, Señor Ramos?"

Caballuco mumbled some words.

"Enough, enough," said Doña Perfecta, laughing. "Don't bother my nephew. Pepe, pay no attention to this rascal . . . Would you like me to tell you the reason for the great Caballuco's anger?"

"Anger?" said the Father Confessor, leaning back in his armchair and laughing loudly and expansively, "I can well imagine!"

"I'd like to say it to Señor Don José," growled the formidable horseman.

"Be quiet, man, for heaven's sake; don't split our eardrums."

"Señor Caballuco, it's no wonder the gentlemen from the Court can cut out the rough riders of these savage lands . . ." declared the canon.

"In a word, Pepe, the point is this: Caballuco is I don't know what—" Laughter prevented him from going on.

"The I don't know what," continued Don Inocencio, "of one of the Troya girls, of Mariquita Juana, unless I'm mistaken."

"He's jealous! The finest creature in the world, after his horse, is Mariquilla Troya."

"Heavens above!" exclaimed the señora. "Poor Cristóbal! Did you think that a man like my nephew . . . ? Come, what were you going to say to him? Speak up."

"Señor Don José and I will talk later," brusquely replied the bravo of the locality.

Without another word he left.

Soon afterward, Pepe Rey went out of the dining-room toward his room. On the veranda he found himself face to face with his Trojan antagonist, and he could not suppress his laughter at the malignant severity of the offended suitor.

"A word with you," said the latter, planting himself insolently in front of the engineer. "Do you know who I am?"

So saying, he laid a heavy hand on the young man's shoulder, with such impudent familiarity that the latter could do no less than shake it off abruptly.

"You don't have to crush me."

The bully, disconcerted for a moment, quickly recovered and stared at Rey with provocative boldness, repeating his refrain:

"Do you know who I am?"

"Yes, I know that you're a brute."

He pushed the man brusquely aside and entered his room. At that moment our unfortunate friend's state of mind was such as to demand action on some short and simple project such as breaking Caballuco's head straightaway; bidding farewell immediately to his aunt, with stern but courteous words which would touch her heart; bidding a frigid good-bye to the canon, embracing the inoffensive Don Cayetano; and finally, winding it all up with a thrashing for Uncle Licurgo. Then to leave Orbajosa that very night and shake the dust from his shoes at the gates of the city.

But in the midst of so much bitterness, the thoughts of the persecuted young man could not leave out of account another unfortunate, who, he imagined, was in a more painful and anxious state than his own. Behind the engineer, a maid entered the room.

"Did you give her my message?"

"Yes, sir, and she gave me this."

Rey took from the girl's hand a slip of newspaper on the margin of which he read these words: "They say you're leaving. I shall die."

When he want back to the dining-room, Uncle Licurgo appeared at the door, asking:

"What time will you need the horse?"

"No time," answered Rey quickly.

"Aren't you going tonight then?" asked Doña Perfecta. "It's better to wait until tomorrow . . ."

"Not then, either."

"Well, when?"

"We shall see," said the young man coldly as he looked at his aunt with imperturbable calm. "At the moment I'm not intending to go away."

His eyes issued a formidable challenge. Doña Perfecta turned first red, then pale. She looked at the canon, who had taken off his gold-rimmed glasses to polish them, and then fixed her gaze successively on the others who were in the room, including Caballuco, who had just entered and seated himself on the edge of a chair. Doña Perfecta looked at them as a general runs his eye over his favorite troops. Then she examined the calm and thoughtful face of her nephew, that enemy who had strategically and unexpectedly reappeared when he was thought to be in utter rout.

Ah! blood, destruction, and desolation! . . . A great battle was shaping up.

XVI

NIGHT

Orbajosa slept. The sad little street lamps were sending forth their last gleams at intersections and in side streets, like tired eyes struggling to sleep. Wrapped in their capes, the vagabonds, the rounders, and the gamblers glided through the feeble light. The still peace of the historic city was broken only by the croaking of a drunk or the song of a lover. Soon the *Ave Maria Purisima*[42] of the wine-soaked watchman sounded like a sickly plaint of the sleeping town.

In Doña Perfecta's house there was silence, too. It was broken only by a conversation in the library between Don Cayetano and Pepe Rey. The savant was seated in repose in the armchair before his desk, which was covered with innumerable papers containing notes, abstracts, and references. Rey's eyes were fixed on the overflowing pile, but his thoughts were doubtless winging to regions far away from that erudition.

"Perfecta," said the antiquarian, "is an excellent woman; but she has the defect of being scandalized by every insignificant thing. My friend, in these provincial towns one pays dearly for the smallest slip. I find nothing out-of-the-way in your going to the Troyas' house. I suspect that under cover of his cloak of benevolence, Don Inocencio is something of a mischief-maker. What business is it of his?"

"Don Cayetano, we've reached a point where it's

---

[42] The beginning of the call of the night watchmen in Spain, announcing the hours.

urgent to take strong measures. I need to see Rosario and talk to her."

"Well, then, see her."

"They won't let me," replied the engineer, striking the desk with his fist. "Rosario is kept a prisoner."

"Kept a prisoner!" cried the savant with incredulity. "In truth I don't like the way she looks, her face, and the stupor in her lovely eyes. She's sad, she hardly speaks, she cries . . . Don José, my friend I'm very much afraid that girl may be the victim of the terrible illness which has claimed so many victims in my family."

"Terrible illness! What is it?"

"Madness . . . or mania, rather. There hasn't been a single one in the family who was free of it. I, I am the only one who has managed to escape it."

"You! . . . Manias aside," said Pepe Ray impatiently, "I want to see Rosario."

"Nothing could be more natural. But the isolation in which her mother keeps her is a health measure, dear Pepe, the only one employed with any success with all the persons in my family. Just consider that the person whose presence and voice must make the deepest impression on the delicate nervous system of Rosarito is the chosen of her heart."

"In spite of all that," insisted Pepe. "I want to see her."

"Perhaps Perfecta will not oppose it," said the savant, turning his attention to his notes and papers. "I don't want to interfere in other people's affairs."

The engineer, seeing that he could not make an ally of the good Polentinos, rose to leave.

"You want to work, and I don't want to disturb you."

"No. I've time enough. Look at the pile of excellent data I've compiled today. Listen . . . 'In 1537 a resident of Orbajosa named Bartolomé del Hoyo went to Civitavecchia in the galleys of the Marquess of Castel-Rodrigo.'

Again: 'In the same year two brothers, also sons of Orbajosa, named Juan and Rodrigo González del Arco, sailed with the six ships which left Maestricht the 20th of February, and in the latitude of Calais encountered an English vessel and the Flemish ones commanded by Van-Owen . . .' In short, that was an important achievement by our Navy. I've discovered that an Orbajosan, a certain Mateo Díaz Coronel, an ensign in the Guard, was the man who in 1709 wrote and had printed in Valencia, the *Metrical Encomium, Funeral Song, Elegiac Lyric, Numerical Description, Glorious Sufferings, and Anguished Glories of the Queen of the Angels.* I own a beautiful copy of this work which is worth all the gold in Peru . . . Another Orbajosan is author of that famous *Treatise on the Various Styles of Horsemanship,* which I showed you yesterday. And, to sum up, I never take a step through the labyrinth of unpublished history without stumbling upon some illustrious fellow-townsman. I intend to rescue all those names from the undeserved obscurity and oblivion where they languish. What an unalloyed joy it is, dear Pepe, to bring back all the luster to the glories, now epic, now literary, of the land of our birth! What better use can a man make of the slight intelligence bestowed by Heaven, of the fortune he may have inherited, and of the brief time that even the most long-lived man can count on . . . Thanks to me, it will be clear that Orbajosa is the illustrious cradle of Spanish genius. But what am I saying? Isn't their illustrious stock already widely recognized in the nobility, the chivalry of the present *urbsaugustine* generation? We know of few localities where the plants and shrubs of the virtues grow more luxuriantly, free from the noxious weeds of vice. Here all is peace, mutual respect, Christian humility. Charity is practiced here as in the times of the Gospel; here envy is unknown; here crimi-

nal passions are unknown, and if you hear talk about
thieves and murderers, you may be sure they are not
sons of this noble land, or if so, that they belong to the
number of those unfortunates who are led astray by
demagogic preachments. You will see here the national
character in all its purity—upright, honorable, incor-
ruptible, clean, simple, patriarchal, hospitable, generous
. . . That is why I so enjoy living in this peaceful
solitude, far from the labyrinths of the city where falseness and vice reign. That is why my many friends in
Madrid have been unable to lure me hence; that is why
I am living in the sweet company of my loyal fellow-
citizens and my books, always breathing this healthful
air of honesty which is disappearing little by little in our
Spain and now exists only among the humble, Christian
cities which have learned how to conserve it through
the virtues they emanate. You wouldn't believe it, dear
Pepe, but this isolation has done a great deal to free me
from my family's terrible congenital disease. Like my
brothers and my father, I used to suffer in my youth
from a dreadful propensity toward the most absurd
manias. But here I am so wonderfully cured that I can
recognize that kind of illness only when I see it in others.
That is why my little niece worries me so much."

"I'm delighted that the air of Orbajosa has preserved
you," said Rey, unable to suppress a mood of mockery
which arose by some strange quirk in the midst of his
sadness. "It has proved so bad for me that I think if I
stay here I'll soon be a madman. With which I shall say
good night, and get a lot of work done."

"Good night."

He went to his room, but feeling no need for sleep
or physical repose, but on the contrary, a strong excitement which drove him to keep moving and wandering,
worrying and prowling, he strode from one end of the

room to another. Then he opened the window which
overlooked the garden, and with his elbows on the
sill, contemplated the immense blackness of the night.
He could see nothing. But a man lost in thought sees
everything, and Rey, with his eyes fixed on the darkness,
stared at the variegated landscape of his misfortunes as
if they were unrolling before him. The shadows denied
him sight of the flowers of the earth and those of the
sky, which are the stars. The absolute absence of light
produced the effect of illusory movement in the mass of
trees which seemed to stretch away, lazily retreating and
curling back like waves on a sea of shadows. A vast ebb
and flow, a struggle between dimly seen forces, shook
the silent sphere. Contemplating that strange projection
of his spirit into the night, the mathematician thought:

"It will be a terrible battle. We shall see who comes
out the winner."

The insect life of the night buzzed in his ears, speaking mysterious words. Here a harsh chirping; there a
clicking like that of the tongue; beyond, sad murmurings;
still farther away, a tinkling like that of a bell hanging
around the neck of a wandering animal. Suddenly Rey
heard a strange sound, a rapid beating note which only
the tongue and lips of humans can make, an exhalation
that pierced his mind like lightning. He felt that rapid
hissing, repeated again and again, growing in intensity
as if it coiled inside him. He stared all around him toward
the upper part of the house, and he thought he saw an
object like a white bird beating its wings at a window.
For an instant the idea of the phoenix, the dove, the
grey heron crossed the excited mind of Pepe Rey . . .
even though the bird was nothing more than a handkerchief.

The engineer vaulted through the window into the
garden. Looking carefully, he saw the hand and face

of his cousin. He thought he could make out the traditional motion imposing silence by a finger to the lips. Then the lovely shadow waved an arm downward, and disappeared. Pepe re-entered his room quickly, and, trying not make any noise, he walked to the veranda, slowly advancing along it. He felt his heart pounding as if a hammer were beating within his chest. He waited a little . . . finally he distinctly heard light footfalls on the treads of the stairs. One, two, three . . . Slippers would make that sound.

He went toward it, wrapped in almost complete darkness, and stretched out his arms to lend aid to the descending girl. A great and exalted tenderness rose in his heart. But, why deny it, beneath that sweet feeling surged another, like an evil inspiration—a terrible desire for revenge. The descending footsteps were nearer. Pepe Rey went forward, and hands groping in the darkness touched him. The four hands joined in a tight clasp.

XVII

LIGHT IN THE DARKNESS

The veranda was long and wide. At one end was the door of the room where the engineer was lodged; in the center, that of the dining-room; at the far end was the stairway and a huge, locked door, with a doorstep at the entrance. That was the doorway to a chapel where the Polentinos kept their family *lares*. Occasionally the holy sacrifice of the Mass was enacted there.

Rosario drew her cousin toward the door of the chapel and let herself sink down on the doorstep.

"Here?" murmured Pepe Rey.

He sensed by the movement of Rosario's right hand that she was crossing herself.

"Rosario, my love, thank you for letting me see you!" he cried, holding her ardently in his arms.

He felt the girl's cold fingers on his lips, enjoining silence. He kissed them frantically.

"You're freezing, Rosario. Why are you trembling so?"

Her teeth were chattering and her whole body was shaking in a feverish tremor. Rey felt the burning warmth of his cousin's face against his cheek and exclaimed in alarm:

"Your forehead is like a volcano. You have a fever."

"A high fever."

"Are you really sick, then?"

"Yes."

"And you came out . . ."

"To see you."

The engineer held her in his arms to warm her; but it was not enough.

"Wait," he said, getting up quickly. "I'm going to my room to fetch a steamer rug."

"Turn out the light, Pepe."

Rey had left the light burning in his room, through the door of which came a faint glow, illuminating the veranda. He returned immediately. The darkness was now deep. By feeling along the walls, he came back to where his cousin was. They met again and he wrapped her carefully from head to foot.

"You're better now, my child!"

"Yes, much better . . . with you."

"With me . . . forever," cried the young man rapturously.

But he felt her withdraw from his arms and get up.

"What are you doing?"

He heard the sound of a small piece of iron. Rosario was fitting a key into the invisible lock, and she cautiously opened the door on the threshold of which they had been sitting. A faint odor of dampness, characteristic of any long-closed room, came from that spot which was as dark as the grave. Pepe Rey felt himself pulled forward by the hand, and his cousin's voice said faintly:

"Come in."

They took several steps. He felt that he was being led into unknown Elysian fields by an angel of the night. She was groping. Finally her sweet voice came again, murmuring:

"Sit down."

They were next to a wooden bench. Both seated themselves. Pepe Rey again took her in his arms. As he did so, he hit his head against some hard object.

"What is this?"

"The feet."

"What did you say, Rosario?"

"The feet of the Divine Jesus, the image of **Christ** crucified, who is adored in my house."

Pepe Rey felt something like a cold lance thrust through his heart.

"Kiss them," said the girl imperiously.

The mathematician kissed the icy feet of the sacred image.

"Pepe," asked the girl, ardently pressing her cousin's hands, "do you believe in God?"

"Rosario! What are you talking about? What nonsense are you thinking?" answered her cousin in perplexity.

"Answer me!"

Pepe Rey felt something wet on his hands.

"Why are you crying?" he said, deeply disturbed. "Rosario, you're killing me with your absurd doubts. Of course I believe in God! Do you doubt that?"

"I don't. But everyone says you're an atheist."

"You'd be diminished in my eyes, you'd lose your halo of purity and esteem, if you were to believe such a stupid thing."

"I've protested from the bottom of my heart against such slander, hearing you called an atheist, even though I couldn't rationally prove the contrary. You couldn't be an atheist. Inside myself, I feel a vivid and strong sense of your faith, as I do of my own."

"How well you've put it! Then, why do you ask me if I believe in God?"

"Because I wanted to hear it from your own lips, and to be glad as I heard you say it. I haven't heard your voice for such a long time! . . . What joy could be greater than to hear it again, after such a long silence, saying, 'I believe in God'?"

"Even men of evil believe in Him, Rosario. If there are atheists, which I doubt, they are the slanderers and schemers with which this world is infested . . . To me, intrigues and slanders matter very little. And if you can rise above them and close your heart to the feeling of discord which some treacherous hand is trying to stir up in you, nothing can prevent our happiness."

"But what is happening to us? Pepe, dear Pepe . . . do you believe in the Devil?"

The engineer was silent. The darkness in the chapel hid from Rosario the smile with which her cousin received such an odd question.

"I'd have to believe in him," he said at last.

"What is happening to us? Mother won't let me see you. But she doesn't speak harshly of you, except about atheism. She keeps telling me to wait; that you will decide; that you're going away, that you'll come back . . . Tell me frankly . . . Have you formed a bad opinion of my mother?"

"Not at all," replied Pepe with a delicacy that matched hers.

"Do you think, as I do, that she loves me very much, that she loves us both, and all she wants is our own good, and that in the end we'll win from her the consent we want?"

"If you think so, I will, too . . . Your mother adores us with all her heart . . . But, Rosario, darling, you must recognize that the Devil has entered this house."

"Don't joke," she answered lovingly. "Oh, Mother is very good. She's never said, even once, that you weren't good enough to be my husband. The only thing she's insistent about is that question of atheism . . . They say I have manias, and that now my mania is to love you with all my heart. In our family, it's the rule not to oppose directly the congenital manias we have, because they get worse if they're combatted."

"Well, I think there are good doctors at your side who've undertaken to cure you, and that they'll finally do it, my adorable little girl."

"No, no; no a thousand times!" cried Rosario, leaning her forehead on her sweetheart's chest. "I'd rather go mad with you. For you I am suffering; for you I am ill; for you I despise life and risk death . . . I can foresee it already. Tomorrow I'll be worse, I'll be sicker . . . I'll die. But I don't care!"

"You're not sick," he answered firmly. "There's nothing wrong with you but an emotional upset which naturally carries with it some slight nervous disorders. There's nothing the matter with you but the pain resulting from this awful violence they're subjecting you to. Your simple, generous heart doesn't understand it. You yield. You forgive those who are hurting you. You feel ill, and you attribute your trouble to dark, supernatural influences. You suffer in silence. You bare your innocent neck to the hangman. You let yourself be killed, and the very knife buried in your throat seems to you the thorn of a flower which pricked you in passing. Rosario, get rid of those ideas. Think of our true situation, which is serious. Look for the cause where it really is, and don't be afraid, don't yield to the mortification being inflicted upon you, sickening you in body and soul. The courage you now lack will restore your health, for you're not really sick, my darling little girl. You're . . . do you want me to tell you? You're frightened, terrified. What's happening to you is what the ancients called witchcraft because they didn't know how else to define it. Rosario, my love, have faith in me! Get up and follow me. I'll say no more."

"Ah, Pepe, my dear cousin, I think you're right," cried Rosario, bathed in tears. "Your words echo in my heart like violent blows that shake me and give me new life. Here, in this darkness where we can't see each other's faces, a light I can't describe comes from you and goes into my heart. What have you done to transform me like this? The moment I saw you, I was suddenly like a new person. Those days when I couldn't see you, I felt myself slipping back into my old insignificant self, into my old cowardice. Without you, my Pepe, I live in Limbo[43] . . . I'll do whatever you tell me to. I'll get up and follow you. We'll go together wherever you want to go. Do you know I feel quite well? You know I haven't any fever now? I feel stronger. I want to run and shout. I'm completely recovered, and I feel as though I'd increased and multiplied a hundredfold just to adore you. Pepe, you're right. I'm not sick. I'm only cowed, or rather, bewitched."

---

[43] In Catholic theology a region between Heaven and Hell, where souls destined to neither of these places exist "without suffering or glory."

"That's it, bewitched."

"Bewitched. Awful eyes look at me and leave me mute and trembling. I'm afraid. But of what? . . . You alone have the strange power to bring me out of it. I revive as I listen to you. I think if I were to die and you were to walk near my grave, I'd feel your steps in the depths of the earth. Oh, if only I could see you now! . . . But you're here, beside me, and I don't doubt that you're you . . . It's been so long since I've seen you. I was crazy. Each day I was alone seemed a century . . . They kept saying tomorrow, tomorrow, always tomorrow. At night, I'd stand at the window and console myself with the light from your room. Sometimes your shadow on the glass was like a divine apparition. I'd stretch my arms out the window, crying and screaming in my mind, but not daring to raise my voice. Then I got your message through the maid. When she gave me your letter telling me that you were going away, I felt very sad. I thought my soul was leaving my body and that I'd die by degrees. I was falling, falling like a bird wounded in flight that dies as it falls . . . Tonight, when I saw you were awake so late, I couldn't bear the longing to see, to talk to you. So I came down. I think I've used up all the daring I'll ever have in my life in a single act, this one, and from now on I'll surely be a coward . . . But you'll give me courage; you'll give me strength; you'll help me. Won't you? . . . Pepe, my dearest cousin, say yes. Tell me I'm strong, and I'll be strong. Tell me I'm not sick, and I won't be sick. I'm not now. I feel so well I could laugh at my ridiculous illnesses."

As she said this, Rosarito felt her cousin's arms clutch her frantically. She heard a cry of pain, not from her lips, but from his, for he had bowed his head and struck it violently against the feet of the Christ. In the darkness he saw stars.

In his frame of mind and with the natural hallucination brought on by dark places, it seemed to Rey not that he had bumped his head on the sacred foot, but that it had moved, admonishing him in the quickest and most eloquent manner. Half in jest, half in earnest, he raised his head and said: "Don't hit me, Lord. I won't do anything wrong."

At the same moment, Rosario took the engineer's hand, pressing it to her heart. An angelic voice, pure, sincere, and deeply stirred, said:

"Lord, whom I adore; Lord God of the world, guardian of my house and my family; Lord whom Pepe also adores, Blessed Christ who died on the Cross for our sins: Before Thee, before Thy wounded body, before Thy head crowned with thorns, I swear that this is my husband, and that after Thee, he is the one most beloved of my heart. I say and I declare that he is mine, and that I will belong to no other until death. My heart and my soul are his. Grant that the world may not oppose our happiness, and grant me the favor of this union, which I swear shall seem good in the eyes of the world as it is in my conscience."

"Rosario, you're mine," cried Pepe with exaltation. "Neither your mother nor anyone else can prevent that."

The girl let her lovely form lie limp upon her cousin's chest. She trembled in his loving, manly arms like a dove in the talons of an eagle.

Through the man's mind flashed the thought that the Devil did indeed exist and that he was it. Rosario shuddered slightly with fear—the tremor of alarm that warns of danger.

"Swear that you won't give up," said Rey worriedly, quieting her movement.

"I swear it by my father's ashes which are—"

"Where?"

"Beneath our feet."

The mathematician felt as though the granite slab under his feet were rising . . . but it was not. He thought he felt it in spite of being a man of science.

"I swear it," repeated Rosario, "by my father's ashes and by God, who is watching over us . . . May our bodies, joined as they are, rest beneath these stones when God sees fit to take us from this world."

"Yes," said Pepe Rey, deeply moved and with an inexplicable uneasiness in his heart.

They were silent for a short time. Rosario had gotten up.

"Who is it?"

She sat down again.

"You're shaking again," said Pepe. "Rosario, you're ill. Your forehead is burning."

"I feel as if I were dying," murmured the girl breathlessly. "I don't know what's the matter with me."

She fell back into her cousin's arms. As he caressed her, he noticed that the girl's face was covered with a cold sweat.

"She really is ill," he said to himself. "It was very foolish of her to come out."

He lifted her in his arms, trying to revive her, but neither her trembling nor the swoon ceased. He therefore decided to take her out of the chapel so that the fresh air might bring her to, which indeed it did. Her senses restored, Rosario displayed uneasiness at being outside her room at such an hour. The cathedral clock was striking four.

"It's very late!" cried the girl. "Let me go, Cousin. I think I can walk. Really, I'm quite sick."

"I'll go up with you."

"Oh, no, not that. I'd sooner drag myself to my room . . . Did you hear a noise?"

They stood still. Absolute silence greeted their anxious concentration.

"Don't you hear anything, Pepe?"

"Not a thing."

"Listen . . . Now I hear it again. It's a sound which may be far, very far off, or near. I don't know. It could be my mother's breathing, or the weather vane turning on the Cathedral tower. Oh, I have very sharp ears."

"Too sharp . . . Come, darling, I'll carry you upstairs in my arms."

"All right. Carry me to the top of the stairs. Then I'll go on alone. After I've rested a while, I'll be as well as ever . . . But don't you hear it?"

They paused on the first step.

"It's a metallic sound."

"Your mother's breathing?"

"No, it's not that. The sound is coming from away off. Can it be a rooster crowing?"

"It might be."

"It seems to be forming two words: 'I'm coming, I'm coming.'"

"Now, now I hear it," murmured Pepe Rey.

"It's a cry."

"It's a horn."

"A horn!"

"Yes. Go upstairs quickly. Orbajosa will be aroused . . . You can hear it clearly now. It isn't a horn, it's a bugle. The soldiers are coming."

"Soldiers!"

"I don't know why I think this military invasion may be lucky for me . . . I'm glad, Rosario. Upstairs, quickly."

"I'm glad, too. Upstairs."

He carried her up in a moment, and the two sweethearts said good-bye speaking so softly in each other's ears that they could hardly be heard.

"I'll go to the window that faces the garden to let you know I've reached my room safely. Good-bye."

"Good-bye, Rosario. Be careful not to stumble over the furniture."

"I know my way here, Cousin. We'll meet again. Come to the window of your room if you want to get my signal."

Pepe Rey did as she asked; but he waited a long time and Rosario failed to come to the window. He thought he heard excited voices on the upper floor.

XVIII

SOLDIERS

The inhabitants of Orbajosa heard that bugle echoing through the dim blur of their last dreams and opened their eyes, saying:

"Soldiers!"

Some of them, talking to themselves, half-awake, half-asleep, were muttering: "They've finally sent us that trash."

Others got up hastily, grumbling: "Let's go and see those confounded rascals."

Someone soliloquized: "We'll have to pay advance taxes . . . They'll want conscripts and contributions: we'll give them sticks and stones."

In another house they cried happily: "If only my son comes with them! . . . If only my brother will come!"

Everyone jumped out of bed, threw on his clothes, opened the windows to see the noisy regiment coming in with the first light of day. The city was sad, silent, old; the army gay, boisterous, young. As the one entered

the other, it seemed as if by some magic the mummy
was receiving the gift of life and was leaping merrily
out of its damp sarcophagus to dance around it. What
movement, what turbulence, what laughter, what joviality! Nothing is more interesting than an army. It is
the nation in all its youth and vigor. All that same nation
may contain of ineptitude, restlessness, sometimes superstition, other times blasphemy, as represented in the
individual, is submerged under the iron pressure of dis-
cipline, which makes a powerful whole of so many
insignificant little parts. At the order to break ranks, the
soldier, that is to say the individual cell, on breaking
away from the parent body, usually retains some of the
peculiar qualities—ordinary or sublime—of the army. But
this is not the rule. Breaking ranks usually means a sudden deterioration. Consequently, if an army means glory
and honor, a gathering of soldiers may be a calamity,
and towns which weep with joy and enthusiasm to see
a victorious battalion enter their confines, will moan
with fear and tremble with foreboding when the soldiers
are at liberty.

That is what happened in Orbajosa, for in those days
there were no glories to sing, no reason whatever to
weave wreaths or print triumphal banners, or record any
deeds of our brave men. For that reason, fear and dis-
trust reigned in the cathedral city, which, although very
poor, was not lacking in such treasures as hens, fruit,
money, and damsels who ran grave risks from the presence of the aforesaid disciples of Mars. Furthermore, the
home town of the Polentinos, a city far from the movement and turmoil which businesses, newspapers, railroads and other well-known agencies bring with them,
had no desire to see its calm existence disturbed.

Each time a suitable opportunity arose, Orbajosa
demonstrated a deep reluctance to submit to the central

authority which governs us for better or for worse. Recalling its ancient rights and ruminating upon them,
as the camel chews the cud of grass it has eaten the pre-
vious day, it boasted of a kind of rebellious independence, regrettable traces of anarchy which on occasion had
caused the governor of the province many headaches.

It must be borne in mind, moreover, that Orbajosa
had rebel antecedents, or better, ancestors. Undoubtedly
it retained in its lifestream certain energetic strains of
the type that in a remote age impelled it to fabulous
feats, according to the enthusiastic opinions of Don
Cayetano. In spite of its decadence, it still felt from
time to time a violent urge to great things, even though
they might prove in the end to be follies and barbarous
acts. Since it had given the world so many distinguished
sons, it doubtless hoped that its present scions—the
Caballucos, Merengues and Pelosmalos—would re-enact
the glorious, epic deeds of their ancestors.

Whenever there were insurrections in Spain, Orbajosa
made manifest that its existence on the face of the earth
had not been in vain, even though it had never served
as the theatre of a real military campaign. Its tempera-
ment, its situation, its history reduced it to the secondary
role of raising rebel bands. It treated the country to this
national fruit during the time of the *Apostólicos* in
1827,[44] during the Seven Years' War,[45] in 1848,[46] and
during other less spectacular periods in the nation's
history. Rebel bands and partisans were always popular,

---

[44] A federation of the most reactionary elements in Spain
aroused certain of the provinces to revolt.

[45] The first of the Carlist Wars. On the death of Ferdinand
VII his brother Carlos, supported by the reactionary forces of the
country, refused to recognize Ferdinand's daughter Isabel II as
heir to the throne, and this gave rise to a series of civil wars.

[46] A year of revolution in all Europe, which in Spain manifested itself in liberal uprisings against the dictatorial regime of
General Narvaez.

an unfortunate circumstance arising from the War of Independence,[47] one of those good things from which come an infinity of detestable results. *Corruptio optimi pessima.*[48] The unpopularity of anything that came to Orbajosa as a manifestation or instrument of the national government coincided with the ever-growing popularity of the rebels and guerrillas. The soldiers were always held in such low esteem there that whenever the old people told of a crime, a robbery, a murder, a rape, or any other outrage, they always added: "This happened when the soldiers came."

And now, after relating this important fact, it would be well to add that the battalions sent there in the days of our story had not come to stroll through the streets of Orbajosa. They had come for a purpose which will later be seen clearly and in detail. As an item of no slight interest, we may note that what is herein related occurred in a year neither very near nor very far from the present; likewise that Orbajosa (*urbs augusta* to the Romans, although some modern scholars considering the *ajosa* are of the opinion that it wears this little appendage because it is the home of the best garlic [*ajos*] in the world) is neither very near nor very far from Madrid; nor can we be certain whether it had its glorious origins in the north or the south, the east or the west, merely that it may be everywhere, or wherever the Spaniards turn their eyes and taste the bite of garlic.

Billeting orders were distributed through the town, and every soldier sought his assigned lodging. They were received with bad grace, and given accommodations in

---

[47] The Peninsular War (1808-1814), in which the British, Spanish and Portuguese joined forces to defeat Napoleon, who had invaded Spain.

[48] "The corruption of the best is the worst corruption." Cf. Shakespeare: "Lilies that fester smell far worse than weeds."

the most atrociously uninhabitable spot in every house. The village girls were not, in fact, altogether unhappy. But a close watch was kept over them, and it was hardly decent for them to show they were pleased at the visit of such rabble. The few soldiers who were local boys were the only ones who lived like kings. The others were considered foreigners.

At eight o'clock in the morning, a lieutenant colonel of cavalry entered the house of Doña Perfecta Polentinos with his billeting orders. The servants received him at the orders of the señora who found herself in such a wretched state of mind that she did not want to go down to meet him. She chose for his room the only available one in the house, it seemed—the one occupied by Pepe Rey.

"Let them get along as best they can," said Doña Perfecta with an expression of gall and vinegar. "And if they don't fit, let them get out into the street."

Was it to annoy the notorious nephew, or was there really no other available room in the house? We do not know, nor do the chronicles whence this true story has been drawn have a word to say on such an important question. What we do know beyond a doubt is that since the two guests were old friends, far from being annoyed at being cooped up together, they were highly pleased. They were both greatly and happily surprised when they met, and they kept asking questions and exclaiming as they marvelled at the strange chance which had brought them together in that place on that occasion.

"Pinzón! You, here! What is this? I'd no idea you were so near . . ."

"I'd heard you were in these parts, Pepe Rey. But I never thought I'd meet you in this horrible, uncivilized Orbajosa."

"A happy chance! This is the greatest, most providential luck . . . Pinzón, between you and me, we're going to do something great in this miserable town."

"And we'll have time to think it out," replied the other, sitting on the bed where the engineer was lying, "because it seems we're both going to be living in this room. What the devil kind of a house is this?"

"It's my aunt's, man. Speak with more respect. Haven't you met my aunt? . . . I'm going to get up."

"That's good, because I'm going to bed, and I sorely need to . . . What a road, friend Pepe, what a road, and what a town!"

"Tell me, are you here to set fire to Orbajosa?"

"Set fire!"

"Tell me, because maybe I'll help you."

"What a town! But what a town!" exclaimed the soldier, taking off his tunic and laying aside his sword and shoulder-straps, dispatch case, and cape. "This is the second time they've sent me here. The third time, I'll ask for my discharge, I swear it."

"Don't speak ill of these good people. But your arrival is so timely! It seems that God sent you in my hour of need, Pinzón . . . I have a big project, an adventure if you want to call it that; a plan, my friend . . . and it would have been very difficult to carry it out without you. Just a moment ago I was going crazy with worry, and I was saying: 'If only I had a friend here, one good friend . . . !' "

"Project, plan, adventure . . . Mr. Mathematician, it's one or the other: either you're going up in a balloon, or it's a love affair."

"It's serious . . . very serious. Go to bed, sleep a while, and later we'll talk."

"I'll go to bed, but I won't sleep. You can tell me all you want to. The only thing I ask is to talk as little as possible about Orbajosa."

"But it's precisely about Orbajosa that I want to talk to you. Are you prejudiced, too, against this cradle of so many illustrious men?"

"Those garlic-eaters! We call them the garlic-eaters. They can be as illustrious as you like. But to me they reek like the local product. Here's a town dominated by people who teach suspicion, superstition and hatred of the whole human race. When we have time, I'll tell you something that happened to me here last year . . . an episode half-funny, half-terrible . . . When I tell you, you'll laugh and I'll send off sparks of anger . . . But, anyhow, let the dead past bury its dead."

"There's nothing funny about what's happening to me."

"But I have several reasons for hating this town. You must know that some ruthless guerrillas murdered my father here in '48. He was a brigadier who had left the service. The governor summoned him, and as he was passing through Villahorrenda on his way to Madrid, he was seized by half a dozen ruffians . . . There were several dynasties of guerrillas here. The Aceros, the Caballucos, the Pelosmalos . . . a prisonful let loose, as it was phrased by someone who knew very well what he was talking about."

"I presume that the arrival of two regiments with some cavalry was not for the pleasure of visiting these lovely gardens?"

"Far from it! We came to search the countryside. There are numerous caches of arms. The Government doesn't care to dissolve most of the Town Councils without first distributing a few companies through these towns. Since there is so much rebel agitation in this section; since two nearby provinces are already infested; and since, moreover, this municipal district of Orbajosa has such a brilliant history in the civil wars, it's feared that the local bravos will take to the roads and plunder everyone they meet."

"A wise precaution! But I believe that unless these people die and are born again, unless rocks can change their shape, there will be no peace in Orbajosa."

"That's my opinion, too," said the soldier, lighting a cigarette. "Don't you see, the rebels are the fair-haired boys of Orbajosa? You'll find all those who laid waste the region in 1848 and at other times, or, if not they, then their sons, ensconced in the inspectors' offices, at the toll gates, in the Town Council, in the mail service. Some of them are constables, sacristans, bailiffs. Some have become formidable political leaders, and they're the ones who rig the elections and exercise power in Madrid; they distribute the spoils . . . In short, it's all enough to make you shudder."

"Tell me, aren't the rebel chiefs likely to carry out some piece of villainy these days? If that should happen, you'd destroy the town, and I'd help you."

"If only it were left to me! . . . They'll play their part," said Pinzón, "because the guerrilla bands in these two provinces are growing like God's curse. And just between us two, friend Rey, I don't see the end of this. Some people laugh and say there can't be another civil war like the past one. They don't know the country; they don't know Orbajosa and its people. I maintain that this thing that's starting now drags a long tail, and that we'll see another cruel and bloody struggle that will last I don't know how long. What do you think?"

"My friend, in Madrid I used to laugh at anyone who talked about the possibility of a civil war as long and terrible as the Carlist Wars; but now, since I've been here . . ."

"You have to bury yourself in these charming places,

see these people close at hand and listen to them talk, to know which way the wind blows."

"You're right . . . Without being able to explain to myself the basis of my ideas, ever since I've been here I have in fact seen things differently, and I believe in the possibility of a long and cruel war."

"Exactly."

"But I'm more worried about a private than a public war here. I'm already in it and I began hostilities a little while ago."

"You said this is your aunt's house? What's her name?"

"Doña Perfecta Rey de Polentinos."

"Oh! I know her by name. She's a fine person, the only one I've never heard the garlic-eaters talk ill about. When I was here before I heard her goodness, her charity, her virtues extolled everywhere."

"Yes, my aunt's a very good woman, very kind," murmured Rey.

For a moment he was thoughtful.

"Now I remember!" exclaimed Pinzón suddenly. "How it all hangs together! . . . Yes, in Madrid, they told me you were going to marry a cousin. Now it comes out. Is she the beautiful, adorable Rosarito?"

"Pinzón, we'll talk about it at length."

"I imagine there are stumbling-blocks."

"Worse than that. There are awful battles. I need powerful, clever friends with initiative and a lot of experience in difficult negotiations—friends with great shrewdness and courage."

"That's even more serious than a challenge to a duel, man."

"Much more serious. It's easy enough to fight another man. But with women, with invisible enemies working in the dark, it's impossible."

"Go on, I'm all ears."

Lieutenant Colonel Pinzón was stretched out to his full length on the bed, resting. Pepe Rey drew up a chair, and leaning his elbow on the bed, head on hand, he began his lecture, consultation, outline of plan, or whatever it was, and he talked for a long time. Pinzón listened to him with profound interest, saying nothing, except for an occasional brief question concerning new facts or the clarification of some obscurity. When Rey had finished, Pinzón looked serious. He lay full length on the bed, stretching himself with the pleasant movements of a man who has not slept for three nights, then said: "Your plan is difficult and risky."

"But not impossible."

"Oh, no, nothing in this world is impossible. Think it over carefully."

"I have."

"And you're determined to go through with it? Things like that aren't customary any more, you know. They usually end badly, and put the one who does them in a poor light."

"I've made up my mind."

"Then even though the matter is risky and serious—very serious—you can count on me to help you in everything and in every way."

"I can count on you then?"

"To the death."

XIX

HEAVY FIGHTING—STRATEGY

The first shots were bound to be fired soon. At the dinner hour, Pepe Rey went to the dining-room, after reaching an agreement with Pinzón regarding his plan. The first condition was that the two friends should pretend not to know each other. In the dining-room he found his aunt, who had just come from the Cathedral where, according to her custom, she had spent the whole morning. She was alone and seemed deeply preoccupied. The engineer noticed that the mysterious shadow of a cloud lay over her face, pale as marble but not without a certain beauty. When she looked up, it regained its sinister radiance, but she seldom looked up. After a quick scanning of her nephew's features, the good lady's face assumed again its expression of studied gloom.

They waited for dinner in silence. They did not wait for Don Cayetano, for he had gone to Mundogrande. As they began to eat, Doña Perfecta said: "Isn't this fine soldier the Government has bestowed upon us today coming in to have dinner?"

"He seems more sleepy than hungry," answered the engineer without looking at his aunt.

"Do you know him?"

"I never saw him before in my life."

"A fine lot of guests the Government sends us. We keep our beds and our table for whenever those scoundrels in Madrid see fit to make use of them."

"They're afraid there may be guerrilla uprisings," said Pepe Rey, feeling a spark of anger run through him. "And the Government has decided to smash the Orbajosans, to exterminate them, to grind them into dust."

"Stop, man, stop, for Heaven's sake, don't grind us into dust," cried the señora sarcastically. "Poor us! Have pity, man, and let these unhappy creatures live. What, are you going to be one of those who'll help the soldiers in their grand work of smashing us?"

"I'm not a soldier. I'll just applaud when I see them destroy once and for all the germs of civil war, insubordination, discord, violence, banditry, and barbarism which exist here to the shame of our time and our country."

"God's will be done."

"Orbajosa, my dear aunt, contains little but garlic and bandits, for those who fling themselves into adventures every four or five years in the name of a political or religious ideal are bandits."

"Thank you, thank you, dear nephew," said Doña Perfecta, turning pale. "So that's all Orbajosa has to offer? There must be something else here that you don't have and that you came looking for among us."

Rey felt the blow. He burned with anger. It was difficult for him to maintain toward his aunt the consideration which her sex, her age, and her position merited. Violence had taken hold of him and he was irresistibly driven to attack his interlocutor.

"I came to Orbajosa," he said, "because you invited me. You made an arrangement with my father."

"Yes, yes, that's true," answered the señora, quickly, interrupting him and striving to regain her usual sweetness. "I don't deny it. The real culprit here is I. I'm to blame for your boredom, for the affronts you've given us, for all the disagreeable things that have happened in my house as a consequence of your coming."

"I'm glad you recognize it."

"On the other hand, you're a saint. Must I also go down on my knees before Your Grace and beg your pardon?"

"Señora," said Pepe Rey gravely, leaving off eating. "I

beg you not to make fun of me in such a cruel fashion.
I can't answer in kind . . . The only thing I said was
that I came to Orbajosa at your invitation."

"That's true. Your father and I did agree that you were
to marry Rosario. You came to meet her. Of course I accepted you as a son . . . You seemed to love Rosario . . ."

"Forgive me," objected Pepe. "I did love and I do love
Rosario. You seemed to accept me as a son. After receiving me with deceitful cordiality, you employed from the
beginning every trick to thwart me and to prevent the ful-
fillment of the promises you made to my father. From the
first day, you set out to irritate me, to wear me down, and
with smiles and loving words on your lips, you have been
trying to destroy me, roasting me over a slow fire. You
have turned loose a swarm of lawsuits, attacking me in
the dark with perfect safety to yourself. You have stripped
me of the official commission I brought to Orbajosa. You
have destroyed my reputation in the town. You have had
me expelled from the Cathedral. You have constantly
kept me away from the girl of my choice. You have tortured your daughter with an inquisitorial confinement
which may cost her her life if God does not intervene."

Doña Perfecta turned scarlet. But that quick flash of
injured pride at the uncovering of her plot faded rapidly,
leaving her pale and sallow. Her lips trembled. Throwing
down the knife and fork with which she had been eating,
she suddenly rose. Her nephew also rose.

"Dear God, Blessed Virgin!" cried the señora, pressing
both hands to her head in a gesture of desperation, "can
I possibly deserve such awful insults? Pepe, my son, is
it you speaking? . . . If I've done what you say, truly I
am a great sinner."

She dropped on the sofa and covered her face with her
hands. Pepe slowly went to her, noting her bitter sob-
bing and the abundant tears she shed. In spite of his

conviction, he could not but be moved, and weakening, he felt some regret for all he had said so harshly.

"Dear Aunt," he said, putting a hand on her shoulder, "if you answer me with tears and sighs, I'll be touched, but I won't be convinced. I need reasoning, not emotions. Speak to me, tell me I'm wrong in thinking what I do, then prove it to me, and I'll acknowledge my error."

"Let me alone. You're not my brother's child. If you were, you wouldn't insult me as you have. So I'm a schemer, an actress, a hypocritical harpy, a cunning spinner of household plots? . . ."

As she spoke, the señora uncovered her face and she looked at her nephew with a saintly expression. Pepe was puzzled. Her tears, the sweet voice of his father's sister, could not fail to reach the young man's heart. Words asking her forgiveness trembled on his lips. Although normally a man of great energy, he could be turned into a child by any appeal to his emotions, anything that moved him. Those are the weaknesses of mathematicians. They say Newton was like that, too.

"I'd like to give you the reasoning you ask for," said Doña Perfecta, inviting him to sit beside her. "I'd like to make amends to you. Then you'd see whether or not I'm good, whether I'm considerate, whether I'm humble . . . ! Do you think I'll contradict you, that I'll deny absolutely the things you've accused me of? . . . No, I don't deny them."

The engineer was dumbstruck.

"I don't deny them," went on the señora. "What I do deny is the malicious intention you attribute to them. What right have you to judge things you know nothing about except through outward appearances and guesswork? Have you the supreme intelligence to pass final judgment on the actions of others and to sentence them? Are you God that you know people's intentions?"

Pepe was even more astonished.

"Isn't it permissible sometimes to use indirect means to achieve a good and honorable end? What right have you to judge my actions when you don't understand them? I confess to you, my dear nephew, with a frankness you don't deserve, that I have indeed availed myself of subterfuges in order to reach a good goal, to accomplish something that will benefit you and my daughter at the same time . . . Don't you understand? You look bewildered . . . Ah, your great grasp of mathematics and German philosophy makes you incapable of understanding these subtleties of a prudent mother."

"You astound me more and more," said Pepe Rey.

"Be as astounded as you like, but admit you're a brute," declared the lady with increasing spirit. "Acknowledge your own hasty and brutal behavior in accusing me as you've done. You're a mere boy with no experience or understanding aside from books, which teach you nothing about the world or the heart. You know nothing except how to build roads and docks. Ah, my young man! One does not gain access to the human heart through railroad tunnels, nor plumb its depths with mine-shafts. One cannot peer into another's conscience with a scientist's microscope, nor decide upon the guilt of his fellow man by measuring ideas with a surveying instrument.

"For God's sake, dear Aunt . . . !"

"Why do you call on God when you don't believe in Him?" said Doña Perfecta in a solemn tone. "If you believed in Him, you wouldn't dare to pass such wicked judgments on my actions. I'm a religious woman. Do you understand? My conscience is clear. Do you understand? I know what I'm doing and why I'm doing it. Do you understand?"

"I understand. I understand. I understand."

"God, in whom you don't believe, sees what you don't

see and can't see—my intention. I'll say no more. I don't
want to go into long explanations, because I don't have
to. You wouldn't understand in any case, if I did tell you
that I wanted to attain my objective without any scandal,
without offending your father, without offending you,
without giving people food for gossip by a definite 'No'
. . . I won't tell you any of this, because you wouldn't
understand that either, Pepe. You're a mathematician.
You can see nothing but what is right before your eyes;
brute Nature, that's all; lines, angles, weights and measures, that's all. You see the effect but not the cause. Anyone who doesn't believe in God can't see causes. God is
the supreme intention of the world. Anyone who doesn't
know Him must necessarily judge everything as you do,
like a fool. You see only destruction in a storm, for example, only ruin in a fire, only poverty in a drought, only
desolation in earthquakes; and yet, my proud young gentleman, one must seek the goodness of the intention in all
these apparent calamities . . . yes, sir, the eternally good
intention of Him who can do nothing evil."

This involved, subtle, and mystical reasoning failed to
convince Rey. But he had no desire to follow his aunt
along the rough trail of such argumentation, and he said,
simply: "Very well, I respect your intentions . . ."

"Now that you seem to recognize your error," went on
the señora, ever bolder, "I'll confess something else to
you, which is that I'm beginning to understand that I did
wrong in adopting such a system, even though my objective was excellent. With your impetuous nature, your
inability to understand me, I should have brought the
question right out into the open and have said: 'Nephew,
I don't want you to be my daughter's husband.' "

"That's the kind of language you should have used
from the beginning," answered the young man, breathing
a deep sigh of relief, like a man shedding a heavy burden.

"Thank you very much for those words. After being knifed in the back, in the dark, this blow in the light of day pleases me very much."

"Well, I'll repeat the blow, then," declared the señora with as much vehemence as displeasure. "You know it now, I don't want you to marry Rosario."

Pepe said nothing. There came a long pause while each stared fixedly at the other, as if to each the other's face were the most finished work of art.

"Don't you understand what I said?" she repeated. "It's all over. There will be no marriage."

"Forgive me if I'm not terrified by your threats, my dear Aunt," said the young man with composure. "Things have come to such a pass that your refusal means little to me."

"What did you say?" screamed Doña Perfecta, in a rage.

"You heard me. I will marry Rosario."

Doña Perfecta rose, indignant, majestic, terrible. She looked like anathema personified. Rey remained seated, calm, resolute, with the passive courage of a profound conviction and an unshakeable resolution. The whole threatening weight of his aunt's anger, her threats, did not make him blink an eyelash. He was like that.

"You are a madman. You, marry my daughter! You, marry my daughter, when I don't want you to!"

The trembling lips of the señora spoke these words in a genuinely tragic tone.

"Even if you don't want it! . . . She is of a different opinion."

"If I don't want it!" repeated the lady. "I say and I repeat: I don't want it. I don't want it."

"She and I want it."

"You fool! Perchance there's no one in the world but

she and you? Aren't there parents? Isn't there society? Isn't there a conscience? Isn't there a God?"

"Just because there is society, because there is conscience, because there is a God," declared Rey gravely, getting to his feet and raising an arm to heaven, "I say and I repeat that I will marry her."

"Wretch! Conceited fool! Do you think there are no laws to halt your violence if you try to trample everything underfoot?"

"Because there are laws, I say and I repeat that I will marry her."

"You have no respect for anything."

"Not for anything unworthy of respect."

"What about my authority, and my wishes . . . What about me? Am I nothing?"

"To me, your daughter is everything. The rest is nothing."

Pepe Rey's firmness was like the manifestation of an irresistible force, perfectly aware of itself. He dealt sharp, stunning blows, without any attempt to soften them. His words seemed like a merciless artillery barrage, if the comparison may be allowed. Doña Perfecta again sank down on the sofa; but she did not weep, and a nervous twitching shook her limbs.

"So, to this wretched atheist," she cried with open fury, "there are no social conventions, there is nothing but personal whim! You're moved by base avarice. My daughter is rich!"

"If you think you can hurt me with that subtle weapon, twisting the question around and giving a distorted meaning to my feelings to offend my dignity, you're wrong, dear Aunt. You can call me avaricious. God knows I am not."

"You have no dignity."

"You're entitled to your opinion. The world may con-

sider you infallible. I don't. I'm far from thinking that
the sentence you pass can have no appeal before God."

"But can what you're saying be true? . . . Do you per-
sist in spite of my refusal? You're trampling everything
underfoot. You're a monster, a bandit."

"I am a man."

"A wretch! Let's put a stop to this. I refuse you my
daughter; I refuse you."

"Then I'll take her. I'll be taking no more than what
is mine."

"Get out of my sight!" screamed the señora, springing
to her feet. "Conceited fool! Do you think my daughter
remembers you?"

"She loves me, the same as I love her."

"Liar, liar!"

"She told me so herself. Forgive me if in this matter
I place more faith in her than in her mother."

"When did she tell you so, if you haven't seen her in
many days?"

"I saw her last night, and she swore to me in front of
the Christ in the chapel that she'll be my wife."

"What a scandal! What loose conduct! . . . What on
earth is this? Good God, what a disgrace!" cried Doña
Perfecta, again pressing her head between her hands and
pacing the floor. "Rosario left her room last night?"

"She came out to see me. It was high time she did."

"What vile behavior on your part! You've behaved like
a thief, you've acted like a common seducer."

"I was taking a leaf from your book. My intention was
good."

"And she came downstairs! . . . Oh, I suspected it. I
found her in her room, all dressed, at daylight this morning. She told me she'd gone out for something, I don't
know what . . . But the real culprit is you, you! . . . This
is a disgrace. Pepe, I expected anything of you, anything

but an outrage of this kind . . . This is the end . . . Get out! For me, you no longer exist. I'll forgive you only on condition that you go . . . I won't say a word about this to your father . . . What shocking selfishness! No, there's no love in you. You don't love my daughter!"

"God knows that I adore her, and for me that's enough."

"Don't take the name of God in vain, you blasphemer, and hold your tongue," cried Doña Perfecta. "In the name of God, whom I have a right to invoke because I believe in Him, I tell you that my daughter will never be your wife. My daughter will be saved, Pepe; my daughter will not be condemned to a hell on earth, for marriage with you would be hell."

"Rosario will be my wife," repeated the young man with moving serenity.

The señora grew more and more enraged at the calm assurance of her nephew. Her voice breaking, she said: "Don't think you can frighten me with your threats. I know what I'm talking about. Do you think you can trample underfoot a home, a family? Do you think you can trample over human and divine authority?"

"I'll trample over everything," said the young man, beginning to lose his calm and expressing himself with more emotion.

"You'll trample over everything! Ah, it's apparent that you're a barbarian, a savage, a man to whom violence is law."

"No, my dear Aunt. I am gentle, upright, honest, and I hate violence. But between you and me, between you, who represent the law, and me, a man who is supposed to respect it, there is a poor, tortured creature, an angel of God held in an iniquitous martyrdom. This spectacle, this unheard-of violence, this injustice, is the thing that has changed my uprightness into barbarity, my reason into force, my honesty into the violence of murderers and robbers. This spectacle, my lady, is what drives me to disrespect for your law, what impels me to set it aside and trample over everything. This, which seems folly to you, is a law that brooks no opposition. I'm doing only what societies do when brute power, as illogical as it is exasperating, stands in the way of their progress. They ride over it and destroy everything in a ferocious assault. That's the state I am in now. I hardly know myself. I was reasonable, and now I'm a brute. I was respectful, and now I'm insolent. I was civilized, and now I find I'm a savage. You have brought me to these terrible extremes, thwarting me and driving me from the path of decency along which I had been peacefully travelling. Whose fault is it, mine or yours?"

"Yours! Yours!"

"Neither you nor I can determine that. I think we're both wrong. You are violent and unjust. I am unjust and violent. One of us has come to be as uncivilized as the other, and we're fighting and tearing at each other without any mercy. God is permitting this to happen. My blood will be on your conscience, yours on mine. Enough, now, señora. I don't want to annoy you with futile words. Now we'll change over to deeds."

"All right, deeds, then!" said Doña Perfecta, roaring rather than speaking. "Don't think for a moment there are no police in Orbajosa."

"Good-bye, señora. I'm leaving this house. I think we'll meet again."

"Get out! Get out, get out, now!" she screamed, pointing to the door with a violent gesture.

Pepe Rey left. Doña Perfecta fell into an armchair after some incoherent words which were all she could utter in her rage. She showed signs of exhaustion or of a nervous attack. The servants came running to her.

"Call Señor Don Inocencio," she screamed. "Immediately! . . . Now! Tell him to come!"

Her teeth tore at her handkerchief.

XX

RUMORS, ALARUMS

The day after this lamentable quarrel, a variety of rumors concerning Pepe Rey and his behavior spread from house to house throughout Orbajosa, from circle to circle, from the club to the drugstore, and from the Promenade of the Descalzas to the gate of Baidejos. Everyone was repeating them, and the commentaries grew so voluminous that if Don Cayetano were to collect and compile them, they would form a rich encyclopedia of Orbajosan kindliness. Among the differing reports circulated, there was agreement on some salient points, one of which was that the young man, enraged because Doña Perfecta refused to let Rosario marry an atheist, had raised a hand to his aunt.

The young man was lodging in the Widow Cusco's inn, an establishment furnished, as they say these days, not in the height, but in the depth of the supremely backward fashion of that region. Lieutenant Colonel Pinzón frequently called there in order to discuss their plans, for the efficient accomplishment of which the soldier displayed great talents. He was constantly thinking of new tricks and artifices, hastening, with excellent humor, to convert them from ideas to acts, although he used to say to his friend:

"Dear Pepe, the part I'm playing is not one of the most

gallant. But I'd crawl on all fours for the sake of getting back at Orbajosa."

We don't know what subtle stratagems were employed by the crafty soldier who was a master of worldly wiles. But it is certain that within three days of being billeted in the house, he had made himself well-liked there. His behavior pleased Doña Perfecta, who could not listen unmoved to his encomiums on the stateliness of the house and her own greatness, piety, and august magnificence. He was on an excellent footing with Don Inocencio. Neither the mother nor the Confessor was disturbed when he talked with Rosario (who had been set free after the departure of the ferocious cousin). With his smooth compliments, his clever flattery, and his remarkable skill, he gained ascendency and even familiarity in the Polentinos household. But the target of all his artfulness was a maid, named Librada, whom he seduced (chastely speaking) into carrying messages and notes to Rosario, pretending that he was in love with her. The servant girl could not resist the bribery accomplished with charming words and a good deal of money, for she was unaware of the source of the love letters and of the true intent of such schemes. If she had known that it was all a new piece of devilment on the part of Don José, even though she liked him very much she would not have betrayed the señora for all the money in the world.

One day Doña Perfecta, Don Inocencio, Jacinto, and Pinzón were all in the garden. They were talking of the soldiers and the mission which had brought them to Orbajosa, and the topic gave the Confessor an opportunity to hold forth on the tyrannical conduct of the Government. By chance, Pepe Rey's name came up.

"He's still at the inn," said the young lawyer. "I saw him yesterday, and he asked to be remembered to you, Doña Perfecta."

"Who ever heard of such impudence? . . . Oh, Señor Pinzón, don't be surprised at my using such language in referring to my own nephew. You know him . . . that gentleman who used to have the room you're now occupying."

"Yes, I know about it! I have nothing to do with him. But I know him by sight and reputation. He's an intimate friend of our brigadier."

"An intimate friend of the brigadier!"

"Yes, señora, of the one who's in command of the brigade which came to this part of the country, and which has been distributed among several villages."

"Where is he?" asked the lady.

"In Orbajosa."

"I think he's billeted in the Polavieja house," declared Jacinto.

"That nephew of yours," went on Pinzón, "and Brigadier Batalla are intimate friends; they're very fond of each other, and are seen together in the village streets at all hours."

"Well, that gives me a poor opinion of that officer," replied Doña Perfecta.

"He's . . . he's a sad case," said Pinzón, in the tone of a man who does not want to use a harsher term, out of respect.

"Present company excepted, Señor Pinzón," declared the lady, "it can't be denied that there's all kinds of riff-raff in the Spanish Army."

"Our brigadier was an excellent soldier until he took up spiritualism . . ."

"Spiritualism!"

"That sect that calls up ghosts and goblins by means of table-rapping!" cried the canon, laughing.

"Out of curiosity, only out of curiosity," said Jacintito with emphasis, "I've sent to Madrid for the works of

Allan Kardec.[49] It's just as well to know something about everything."

"But are such absurdities possible . . . ? Good Lord! Tell me, Pinzón, does my nephew belong to that cult of table-tipping?"

"It seems to me it was he who indoctrinated our brave Brigadier Batalla."

"Good Heavens!"

"That's it. When he has a mind to he can talk with Socrates, St. Paul, Cervantes, and Descartes," observed Don Inocencio unable to contain his laughter, "just the way I ask Librada here for a match. Poor Señor de Rey! I told you that head wasn't any too steady."

"Except for that," went on Pinzón, "our brigadier is a fine soldier. If anything, he errs on the side of harshness. He obeys the Government's orders to the letter of the law and to such a point that if people thwart him here, he's capable of razing Orbajosa to the ground. Yes, I'm warning you, they'd better look out."

"Why, a monster like that will cut our heads off. Ah, Don Inocencio, these visitations of soldiers remind me of what I've read in the lives of the martyrs when a Roman proconsul appeared in a Christian village . . ."

"The comparison is not far wrong," said the Confessor, staring at the soldier over his glasses.

"It's sad, but since it's true, it might as well be said," stated Pinzón with an air of benevolence. "So, ladies and gentlemen, you're at our mercy."

"The local authorities still function perfectly," objected Jacinto.

"I think you're mistaken," replied the soldier, who was watching the lady and the Confessor with the keenest

---

[49] The Frenchman Hippolyte-Leon Denizard Rivail (1803-1869), better known by his pseudonym "Allan Kardec," was the author of numerous works on spiritualism.

interest. "An hour ago the mayor of Orbajosa was dismissed."

"By the Governor of the province?"

"The Governor's post has been taken by a delegate from Madrid who was to have arrived this morning. All the town councils were abolished today. That's what the Minister has ordered, because he was afraid, I don't know why, they wouldn't support the Central Government."

"Well, we're in a fine state," murmured the canon, knitting his brows and pushing out his lower lip.

Doña Perfecta was thoughtful.

"They've also removed some judges of the lower courts, among them the one in Orbajosa."

"The Judge! Periquito! . . . Periquito isn't the Judge any more?" cried Doña Perfecta with the gesture and voice of one who has had the misfortune to be bitten by a snake.

"The one who was judge in Orbajosa isn't any more," said Pinzón. "Tomorrow the new man will come."

"A stranger!"

"An outsider!"

"Perhaps a rascal . . . The old one was so honest!" said the señora anxiously. "I never asked him for a thing he didn't grant me immediately. Do you know who the new mayor will be?"

"They say a Chief Magistrate is coming."

"You might as well say right now that the Deluge is on its way and we'll be finished," declared the canon, rising.

"Then we're at the mercy of the brigadier?"

"For a while, at least. Don't get angry with me. In spite of my uniform, I'm not fond of militarism. But they order us to strike . . . and we strike. There can't be a baser calling than ours."

"It's all of that; it's all of that," said the señora, her

fury poorly concealed. "Now that you've admitted it . . .
So we have neither mayor nor judge."

"Nor a governor of the province."

"Why don't they take away our Bishop, too, and send
us some acolyte in his place?"

"That's all that's lacking . . . If they let them do it
here," murmured Don Inocencio, lowering his eyes, "they
won't stop at trifles."

"And all because they're afraid of a rebel uprising in
Orbajosa," cried the señora, folding her hands and raising
and lowering them from chin to knee. "Frankly, Pinzón,
I don't know why even the stones don't rise up. I don't
wish you the slightest harm, but it would be only fair if
the water they drink should turn into mud . . . Did you
say my nephew is an intimate friend of the brigadier?"

"So intimate they're together all day long; they were
school chums. Batalla loves him like a brother and does
everything he can to please him. In your shoes, señora,
I wouldn't be at all easy."

"Oh! Dear Lord! I'm afraid there'll be some outrage! . . ." she cried, greatly upset.

"Señora," declared the canon vehemently, "rather than
permit an affront to this honored house; rather than consent to the slightest annoyance to this noble family, I . . .
my nephew . . . all your neighbors in Orbajosa . . ."

Don Inocencio could not finish his speech. His anger
was so intense that the words stuck in his mouth. He took
a few martial strides, then sat down again.

"It seems to me your fears are not without foundation,"
said Pinzón. "In case of necessity, I . . ."

"And I . . ." cried Jacinto.

Doña Perfecta had her eyes fixed on the glass door of
the dining-room, through which a charming figure could
be seen. As she stared, it seemed as though the dark
clouds of fear grew darker on the señora's face.

"Rosaria! Come here, Rosario," she said, going to meet her. "It seems to me you look better today, and that you're livelier, yes . . . Doesn't it seem to you gentlemen that Rosario looks better? She looks like another person!"

They all agreed that her face mirrored the most radiant happiness.

XXI

ARISE! TO ARMS!

During those days, the newspapers in Madrid published the following reports:

"It is not true that any rebel group has taken up arms in the vicinity of Orbajosa. We have had word from that locality that the countryside is so little disposed to adventures that the presence of Brigadier Batalla in that town is considered unnecessary."

"It is said that Brigadier Batalla will leave Orbajosa since there is no need for armed forces there, and that he will go to Villajuan de Nahara where some rebel bands have appeared."

"It has been ascertained that some mounted men of the Aceros band are overrunning the district of Villajuan, adjoining the judicial district of Orbajosa. The Governor of the Province of X— has wired the central government saying that Francisco Acero entered Las Roquetas where he collected six months' taxes and demanded rations. Domingo Acero (*Faltriquera*), was ranging the Jubileo Mountains, actively pursued by the Civil Guards, who killed one of his men and captured another. Bartolomé

Acero was the man who burned the civil registry office in Lugarnoble, carrying off the mayor and two of the leading landowners as hostages."

"Complete calm reigns in Orbajosa, according to a letter we have received, and the villagers have no thought but to prepare their land for the new garlic crop, which promises to be magnificent. It is true that the nearby regions are infested with rebels, but the Batalla Brigade will make short work of them."

Orbajosa was in fact calm. The Aceros, that guerrilla dynasty worthy, according to some, of figuring in the *Romancero,*[50] had seized the neighboring province. But within the limits of the cathedral city, the uprising had not spread. It might be thought that modern culture had finally won its battle with the rebellious habits of the factions, and that it was now savoring the joys of a lasting peace. And certainly it is true that Caballuco himself, one of the most outstanding figures in the rebel history of Orbajosa, was proclaiming loudly that he did not want to "quarrel with the Government," or to "stick his nose into things" that might cost him dear.

Say what you will, the reckless character of Ramos had quieted down with the years. The fiery temper he had inherited from his Caballuco forebears, the best breed of rebel fighters that ever scourged the earth, had cooled off. Furthermore, it was said that the new provincial governor had held a conference with this important personage during those days, and *had received from his own lips the most binding assurances* that he would help to keep the public peace and avoid any occasion to break it. Unimpeachable sources stated that they had witnessed him in amicable companionship with the soldiers, hobnobbing with this one or that one in the tavern, and they even went so far as to declare that he was about to be given

---

[50] The name given to the collection of historic Spanish ballads.

a good post in the Town Council of the capital of the province. Ah, how difficult it is for the historian who tries to be impartial to filter the truth through the opinions and intentions of the eminent personages whose names have resounded throughout the world! One scarcely knows what to believe, and the lack of verifiable data gives rise to lamentable errors. What psychologist or historian can fathom what went on, before or afterward, in the minds of Bonaparte, Charles V, or Titus, when he notes such conclusive facts as the incident of the Brumaire,[51] the sack of Rome by Bourbon,[52] or the ruin of Jerusalem?[53] What an immense responsibility ours is! To escape it in part, we shall quote words, phrases, and even speeches by the emperor of Orbajosa himself, and in this way each may form the opinion he judges most trustworthy.

There can be no doubt that Cristóbal Ramos left his house after nightfall, and passing through Condestable Street, he saw three peasants riding toward him on their mules. When he asked them where they were going, they replied that they were on their way to Doña Perfecta's house to bring her some first fruits of the orchards and some rent money which had fallen due. They were Señor Pasolargo, a boy called Frasquito González and the third, middle-aged and of ruddy complexion, answered to the name of Vejarruco, although his real name was José Estéban Romero. Caballuco turned back, attracted by the good company of those men with whom he had kept

---

[51] In the calendar introduced by the French Revolution the second month beginning October 22 and ending November 20. On November 9, 1799, Napoleon overthrew the Directory by a coup d'état and made himself head of the French government.

[52] The armies of Charles V, under the Constable of Bourbon, sacked Rome in 1527.

[53] The Roman emperor Titus besieged and laid waste Jerusalem in 70 A.D.

up an old and close friendship. With them, he entered the señora's house. According to the most incontrovertible data, this happened at nightfall, two days after Doña Perfecta and Pinzón had discussed what the reader of the preceding chapter already knows. The great Ramos occupied himself in giving Librada certain messages of slight importance which a neighbor woman had entrusted to his good memory. When he entered the dining-room, the three aforementioned peasants and Señor Licurgo, who by a strange coincidence was also present, were engaged in a conversation having to do with the harvest and the house. The lady was in a vile humor. She found fault with everything and scolded them roundly for the lack of rainfall and the infertility of the earth, phenomena for which the poor devils were not responsible. The Father Confessor witnessed the scene. When Caballuco entered, the good canon hailed him affectionately, pointing to a seat at his side.

"Here's the great man," said the lady with disdain. "It seems impossible there can be so much talk about a man of so little courage! Tell me, Caballuco, is it true that some soldiers cuffed you about this morning?"

"Me? Me?" said the Centaur, rising indignantly like a man who has just received the grossest insult.

"That's what they say," continued the señora. "Isn't it true? I believed it, because you think so little of yourself . . . They'll spit on you and you'll think yourself honored by the soldiers' saliva."

"Señora!" shouted Ramos violently. "But for the respect I owe you, who are my mother, more than my mother, my lady, my queen . . . Well, I say, but for the respect I owe to the person who has given me everything I have . . . But for the respect . . ."

"What? . . . You seem to have a lot to say but you don't say anything."

"Well, I say that but for the respect, that business about being hit is a slander," he went on, expressing himself with extreme difficulty. "Everybody talks about me: whether I come or go, whether I go out or come in . . . Why is that? Because they want to use me as a figurehead to stir up the country. I believe in letting well enough alone, ladies and gentlemen. So the soldiers have come? . . . That's bad. But what can we do about it? . . . So they've fired the mayor and the secretary and the judge? . . . That's bad. I wish the stones of Orbajosa would rise up against them. But I gave my word to the Governor, and up to now I . . . ."

He scratched his head, knitted his gloomy brow, and went on, with a more and more confused tongue: "I may be stupid, dull, ignorant, touchy, stubborn, or anything else you like. But as a gentleman, I don't take a back seat for anybody."

"A fine kind of Cid Campeador!"[54] said Doña Perfecta with the greatest scorn. "Don't you agree with me, Señor Confessor, that there's not a single man in Orbajosa with any shame?"

"That's a pretty strong opinion," replied the canon, not looking at his friend nor removing his chin from the hand on which he rested his thoughtful face. "But it does seem to me that this vicinity has accepted the heavy yoke of militarism with excessive meekness."

Licurgo and the three peasants were laughing to burst their sides.

"When the soldiers and the new authorities," went on the señora, "have taken our last cent, after humiliating the village, we'll send all the brave men of Orbajosa to Madrid in a crystal urn, so they can be put into a museum or shown through the streets."

"Hurray for the señora!" cried the one called Vejarruco

---

[54] Rodrigo Díaz de Vivar, the Cid, the national hero of Spain.

with animation. "Her words are pure gold. They can't say there are no brave men on my account, though I'm not with the Aceros because a fellow with three kids and a wife has to watch what he does. But if it weren't for that . . ."

"But you haven't given your word to the Governor?" asked the señora.

"To the Governor?" cried the so-called Frasquito González. "There isn't a rascal in the whole country that deserves shooting more than he does. Governor and Government, they're all alike. On Sunday the priest preached a lot of high-flown things about heresies and offenses against religion in Madrid . . . Oh! You should have heard him . . . Finally he began shouting from the pulpit that religion has no defenders today."

"Here's the great Cristóbal Ramos," said the señora, giving the Centaur a whack on the shoulder. "He gets on his horse; he rides around the plaza and along the highway so the soldiers will notice him. As soon as they see him, they're terrified of our hero's fierce looks and they run away, scared to death."

The señora finished her speech with an exaggerated laugh, made the more shocking by the deep silence of those who heard it. Caballuco went pale.

"Señor Pasolargo," went on the lady, turning serious, "when you get home send your son Bartolomé here to spend the night. I need trustworthy people in the house. Even so, it might well happen that some fine day my daughter and I will find ourselves murdered in our beds."

"Señora!" they all exclaimed.

"Señora!" shouted Caballuco, getting to his feet. "Is that a joke, or what is it?"

"Señor Vejarruco, Señor Pasolargo," continued the señora without looking at the local bravo, "I'm not safe in my own house. No Orbajosan is, and least of all I.

I live in constant fear. I daren't close my eyes all night long."

"But who? Who would dare . . . ?"

"Come," said Licurgo, full of fire, "old and feeble as I am, I'd take on the whole Spanish Army if they touched a hair of the señora's head."

"Señor Caballuco by himself," noted Frasquito González, "is more than enough."

"Oh, no!" replied Doña Perfecta with cruel irony. "Can't you see that Ramos has given his word to the Governor . . . ?"

Caballuco sat down again, and crossing his legs, he folded his hands over them.

"A coward is enough for me," added the lady, "provided he has given no pledges. Things may come to such a pass that I'll see my house attacked, my darling daughter torn from my arms, myself trampled underfoot and insulted in the vilest way . . ."

She could not go on. Her voice caught in her throat and she burst into disconsolate weeping.

"Señora, for God's sake, calm yourself! Come . . . there's no reason yet . . ." Don Inocencio broke in with the voice and countenance of deep distress. "Besides, a little resignation is called for to bear the calamities that God sends us."

"But, who . . . señora? Who would dare to commit such outrages?" asked one of the four. "The whole of Orbajosa would stand as one man to defend the señora."

"But who? Who?" they all asked again.

"Come, don't bother her with troublesome questions," said the Confessor officiously. "You may go."

"No, no, let them stay," declared the señora, quickly drying her tears. "The company of my good servants is a great consolation to me."

"Why, I'll be damned if all these nasty tricks aren't

the work of the señora's very own nephew," said Tío Lucas, striking his fist on his knee.

"Of Don Juan Rey's son?"

"Ever since I laid eyes on him at the station in Villahorrenda and he started talking to me in that honeyed voice of his, with his airs of a dude at the Court," declared Licurgo, "I took him for a big . . . I won't go on out of respect for the lady . . . But I knew him . . . I caught on to him from that day, and I wasn't wrong, no, sir. I know very well you can tell the yarn by the thread and the cloth by the sample, and the lion by his claws, as they say."

"Don't you speak ill of that unfortunate young man in my presence," said the Señora de Polentinos gravely. "However great his faults may be, charity forbids us to speak of them and to spread the word around about them."

"But," declared Don Inocencio firmly, "charity doesn't prevent us from protecting ourselves against evil men, and that's what we're talking about. Now that courage and character have so declined in poor Orbajosa, now that people seem ready to hold up their faces for four soldiers and a corporal to spit on, let's try to put up some sort of defense by uniting."

"I'll defend myself as best I can," said Doña Perfecta, folding her hands resignedly. "Let the Lord's will be done!"

"What an uproar about nothing . . . Heavens! Everyone in this house is scared to death!" exclaimed Caballuco, half serious, half jovial. "Anyone would think Don Pepito was a legion of devils. Don't be afraid, señora. My little nephew Juan, thirteen years old, will guard the house, and we'll see, nephew for nephew, which is the better man."

"We know by now how much your boasting and bragging amounts to," replied the lady. "Poor Ramos! You'd like to make yourself out a big hero, but it's plain to see that you're no good for anything!"

Ramos paled a little and turned on the señora a strange look which combined fear and respect.

"Don't look at me like that, man. You know I'm not afraid of bugaboos. Do you want me to speak plainly for once? All right, you're a coward."

Ramos, squirming like a man stung all over his body, displayed enormous discomfort. He breathed in and out through his nostrils like a horse. Within that big body a storm, a passion, a cataclysm was struggling to burst forth, roaring and smashing. After half uttering some words, chewing up others, he rose and howled: "I'll cut Señor Rey's head off."

"What foolishness! You're as stupid as you are cowardly," she said, blanching. "Who's talking about killing? I don't want anyone to be killed, much less my nephew whom I love in spite of his villainies."

"Murder! What a crime!" cried Don Inocencio, scandalized. "The man is insane."

"Killing! . . . The very idea of a murder horrifies me, Caballuco," said the señora, closing her gentle eyes. "Poor man! As soon as you want to show how brave you are, you begin howling like a man-eating wolf. Go away, Ramos. You're horrifying me."

"Didn't the señora say she was afraid? Didn't she say they'll trample her house underfoot, they'll carry off her girl?"

"Yes, I'm afraid of it."

"And one man is going to do all this!" said Ramos with scorn, as he sat down again. "Don Pepe Piddler with his mathematics. I was wrong to say I'd cut off his head. A store-window dummy like that, you take him by the ear and duck him in the river."

"All right, laugh now, idiot. Alone, my nephew wouldn't commit those crimes you've mentioned and which I fear, for if he were alone he wouldn't dare to. All I'd have to do would be to order Librada to stand at the door with a gun . . . it would be enough . . . It isn't he alone, no."

"Well then, who . . . ?"

"Don't be stupid. Don't you know my nephew and the brigadier who commands these cursed soldiers are in collusion . . . ?"

"Collusion!" exclaimed Caballuco, clearly not understanding the expression.

"They're in cahoots," noted Licurgo. "They're in 'lusion means they're in cahoots. I've already caught on to what the señora's saying."

"It all comes down to the fact that the brigadier and the officers are blood brothers with Don José, and what he wants those soldiers will do, and they'll commit any kind of atrocity or barbarity because that's their business."

"And we have no mayor to help us."

"Nor judge."

"Nor governor. That means we're at the mercy of this vile rabble."

"Yesterday," said Vejarruco, "some soldiers enticed away the youngest daughter of Tío Julián, and the poor child didn't dare go back home; they found her crying and barefooted near the old fountain, picking up the pieces of her water jar."

"Poor Don Gregorio Palomeque, the notary at Naharilla Alta!" said Frasquito. "Those rascals robbed him of all the money he had in the house. But when the brigadier was told about it, he said it was a lie."

"Tyrants, real tyrants, every mother's son of them," declared the other. "I tell you for two cents I'd go with the Aceros . . . !"

"And what about Francisco Acero?" asked Doña Perfecta meekly. "I'd be sorry if any harm were to come to him. Tell me, Don Inocencio, wasn't Francisco Acero born in Orbajosa?"

"No. Both he and his brother are from Villajuan."

"I regret it for Orbajosa's sake," said Doña Perfecta. "This poor city has fallen upon evil days. Do you know whether Francisco Acero gave his word to the Governor that he wouldn't interfere with the poor little soldiers in their raping of young girls, their sacrileges, or their dirty thieveries?"

Caballuco gave a start. This time he did not feel that he had been pricked, rather that he was wounded by a terrible saber stroke. His face burned, and eyes blazing, he shouted: "I gave my word to the Governor because the Governor told me they were here for a good purpose."

"Don't shout, you oaf. Speak like a human being, and we'll listen."

"I promised him that neither I nor any of my friends would join in any rebellion in the territory of Orbajosa . . . I've told anyone and everyone who wanted to get into it and was itching to fight: 'Go with the Aceros, we're not rising here' . . . But I've got a lot of honorable people, yes, señora; and good people, yes, señora; and brave people, yes, señora, scattered through the hamlets and villages, through the hills and woods, each in his own house, eh? And the moment I give them the slightest hint, eh? Right away they'll be taking down their guns, eh? And breaking into a dead run on foot or on horseback to wherever I send them . . . And don't give me any of your big words, for if I gave my word, it was because I gave it. And if I'm not rising, it's because I don't want to rise. And if I want rebels, there'll be rebels. And if I don't want them, no. For I am who I am, the same man as ever, as all of you well know . . . And I tell you again not to come it over me with your big words. Is that clear? And don't say things to me backwards. Is that clear? And if you want me to start a rising, tell me so in plain words. Is that clear? That's what God gave us tongues for: to say this and that. The señora knows full well who I am, as I know full well that I owe her the shirt on my back, and the bread I put in my mouth, and the coffin they buried my father in when he died, and the medicine and the doctor who fixed me up when I was sick. And the señora knows full well that if she tells me, 'Caballuco, break your head,' I'll go over to that corner and break it against the wall. The señora knows full well that if she says to me right now that it's day, I'll believe I'm wrong and that it's broad daylight, even though I can see it's night. The señora knows very well that she and what's hers come before my own life, and that if a mosquito bites her in front of me, I'll forgive it only because it's a mosquito. The señora knows very well that I love her more than anything under the sun . . . All she has to say to a man who feels like I do about her is: 'Caballuco, you brute, do this, that, or the other'; and never mind the fancy lingo, never mind jabbing at me with words and preaching one thing but meaning another, and pricking here and pinching there."

"Come, man, calm down," said Doña Perfecta graciously. "You've got as hot as those republican orators who came here preaching freethinking, free love, and I don't know what all . . . Bring him a glass of water."

Caballuco made a knot or a kind of ball of his handkerchief and rubbed it over his broad forehead and the back of his neck to mop up the sweat which covered them. They brought him a glass of water, and the canon, with a meekness which accorded perfectly with his priestly character, took it from the servant girl's hands to give it to him and to hold the plate while he drank. The water poured down Caballuco's throat, gurgling as it ran.

"Now bring me another, Libradita," said Don Inocencio. "I've got a little fire inside me, too."

XXII

AWAKE!

When they had finished drinking, Doña Perfecta said, "With regard to the rebels, I only tell you to do whatever your conscience bids you."

"I don't know anything about bidding," shouted Ramos. "I'll do whatever the señora wants me to."

"Well, I won't give you any advice whatsoever in such a delicate matter," she answered with the circumspection and good breeding which so became her. "This is very serious, extremely serious, and I can't advise you at all."

"But your opinion is . . ."

"My opinion is that you ought to open your eyes and see, open your ears and hear . . . Consult your heart . . . I'll grant that you have a great heart . . . Consult that judge, that advisor which knows so much, and do as it commands you."

Caballuco meditated; he thought as much as a sword can think.

"We in Naharilla Alta," said Vejarruco, "counted up yesterday, and we were thirteen, all ready for any big undertaking . . . But since we were afraid the señora would be angry, we didn't do anything. Now it's time for the shearing."

"Don't worry about the shearing," said the señora.

"There's time enough. It won't fail to be done for lack of time."

"My two boys," declared Licurgo, "were fighting with each other yesterday because one of them wanted to go with Francisco Acero and the other one didn't. I said to them, 'Easy, my sons, easy, all in good time. Wait, for the bread they make here is as good as in France.' "

"Last night Roque Pelosmalos said to me," said Tío Pasolargo, "that the moment Señor Ramos gives the least word, they're all ready, weapons in hand. What a pity the two Burguillos brothers have gone to work around Lugarnoble!"

"Go and get them," said the lady quickly. "Lucas, have a horse ready for Tío Pasolargo."

"I'll go to Villahorrenda to see if Robustiano, the forest guard, and his brother Pedro want to join up too, if the señora and Señor Ramos tell me to."

"It seems to me a good idea. Robustiano is afraid to come to Orbajosa because he owes me a trifling sum. You can tell him I'll forget about the six and a half dollars . . . These poor people are content with so little, but they know how to sacrifice themselves generously for a good cause . . . Isn't that so, Don Inocencio?"

"Our good Ramos here," replied the canon, "tells me that his friends are dissatisfied with him and his luke-warmness; but as soon as they see he's made up his mind they'll all put on their cartridge belts."

"But what is this? Have you decided to take up arms?" said the señora to Ramos. "I haven't advised you to do any such thing, and if you do it, it's entirely your own decision. Neither has Don Inocencio said a word to you on this subject. But if and when you do decide to do it, you'll have justice on your side . . . Tell me, Cristóbal, do you want supper? Would you like something to drink? . . . Speak out . . ."

"In the matter of my advising Señor Ramos to fling himself into the fray," said Don Inocencio, gazing over his glasses, "the señora is right. As a priest, I cannot advise any such thing. I know there are some priests who do it, and even take up arms;[55] but this seems to me improper, very improper, and I shall not be one to emulate them. I carry my own scruples to the point of refusing to say a word to Señor Ramos on the delicate subject of his rising up in arms. I know that Orbajosa wishes it. I know that all the inhabitants of this noble city will call him blessed. I know we're going to see deeds here worthy of going down in history. But, neverthless, I can only permit myself a discreet silence."

"That's very well said," added Doña Perfecta. "I don't like to see priests get mixed up in any such business. An outstanding clergyman should conduct himself as you do. We know full well that priests play their part, arousing men to battle and even joining in it in solemn and serious times, as for example when the country and our faith are in peril. Since God Himself has fought in famous battles, in the form of angels or saints, His vicars may well do likewise. During the wars against the infidels, how many bishops led the Spanish troops?"

"Many of them, and some were outstanding soldiers. But these are other times, señora. It is true that if we were to study things closely, our faith is in greater danger now than before . . . What do those armies occupying our city and the nearby towns represent? What do they represent? Are they anything but the base tools of which the atheists and Protestants infesting Madrid avail themselves for their wicked conquests and for the extermination of our beliefs? . . . We all know it very well. In that

---

[55] During the Carlist wars many priests took up arms in support of the Pretender Don Carlos, and even headed guerrilla bands.

cesspool of corruption, of scandal, of antireligion and unbelief, a handful of evil men, bought by foreign gold, have set themselves to destroy the seeds of the faith in our Spain . . . What do you think, then? They permit us to say mass and you to hear it because they retain a tag-end of consideration and of shame . . . But some fine day . . . As for me, I am calm. I'm a man unmoved by temporal and mundane interests. Doña Perfecta is well aware of it, all those who know me are aware of it. I'm calm, and I'm not afraid of the triumph of evil. I know very well that terrible days await us, that the lives of all of us who wear clerical garb are hanging by a hair, for Spain, make no mistake about it, will witness scenes like those of the French Revolution when thousands of devout priests perished in a single day . . . But I'm not worried. When it comes time for heads to roll, I'll lay mine on the block. I've lived long enough. What am I good for? For nothing, for nothing."

"May I be thrown to the dogs," shouted Vejarruco, clenching a fist hardly less strong and hard than a hammer, "if we don't finish off that thieving rabble quickly."

"They say they're going to start tearing down the Cathedral next week," declared Frasquito.

"I suppose they'll tear it down with pickaxes and hammers," said the canon, smiling. "But there are craftsmen who lack such tools, and yet build more rapidly. You all know that, according to a pious legend, our beautiful Sagrario chapel was razed by the Moors in a month and rebuilt by angels in a single night . . . Let them, let them destroy."

"According to what the priest in Naharilla told us the other night," said Vejarruco, "there are so few churches left now in Madrid that some priests have to say mass in the middle of the street, and a lot of them don't want to say it because they're mauled and insulted and even spat upon."

"Fortunately, my sons," declared Don Inocencio, "we've not yet had any scenes of that kind here. Why? Because they know what kind of people you are; because they've heard about your ardent piety and your courage . . . I wouldn't answer for the consequences to the first one who lays a hand on our priests and our religion . . . Of course, it must be admitted that if they aren't halted in time, they'll wreak deviltries. Poor Spain, so holy, so humble, and so good! Who would have said that she'd find herself in such straits! . . . But I maintain that god-lessness will not triumph, no, sir. There are still brave men, there are still men like those of old. Isn't that so, Señor Ramos?"

"There still are, yes, sir," replied Ramos.

"I have a blind faith in the triumph of God's law. Some-one must go forth in defense of it. If some won't, others will. Someone will carry off the palm of victory and with it eternal glory. The evil will perish, if not today, then tomorrow. He who goes contrary to the will of God will fall, there's no escaping it. Whether by this means or that, in the end he must fall. Neither his sophistries, nor his evasions, nor his tricks will save him. God's hand is raised above him, and it will strike him without fail. Let us have pity on him and long for his repentance . . . As for you, my sons, don't expect me to say a word about the step you're surely going to take. I know that you are good men. I know that your generous resolution and the noble end which guides you will wash out any stain of sin caused by the shedding of blood. I know that God blesses you; that your victory, as well as your death, will exalt you in the eyes of God and of men. I know that you merit the palm and all manner of praise and honors. But despite this, my sons, my lips will not incite you to arms.

I have never done that in my life and I shall not do it now. Act according to the bidding of your noble hearts. If your heart commands you to remain in your houses, stay in them. If it orders you to go forth, go forth and so be it. I resign myself to being a martyr and to bowing my neck before the headsman if these miserable soldiers stay on here. But if an honorable, ardent, and pious impulse on the part of the sons of Orbajosa leads them to help in the great work of extirpating the misfortunes of our country, I shall consider myself the most fortunate of men merely in being your compatriot, and my whole life of study, penance, and resignation will seem to me a less meritorious claim to Heaven than one single day of your heroism."

"No one could say more or say it better!" cried Doña Perfecta, overcome with enthusiasm.

Caballuco had been leaning forward in his seat, his elbows on his knees. When the canon had finished speaking, he seized his hand and kissed it with fervor.

"A better man was never born of woman," said Uncle Licurgo, squeezing out, or pretending to wipe away, a tear.

"Long live the Father Confessor!" shouted Frasquito González, rising to his feet and tossing up his cap.

"Quiet!" said Doña Perfecta. "Sit down, Frasquito. You're one of those who cackle without laying an egg."

"God bless my soul, you've got a golden tongue," exclaimed Cristóbal, on fire with admiration. "What a pair I see before me! As long as they're both alive, who'd want another world? . . . Everyone in Spain ought to be like them . . . But how are they going to be like them if they're all knaves and rascals! In Madrid, it's all thievery and farce, and that's the place our laws and orders come from. What they've done to our poor religion! . . .Wherever you look, you see nothing but sin . . . Señora Doña

Perfecta, Señor Don Inocencio, by the soul of my father,
by the soul of my grandfather, by my hopes of salvation,
I swear I'd like to die."

"To die!"

"Let those dirty dogs kill me. I say let them kill me,
because I can't draw and quarter them. I'm not big
enough."

"Ramos, you're big," said the lady solemnly.

"Big, big? . . . My heart is big, yes. But have I got
forts? Have I got cavalry? Have I got artillery?"

"That's one thing, Ramos," said Doña Perfecta, smiling, "that I wouldn't worry about. Hasn't the enemy got
whatever you need?"

"Yes."

"Well, then, take it away from him."

"We'll take it away from him, yes, señora. When I say
that we'll take it away from him . . ."

"Dear Ramos," declared Don Inocencio. "What an
enviable position you're in . . . To be able to distinguish
yourself, to rise above the mob, to make yourself the equal
of the greatest heroes in the world . . . to be able to say
that the hand of God is guiding your hand! . . . Oh, what
glory and honor! My friend, I'm not flattering you. What
breeding, what chivalry, what gallantry! . . . Men of such
mettle can't die! The Lord is with them, and enemy bul-
lets and enemy steel are turned aside . . . they fall short
. . . how could they dare hit home when they're fired
from artillery in the hands of heretics? . . . Dear Caballuco, just to look at you, just to see your courage and
chivalry, I am reminded suddenly of the verses of that
ballad on the conquest of the Empire of Trebizond:

> "Then came the valiant Roland,
>   Armed in full panoply,
>   Mounted on strong Briador,

His mighty war-charger,
With his powerful sword Durandel
Girt to his side;
His lance pointed straight as a spar,
Invincible shield on his arm;
His helmet flashed fire
Through the visor and
Quivered the length of his lance
Like a reed that is bent by the wind
As he faced the enemy's ranks
Like a flambeau ablaze."

"Very good," shouted Licurgo, clapping. And like Don Rinaldo, I say:

"Let no one who longs to go free
    Touch one hair of Rinaldo;
The man who invokes a harsh fate
    Will be paid in such coin
    That none of the rest shall
    Slip through my hands,
    But as crushed fragments
    Or cruelly chastened."[56]

"Ramos, you surely want some supper, or something to eat, don't you?" said the señora.

"Nothing, nothing," replied the Centaur. "Unless you happen to have a dish of gunpowder."

On saying this, he burst into a strident laugh, took several turns around the room, closely watched by the others, and, pausing near the group, he fixed his eyes on Doña Perfecta, and, in a voice of thunder, he uttered these words:

"I say there's nothing more to be said. Long live Orbajosa, death to Madrid!"

---

[56] These are fragments from an old Spanish ballad which recounts episodes from the epic legends of France.

He brought his hand down on the table with such force that the floor of the house shook.

"What a great spirit!" murmured Don Inocencio.

"What a pair of fists . . ."

They all stared at the table, which had broken into two pieces.

Then their eyes moved to the never sufficiently admired Rinaldo, or Caballuco. Undoubtedly there was a kind of air of greatness, a vestige, or rather an echo, of the great races which have ruled the world in his handsome face, his green eyes alight with a peculiar feline glare, his black hair, his herculean body. But his general appearance reflected a pitiful degeneration, and it was difficult to see traces of his noble and heroic stock in his present brutishness. He resembled Don Cayetano's great men as a mule resembles a horse.

XXIII

A MYSTERY

The meeting went on long after the events already related, but we shall omit the rest of it, for it is not indispensable to a clear understanding of this tale. Finally the men left, Don Inocencio last, as usual. There had not been time for the señora and the canon to exchange views, when an old and trusted servant woman, Doña Perfecta's right arm, entered the dining-room, and seeing her disturbed and upset, her mistress, too, became upset, suspecting that something bad had happened in the house.

"I can't find the señorita anywhere," said the servant in response to the señora's questions.

"Good Lord! Rosario! . . . Where is my daughter?"

"Bless me, Our Lady of Perpetual Help!" cried the Confessor, putting on his hat and making ready to run after the señora.

"Look everywhere for her . . . But wasn't she with you in her room?"

"Yes, señora," answered the old woman, trembling. "But the Devil tempted me and I fell asleep."

"Damn your slumber! . . . Dear God! . . . What's happened? Rosario! Rosario! . . . Librada!"

They went upstairs; they came downstairs; they went up and down again, carrying lights and searching every room. At last they heard the voice of the Confessor on the stairway, crying out joyously: "Here she is, here she is! She just arrived."

A moment later mother and daughter came face to face in the hallway.

"Where were you?" asked Doña Perfecta in a stern tone, searching her daughter's face.

"In the garden," murmured the girl, more dead than alive.

"In the garden at this time of the night! Rosario!"

"I was too warm, I went to the window. I dropped my handkerchief and went down to look for it."

"Why didn't you tell Librada to fetch it for you? . . . Librada! . . . Where is that girl? Has she gone to sleep, too?"

Finally Librada appeared. Her pale face indicated the dismay and anxiety of guilt.

"What's going on? Where were you?" demanded the lady with terrible anger.

"But, señora . . . I went downstairs to look for the clothes in the room that faces on the street . . . and I fell asleep."

"Everyone's falling asleep tonight. It seems to me that

somebody is not going to sleep in this house tomorrow. Rosario, you may go to bed."

Realizing that the situation called for speed and energy, the lady and the canon started their investigations with no delay. Questions, threats, entreaties, promises were employed with consummate skill to seek the truth behind the occurrence. The old servant was found to be without a trace of guilt. But Librada, between sobs and sighs, fully confessed all her knavery.

What it came down to was that soon after being billeted in the house, Señor Pinzón began to make eyes at Rosario. He paid Librada, she said, to use her as a bearer of messages and love notes. The young lady had not appeared to be angry; on the contrary, she was well pleased, and thus several days went by. Finally, the servant stated, Rosario and Señor Pinzón had agreed to meet that night and talk through the window of the latter's room which faced on the garden. They confided their intention to the girl, who offered to stand guard in consideration of a sum they paid her on the spot. According to the agreement, Pinzón was to leave the house at his usual time and come back secretly at nine to go to his room which he would leave again clandestinely to return openly at his customary late hour. Thus no suspicion would fall on him. Librada waited for Pinzón, who came in wrapped in his cloak, without a word. He entered his room at the very moment the girl came down into the garden. During the interview, the servant girl, who was not present, acted as a sentinel on the veranda to warn Pinzón of any danger which might arise; and at the end of an hour he went out as before, tightly wrapped in his cloak, without a word. At the end of the confession, Don Inocencio asked the hapless girl:

"Are you sure that the man who came in and went out was Señor Pinzón?"

The culprit made no reply and her face showed great perplexity. The señora turned green with rage.

"Did you see his face?"

"But who could it be but him?" replied the girl. "I'm certain it was he. He went straight to his room . . . he knew the way very well."

"That's strange," said the canon. "He didn't need to use such subterfuges since he lives in the house . . . He could have pretended to be ill and stayed at home . . . Isn't that true, señora?"

"Librada!" she exclaimed in a paroxysm of rage, "I swear to God that you'll go to jail."

She clenched her hands, the fingers locked together so tightly they almost bled.

"Don Inocencio," she declared. "Let's die . . . There's nothing to do but to die."

Then she burst into disconsolate weeping.

"Courage, my deal lady," said the priest in the voice of a stricken man. "You must be very brave . . . Now is when you need all the courage you have. This calls for serenity and a stout heart."

"Mine is very stout," said the Señora Polentinos amid sobs.

"Mine is weak . . . but we'll do what we can."

XXIV

THE CONFESSION

Meanwhile, Rosario was on her knees in her room until far into the night, her hands crossed, her feet bare, her burning head resting on the edge of the bed. She was alone, silent, in the dark, her heart in shreds, yet unable to weep, to regain calm or tranquillity, transfixed by the cold steel of an immense suffering. Her mind shuttled back and forth from the world to God and from God to the world. She was careful not to make the slightest sound so as not to attract the attention of her mother who was asleep—or feigning sleep—in the adjoining room. She raised her disordered thoughts to heaven.

"Lord God, why is it that I never knew how to lie before, but now I do? Why did I never know how to deceive before, and now I do? Am I a wicked woman . . . ? Is what I feel and what's happening to me the downfall from which I can never rise again? Have I stopped being good and honorable . . . ? I no longer recognize myself . . . Am I the same girl, or has someone else taken my place . . . ? What terrible things have happened in such a short time! So many new emotions! My heart is being consumed with so much feeling . . . ! Dear Lord, dost Thou hear my voice, or am I condemned to pray eternally without being heard . . . ? I am good. No one can ever convince me that I'm not. Is it a sin to love, to love so much . . . ? No . . . this is an illusion, a trap. I am worse than the worst women on earth. A huge serpent inside me is biting me and poisoning my heart . . . What is this I feel? Why dost Thou not kill me, my God? Why dost Thou not cast me into Hell for all eternity . . . ? It's frightful; but I confess it. I confess it to God here alone, to Him, Who hears me, and I will confess it to the priest. I abhor my mother. Why? I can't explain it to myself. He has never said one word against my mother. I don't know how this has happened to me . . . How wicked I am! Devils have taken possession of me. Lord, come to my aid, for without Thy help, I can't conquer myself. An awful impulse is drawing me out of this house. I want to flee, to run away from here. If he doesn't take me

away, I'll go after him, dragging myself along the roads
. . . How can this divine happiness that is struggling in
my heart be mingled with such bitter pain . . . ? Lord
God the Father, show me the way. I want only to love.
I can't stand this hatred that's devouring me. I can't
stand hiding my feelings, lying, deceiving. Tomorrow I'll
go out into the street and shout from the middle of it to
everyone going by: I love, I hate . . . That would be
the way to get this weight off my heart . . . How wonderful it would be to be able to reconcile everything, to love
and respect everyone! May the Holy Virgin protect me
. . . That awful idea again. I don't want to think it, but
I do think it. I don't want to feel like this, but I do. Ah!
I can't deceive myself about this. I can't root it out or
soften it . . . but I can confess it, and I do. I tell Thee:
'Lord, I abhor my mother!' "

At last she fell into a doze. In her restless dreaming,
her imagination re-created all that had happened that
night, distorting it, but not changing its essence. She
was hearing the Cathedral clock strike nine. She was
seeing with delight that the aged servant was sleeping
the sleep of the just, and she was going out of her room
very softly so as not to make any noise; she was descending the stairs so quietly that she dared not move a foot
until she was sure not to make the slightest sound. She
was going out into the garden, around the room shared
by the cook and the servant girls. She was pausing for
a moment in the garden to gaze at the sky, sprinkled
with stars. The wind was still. Not a sound broke the
deep serenity of the night. She seemed to feel within
her a silent, fixed attention, like that of eyes that stare
without blinking and ears which strain in wait for some
important event . . . The night was watching.

Then she was approaching the French door to the
dining-room, staring in cautiously from a distance for

fear that the people within might hear her. By the light
of the dining-room lamp, she could see her mother's
back. The Father Confessor was at her right hand, and
his profile looked oddly distorted. His nose seemed to
have grown until it resembled the beak of some unlikely
bird, while his whole figure became a foreshortened
shadow, thick and black, angular in places, grotesque,
disembodied, and thin. Caballuco was facing her, more
like a dragon than a man. Rosario could see his green
eyes like two great lanterns with convex panes. That
glow and his imposing animal figure struck fear in her.
Uncle Licurgo and the other three looked like grotesque
figurines. Somewhere she had seen such stupid smiles,
such rude forms, and such idiotic faces, probably on
the clay dolls at the fairs. The dragon was waving his
arms; like the blades of a windmill, they turned instead
of making meaningful gestures. His green lantern bulbs,
much like the colored globes in a drugstore, moved from
side to side. His stare was blinding . . . The conversation seemed to be interesting. The Father Confessor was
flapping his wings. He looked like a bird that wanted
to fly and could not. His beak seemed to elongate and
to curve downward. He ruffled his feathers excitedly,
then pulling himself together and calming down, he
tucked his bald head under his wing. Next the clay
figurines moved about, trying to be human, and Frasquito
González strove hard to be a man.

Rosario felt an inexplicable terror at witnessing that
friendly conclave. She retreated from the window and
went ahead step by step, looking all about her in case
she might be observed. She felt a million eyes fixed on
her, although she saw no one . . . But her fears and
her sense of guilt suddenly vanished. A blue man
appeared at the window of the room where Señor Pinzón
lodged. The buttons on his clothing shone like strings of

little lights. She went to him. Immediately she felt arms trimmed with braid lift her up like a feather, carrying her in one swift movement into the room. Everything was transfigured. Suddenly there came a crash, a violent blow which shook the house to its foundations. No one knew the cause of the noise. They trembled and were silent.

It was the moment when the dragon broke the dining-room table.

XXV

UNFORESEEN HAPPENINGS—A PASSING DISAGREEMENT

The scene changes. Behold a handsome room—bright, simple, gay, comfortable, and of an astonishing neatness. A fine matting covers the entire floor, and the white walls are decorated with fine prints of saints and some sculptures of dubious artistic merit. The old mahogany of the furniture gleams from its Saturday rubbings, and the altar, where a pompous Virgin, garbed in blue and silver, receives the adoration of the household, is covered with charming knicknacks, some sacred, some profane. Moreover, there are little pictures done in beads, holy water fonts, a clock case with an *Agnus Dei*,[57] a withered palm from Palm Sunday, and several vases of scentless artificial roses. A massive oak bookcase holds a rich and well-chosen library; Horace, the Epicurean and sybarite,

---

[57] "Lamb of God." A medal blessed by the Pope and bearing the figure of a lamb.

side by side with the gentle Virgil, in whose verses the
ardent Dido's heart quivers and flames with love; Ovid,
the long-nosed—sublime, obscene, and ingratiating in
equal parts, next to Martial, the impudent and witty
rascal; Tibullus, the passionate, with Cicero, the great.
The severe Titus Livius with the terrible Tacitus, the
scourge of the Caesars. Lucretius, the pantheist; Juvenal,
who could flay with his pen; Plautus, who conceived the
greatest comedies of the ancient world while turning a
mill. Seneca, the philosopher, of whom it was said that
the greatest act of his life was his death. Quintilian, the
rhetorician; Sallust, the rascal who speaks so highly of
virtue; both Plinys, Suetonius, and Varro. In short, all
of Latin letters, from the day they stammered their first
word with Livius Andronicus until they breathed their
last sigh with Rutilius.[58]

But while making this rapid inventory, we have failed
to note that two women have entered the room. It is
very early; but in Orbajosa everyone gets up with the
dawn. The little birds are singing in their cages with
all their might; the church bells are ringing for mass, and
the goats which are to be milked at the doors of the
houses jingle their neck-bells.

The two ladies have just heard mass. They are dressed
in black, and each carries in her right hand her missal
and her rosary, wound around her fingers.

"Your uncle should be here soon," said one of them.
"We left him beginning the mass, but he says it quickly,
and by now he must be taking off his chasuble in the
sacristy. I would have stayed to hear his mass, but I'm
very tired today."

"Today I heard only the prebendary's mass," said the
other. "The prebendary says them in a single breath,
and I don't think I got much good from it, for I was

---

[58] These names are those of great Roman writers.

worried and I couldn't take my mind off these awful
things that are happening to us."

"What can we do! . . . We must be patient . . . Let's
see what your uncle advises."

"Oh!" cried the second lady, heaving a deep sigh. "It
makes my blood boil."

"God will take care of us."

"To think that a lady like you should find herself
threatened by a . . . ! And he goes right on with his
schemes . . . Last night, Señora Doña Perfecta, I went
back to the Widow Cusco's inn and asked for the latest
news, as you told me to. Don Pepito and Brigadier Batalla
are forever putting their heads together . . . Ah, Jesus,
Our Lord and God! They're conferring together over
some devilish scheme and tossing off bottles of wine.
They're two drunks, two lost souls. Undoubtedly, they're
plotting some great wickedness. Since I was so concerned
about you, last night when I was at the inn, I saw Don
Pepito go out and I followed him . . ."

"Where did he go?"

"To the Club. Yes, señora, to the Casino," replied the
other, somewhat upset. "Later he went back home. Oh,
how my uncle would scold me for going around spying
at all hours . . . but I can't help it . . . Dear God, help
me! I can't help it, and I nearly go crazy to see someone
like you in such a dangerous predicament . . . Dear, dear.
Señora, I can plainly see that those rascals are quite likely
to storm your house and carry off Rosarito . . ."

Doña Perfecta meditated for a long while, staring at
the floor. She was pale and frowning. Finally she said:
"But I don't see how I can stop him."

"I can see how," said the other quickly. She was the
Confessor's niece and Jacinto's mother. "I can see a very
simple way to do it. What I've already told you, but
you don't like it. Ah, señora, you're too good. At times

like this it's best to be a little less perfect . . . to lay aside your scruples. Would that offend God?"

"María Remedios," replied the señora haughtily, "don't talk nonsense."

"Nonsense! . . . You with all your wisdom, you don't know how to teach that nephew of yours a lesson. What could be simpler than the thing I'm suggesting? Since there's no justice to protect us these days, we'll have to take justice into our own hands. Aren't there men in your house who'll do anything whatsoever for you? Well, call them and tell them: 'See here, Caballuco, Pasolargo, or whoever it is, wrap yourself up well tonight so no one will know you, take some good friend of yours with you, and go stand on the corner of Santa Faz Street. Wait a while, and when Don José Rey comes down Tripería Street on his way to the Club, where he's bound to go— Understand? As he goes by, stop him, and give him a good scare . . .'"

"María Remedios, don't be such an idiot," said the señora with queenly dignity.

"Just a scare, that's all, señora. Mark my words, just a scare. Well, am I the sort to advise anyone to commit a crime . . . ? As God is my Redeemer, the very idea of such a thing fills me with horror, and I can almost see blood and fire before my eyes. No such thing, señora . . . A scare, and nothing but a scare, so that ruffian will know that we aren't defenseless. He always goes alone to the Club, señora, entirely alone, and there he meets his fine friends with their sabers and helmets. Just suppose he gets a good scare, and even a few broken bones, but of course no serious wounds . . . Well, in that case, either he'll turn coward and leave Orbajosa, or he'll have to stay in bed a couple of weeks. Of course it must be understood that it's a real good scare. No killing . . . nothing like that, but a good beating."

"María," said Doña Perfecta haughtily, "you're incapable of a noble idea, or of any great and redeeming decision. What you're advising me to do would be a cowardly indignity."

"All right, then, I'll keep still . . . Oh, dear, what a fool I am," muttered the Confessor's niece humbly. "I'll keep my fool words to console you with after your daughter is lost to you."

"My daughter! . . . My daughter lost to me!" cried the lady in a sudden burst of anger. "It drives me crazy just to hear that. No, they won't take her away from me. If Rosario doesn't hate that lost soul, as I wish she would, she will. A mother's authority is worth something . . . We'll uproot that passion of hers, or rather that whim, like a tender blade of grass that hasn't had time to put down roots . . . No, this can't go on, Remedios. Come what may, it shall not be! That madman with all his evil means shall not prevail. Rather than see her the wife of my nephew, I'll accept the worst, even death."

"It would be better to see her dead, to see her buried and food for the worms," declared Remedios, clasping her hands as though praying, "than to see her in his power . . . Ah, señora, don't be offended if I tell you something. It would be a great weakness to give in because Rosarito has had some secret meetings with that bold rascal. That business of last night, as my uncle told it, seems to me a low trick on the part of Don José to gain his ends by causing a scandal. Lots of them do it . . . Ah, dear God, I don't know how anyone can look any man in the face unless he's a priest."

"Be still, be still," said Doña Perfecta vehemently, "Don't talk about last night. What a terrible thing to happen! María Remedios . . . I can understand how wrath can cause a person to lose his soul forever. My blood boils . . . Oh, how awful it is to see such things going on and not to be a man! . . . But to tell the truth about that business of last night, I still have my doubts. Librada swears by all that's holy that it was Pinzón who went in . . . My daughter denies the whole thing, and my daughter has never lied! . . . But I still have my suspicions. I think Pinzón is a rascally go-between, but nothing more . . ."

"It comes back to the same thing always—that the author of all these wicked things is that blessed mathematician . . . Oh, I made no mistake the first time I saw him . . . Well, señora, resign yourself to seeing even worse things unless you make up your mind to call Caballuco and tell him, 'Caballuco, I hope that . . .'"

"There you go, back to the same thing; but you're a simpleton."

"Oh, I'm a simpleton, I know it; but if I can't help it, what can I do? I say whatever comes into my mind, without any real wisdom."

"What occurs to you, that vulgar nonsense about a beating and a scare, would occur to anyone. You haven't an ounce of sense, Remedios. When you're faced with a serious problem, you come out with nonsense like that. I can imagine measures worthier of well-bred and well-born people. A beating! How stupid! Furthermore, I don't want my nephew to get a scratch by my orders. By no means. God will send him his punishment by one of His own admirable means. The only thing we can do is to work to remove any obstacles to God's designs, María Remedios. In matters such as this we must go directly to the causes of things. But what do you know of causes . . . you can see nothing but trifles."

"Perhaps so," said the priest's niece humbly. "Why did God make me so stupid that I can't understand anything about such big, important ideas."

"We must go to the root of it, the root, Remedios. Don't you understand me, either?"

"No."

"My nephew is not my nephew, woman. He is blasphemy itself, sacrilege, atheism, demagoguery . . . Do you know what demagoguery is?"

"Something like those people who burned up Paris with kerosene, and the ones who tear down the churches and shoot images . . . I understand you so far."

"Well, my nephew is all of that . . . Ah, if only my nephew were alone in Orbajosa! . . . But he's not, dear. Through a series of coincidences, each of which constitutes proof of the passing evils which God sometimes permits in order to punish us, my nephew is the equivalent of an army, of the Government's authority, of the mayor, of the judge . . . My nephew is not my nephew; he's the officialdom of the nation, Remedios; he's that nation within a nation made up of the damned souls who rule in Madrid, and who have made themselves masters of material power; of that seeming nation, for the real nation consists of those who keep silent, pay, and suffer; of that fictitious nation which signs decrees, spouts speeches, and makes a farce of government, a farce of authority, and a farce of everything. Today that is my nephew. You must learn to see what is behind the things that happen. My nephew is the Government, the brigadier, the mayor, the new judge, for they all favor him because they all think alike; because they're hand in glove, all wolves of the same pack . . . Mark my words. We must defend ourselves from all of them, for they are all for one, and one for all. We must attack them in unison, not with street-corner beatings, but as our forebears attacked the Moors—the Moors, Remedios . . . You must understand this well, my dear. Open your mind and let in some idea that is not vulgar . . . Rise above yourself. Lift your thoughts, Remedios."

Don Inocencio's niece was awestruck by this exhortation. She opened her mouth to say something in keeping with such lofty thoughts; but all she could do was to sigh.

"As in the days of the Moors," repeated Doña Perfecta. "This is a question of Moors and Christians. And you thought it could all be settled by scaring my nephew! . . . How stupid you are! Can't you see that his friends are helping him? Can't you see we're at the mercy of that rabble? Can't you see that some insignificant lieutenant may set fire to my house if he takes a notion to? . . . Can't you grasp this? Don't you understand that it's necessary to get to the roots? Don't you understand the size, the terrible scope of my enemy, who is not one man, but a whole sect? . . . Don't you understand that my nephew, as he defies me today, is not merely a calamity, but a plague? . . . We shall have to rally against it, dear Remedios, a battalion of God here to annihilate the infernal militia of Madrid. I tell you, it will be great and glorious . . ."

"If in the end it could be . . ."

"Do you doubt it? We're going to see some terrible things here today . . ." said the lady impatiently. "Today, today! What time is it? Seven o'clock . . . So late, and nothing has happened yet!"

"Perhaps my uncle will know something about it. He's here now. I hear him coming up the stairs."

"Thank God . . ." added Doña Perfecta, getting up to go and meet the Confessor. "He'll have news for us."

Don Inocencio hurried in. His disturbed appearance showed that that soul of his, consecrated to piety and Latin studies, had lost its accustomed calm.

"Bad news," he said, putting his hat on a chair and untying the strings of his cape.

Doña Perfecta turned pale.

"They're arresting people," added Don Inocencio, lowering his voice as though a soldier lurked under every chair. "Undoubtedly they suspect that the people here aren't going to put up with their bad jokes, and they've gone from house to house, laying hands on everyone with a reputation for courage . . ."

The señora threw herself into a chair and gripped the wooden arms tightly.

"If they've let themselves be taken . . ." put in Remedios.

"Many of them, many, had time to get away, and have gone to Villahorrenda with guns and horses," said Don Inocencio, speaking to the señora, with approving gestures.

"What about Ramos?"

"They told me in the Cathedral that he's the one they're most eager to get their hands on . . . Oh, dear Lord! To arrest like that some poor souls who haven't done a thing yet . . . I don't see how good Spaniards keep their patience. My dear Doña Perfecta, while I was talking about this matter of the arrests, I forgot to tell you that you ought to get home at once."

"Yes, right this minute . . . Are those bandits going to search my house?"

"Perhaps. Lady, we've fallen upon evil days," said Don Inocencio in solemn and emotional tones. "May God have pity on us."

"I have half a dozen well armed men in my house," replied the lady, greatly agitated. "What iniquity! Will they go so far as to arrest them, too? . . ."

"Most certainly Señor Pinzón won't have been lax about informing on them. Señora, I repeat that we've fallen upon evil days. But God will protect the innocent."

"I must go. Don't fail to come to see me."

"Señora, as soon as I've dismissed the class . . . and I imagine that with all the excitement there is in the town, all the boys will be playing truant today. But class or no class, I'll go to your house later . . . I don't want you to go out alone, señora. Those good-for-nothing soldiers are walking the streets and putting on such airs . . . Jacinto, Jacinto!"

"It's not necessary . . . I'll go alone."

"Let Jacinto go with you," said his mother. "He must be up by now."

They heard the quick steps of the little savant who ran downstairs full speed from the upper floor. His face was red and he was out of breath.

"What's the matter?" asked his uncle.

"In the Troyas' house, in the house . . ." said the youth, "well . . ."

"Out with it!"

"Caballuco is there."

"Up there? . . . In the Troyas' house?"

"Yes, sir . . . He spoke to me from the terrace. He told me he's afraid they'll arrest him there."

"Oh, that brute! . . . That fool will let himself be arrested," exclaimed Doña Perfecta, stamping an impatient foot.

"He wants to come down here so we can hide him in the house."

"Here?"

The canon and his niece stared at each other.

"Let him come down!" said Doña Perfecta imperiously.

"Here?" repeated Don Inocencio, looking very ill-humored.

"Here," replied the señora. "I don't know of a house where he will be safer."

"He can easily come in through the window in my room," said Jacinto.

"Well, if it's absolutely necessary . . ."

"María Remedios," said the señora, "if they take that man from us, everything is lost."

"I may be a simpleton and a fool," replied the canon's niece, putting her hand to her breast and pressing back the sigh that was doubtless about to issue forth. "But they won't take him."

The señora left quickly, and soon afterward the Centaur was making himself comfortable in the armchair where Don Inocencio was accustomed to sit to write his sermons.

How it came to the ears of Brigadier Batalla we cannot say, but the fact remains that this alert soldier received information that the Orbajosans had changed their minds, and on the morning of that day he ordered the arrest of those who in our rich language of rebellion are known as *marked men.* The great Caballuco was miraculously saved by taking refuge in the Troyas' house; but believing he was not safe there, he went down, as we have seen, to the inviolable dwelling of the canon, which was above suspicion.

The soldiers, occupying various points in the village, maintained a close watch over those who entered and left by night; but Ramos succeeded in eluding them, evading, or perhaps not evading, the military precautions. This completed the work of inflaming the minds of the citizenry, and a number of them met by night to conspire in the hamlets near Villahorrenda, dispersing by day, to lay the ground for the arduous task of the uprising. Ramos scoured the environs, rallying people and arms, and as the flying columns of soldiers were pursuing the Aceros in the region of Villajuan de Nahara, our knightly hero accomplished a great deal in a short time.

With consummate audacity he risked entering Orbajosa at night, availing himself of astute strategems, or perhaps of bribes. His popularity and the protection he was given inside the town acted in some degree as a safeguard, and it would not be rash to say that the soldiers failed to display the same zeal toward that daring champion as toward the insignificant men of the locality. In Spain, and especially in time of war, always demoralizing here, such base tolerance toward the powerful is frequent, while the little fellows are persecuted mercilessly. Aided, then, by his boldness, by bribery, or whatever it might have been, Caballuco entered Orbajosa, recruited more men, gathered arms, and raised money. In order to cover his steps, and for his own greater safety, he never set foot in his own house, and seldom went to Doña Perfecta's to discuss important matters. As a rule, he supped with one or another of his friends, always preferring the respected dwelling of some priest, and mainly that of Don Inocencio where he had been given asylum on the black morning of the arrests.

Meanwhile, Batalla had telegraphed the Government, saying that after discovering a rebel conspiracy, he had taken the instigators of it into custody, and that the few who had managed to escape were scattered and in flight, actively pursued by our columns.

XXVI

MARÍA REMEDIOS

Nothing is more entertaining than to seek out the origin of notable events which astonish or perturb us, and nothing more gratifying than to discover it. When we see violent passions in open or hidden conflict, and, following the natural impulse to reason inductively which always attends human observation, we succeed in locating the hidden fount whence come the waters of that turbulent river, we experience a joy like that of geographers and explorers.

God has granted us this joy now, for in exploring the hidden recesses of the hearts which beat through this story, we have uncovered a fact which is surely the progenitor of the most important events herein narrated: a passion which constitutes the first drop of water of this rushing torrent whose course we are following.

Let us, then, go on with the story. Let us leave Señora de Polentinos without concerning ourselves with what may have happened to her on the morning of her dialogue with María Remedios. Filled with misgivings, she went home where she was obliged to endure the apologies and courtesies of Señor Pinzón, who assured her that as long as he was alive, the señora's house would not be searched. Doña Perfecta answered him haughtily, not deigning to look at him; and when he urbanely asked the reason for her displeasure, she replied by requesting Señor Pinzón to leave her house, deferring until a more opportune moment the accounting due her of his treacherous conduct in her home. Don Cayetano arrived and he and Pinzón exchanged words as one gentleman to another. But since another matter interests us more, let us leave the Polentinos and the lieutenant colonel to compose their differences as best they may, and go on to scrutinize the historic sources mentioned above.

Let us fix our attention on María Remedios, that estimable woman to whom we must devote a few lines. She was a lady, truly a lady, for despite her humble origin the virtues of her uncle, Don Inocencio (also of humble origin, but elevated by holy orders as well by his learning and respectability) had shed a refulgent light upon the entire family.

The love of Remedios for Jacinto was one of the most vehement of the passions a mother's heart can contain. She loved him devotedly; she placed the welfare of her son above all human considerations; she believed he was the most perfect model of beauty and talent ever created by God, and to see him happy and highly placed she would have given her entire life, and even a portion of eternal glory. Noble and sanctified as it is, maternal feeling is the only sentiment which is permitted exaggeration; the only one not debased by excess. However, a not infrequent phenomenon is that if this exaltation of maternal love is not accompanied by complete purity of heart and by perfect honesty, it may run wild and become transformed into a frenzy which, like any other uncontrolled passion, can lead to great errors and catastrophes.

In Orbajosa, María Remedios was considered a model of virtue and a model niece; perhaps, indeed, she was. Her help was available to all who needed her. She never gave cause for tittle-tattle and evil gossip. She never mixed into intrigues. She was pious, even if quite sanctimonious; she practiced charity; she ran her uncle's house with great skill; she was well received, admired, and praised everywhere, despite the feeling of almost unbearable suffocation she induced by her habit of continually sighing and always talking in a complaining tone.

But in Doña Perfecta's house, that excellent lady suffered a kind of eclipse or loss of prestige. Back in difficult times for the family of the good Confessor, María Remedios (why not say it, since it's the truth?) had been a laundress in the Polentinos household. It was not that Doña Perfecta was haughty toward her; not at all; she displayed no pride; she felt a sisterly affection for her. They ate together, prayed together, shared each other's troubles; they worked side by side on their charities and

in their devotions, as well as in household matters . . .
But, nevertheless, it must be admitted that there was
always something, always an invisible line that could
not be crossed, between the elevated lady and the born
lady. Doña Perfecta spoke familiarly to María, while the
latter could never erase a certain formality in speaking
to the señora. Don Inocencio's niece felt so small in the
presence of her uncle's friend that her native humility
took on a certain curious tinge of sadness. She observed
that the good canon was a kind of perpetual royal coun-
selor in Doña Perfecta's house; she beheld her idolized
Jacintillo on familiar, almost loving terms with the
señorita, and yet the poor niece and mother visited the
house as seldom as possible. María Remedios felt herself
reduced in rank beside Doña Perfecta, and this was
most disagreeable to her, for there was a spark of pride
in that sighing soul, as there is in every living being . . .
To see her son married to Rosarito; to see him rich and
powerful; to see him related to Doña Perfecta, to the
lady! . . . Ah, for María Remedios that would be heaven
on earth, the best of both worlds, the reason for her existence. Her mind and her heart had been filled with that
sweet glow of hope for many years. For this she was
good or bad; religious and humble, or bold and terrible;
for this she was whatever she needed to be. For without
that dream, María, who was the very incarnation of her
own plan, would not have existed.

In appearance, María Remedios could not have been
more insignificant. Her only distinction was a surprising
freshness which seemed to give the lie to her years, and,
even though her widowhood was now an old, old story,
she always dressed in mourning.

Five days had gone by since Caballuco had first entered
the Confessor's house. Night was falling. Remedios went
to her uncle's room with a lighted lamp, and after plac-

ing it on the table, she sat down facing the old man
who had remained motionless and thoughtful in his armchair since the middle of the afternoon, as though he had
been nailed to it. His hand supported his chin, his
swarthy skin was lined, and he had not shaved for
three days.

"Is Caballuco coming here for supper tonight?" he
asked his niece.

"Yes, sir, he's coming. The poor fellow is safest in these
respectable homes."

"Well, in spite of the respectability of my house," replied the Confessor, "I'm not altogether easy in my mind.
The risks that brave Ramos runs! . . . And they tell me
that in Villahorrenda and the surrounding country there
are many men . . . I don't know how many men . . .
What have you heard?"

"That the soldiers are committing atrocities . . ."

"It's a miracle that those cannibals haven't searched
my house! I swear that if I saw one of them in their
red pants come in here, I'd be struck speechless."

"A fine thing! We're in a fine fix," said Remedios,
bringing up half her soul in a sigh. "I can't get Doña
Perfecta's troubles out of my mind . . . Ah, Uncle, you
ought to go to her."

"Go there tonight? . . . The soldiers are patrolling the
streets. Just think if one of them should take it into
his head . . . The señora is well protected. They searched
her house the other day and arrested the six armed men
she had there; but later they turned them loose. We've
no one to defend us in case of some outrage."

"I've sent Jacinto to stay a while with the señora. If
Caballuco comes, we'll tell him to go, too . . . I can't
get it out of my head that those rascals are planning some
piece of villainy against our friend. Poor lady, poor
Rosarito! . . . When one thinks that this could have been

avoided by doing what I suggested to Doña Perfecta
two days ago . . ."

"My dear niece," said the Confessor phlegmatically,
"we've done everything humanly possible to accomplish
our blessed project . . . Now there's nothing more to be
done. Remedios, we've failed. Get this through your
head, and don't be stubborn: Rosarito can't be the wife
of our idolized Jacintillo. Your rosy dream, your ideal of
happiness which seemed to us feasible at one time, and
to which, like a good uncle, I dedicated all the resources
of my mind, has turned into a chimera, and has blown
away like smoke. Serious obstacles, the evil of one man,
the unquestionable passion of the girl, and other things
I need not mention, have knocked the bottom out of
everything. We were on the way to winning, and now
suddenly we've lost. Ah, niece, make up your mind to
one thing. As matters now stand, Jacinto deserves much
better than that crazy girl."

"Whims and obstinate notions," replied María with
disrespectful irritation. "That's a fine thing you come up
with now, Uncle! A fig for all your great minds! . . . Doña
Perfecta with her lofty ideas and you with your hair-
splitting, are both good for nothing. It's a pity God made
me so stupid, with this brick and mortar brain of mine,
as the señora calls it, for if it were otherwise, I'd settle
the thing."

"You?"

"If you and she had let me go ahead, it would be
settled right now."

"With a beating?"

"Don't be so scared, and don't open your eyes, for I'm
not talking about killing anyone . . . Come, come!"

"Beating," said the canon, smiling, "is like scratching
. . . Once you start . . ."

"Bah! . . . Go on, you, too. Call me cruel and blood-

thirsty . . . I haven't the heart to kill a fly, as you very
well know . . . How would I wish for a man's death?"

"In short, my child, twist and turn it as you will, Don
Pepe gets the girl. It can't be avoided now. He's ready
to use any means, including dishonor. If Rosarito—how
she deceived me with that demure little face and those
angelic eyes!—I say, if Rosario didn't love him . . . well
. . . everything could be arranged. But, alas, she loves
him as the sinner loves sin, she's consumed by an iniquitous fire; she fell, my dear niece, she fell into his devilish
and lustful trap. Let's be honest and fair; let's turn away
our eyes from the ignoble couple, and let's think no
more of either one of them."

"You don't understand women, Uncle," said Remedios
with hypocritical cajolery. "You're a holy man; you don't
understand that this business about Rosarito is nothing
but one of those whims that pass, one of those that can
be cured by a couple of good scoldings or half a dozen
whacks."

"Niece," said Don Inocencio gravely and sententiously,
"when serious things have happened, little whims are
not called little whims, but something else again."

"Uncle, you don't know what you're talking about,"
replied his niece, whose face suddenly flamed. "Why,
are you capable of thinking that Rosarito . . . ? How
awful! I'll defend her, yes, I defend her . . . She's pure
as an angel . . . Come, Uncle, you make me blush with
such things, and you make me angry."

The good priest's face darkened with a tinge of sadness at her words, and he seemed to have aged ten years.

"Dear Remedios," he went on, "we've done all that
was humanly possible and everything that could or
should be done in good conscience. Nothing could be
more natural than our desire to see Jacintillo linked by
marriage to that great family, the foremost in Orbajosa.

Nothing could be more natural than our desire to see
him owner of the seven houses in town, of the ranch of
Mundogrande, of the three orchards of Arriba, of the
Encomienda, and all the other urban and rural property
which that girl owns. Your son is a very worthy lad,
we all know that. Rosarito used to like him, and he,
Rosarito. It seemed a foregone conclusion. The señora
herself seemed well disposed to it, owing to her high
esteem and respect for me, as her confessor and friend,
even though she was not over-enthusiastic, doubtless
because of our origin . . . But suddenly that wretched
man came along. The señora tells me she had made her
brother a promise and that therefore she could not reject
the proposal. A serious conflict! But what did I do in
view of this? Ah, you have no idea. I'm being frank with
you. If I had seen in Señor de Rey a man of high principles, capable of making Rosario happy, I would not have
intervened in the matter. But this particular young man
seemed to me a calamity, and as the spiritual director of
the household it was my duty to take a hand, and I did.
You know that I blocked him at every point. I unmasked
his vices. I uncovered his atheism. I revealed the rotten-
ness of that materialistic heart for all the world to see,
and the señora became convinced that he was leading
her daughter to ruin . . . Ah, the anxiety I went through!
The señora vacillated; I fortified her hesitant mind; I
advised her on the lawful means she must use against
that nephew to get rid of him without any scandal. I
suggested subtle methods. And, as she revealed to me
how her pure conscience was disquieted, I calmed her by
pointing out just how far she could licitly go in the
campaigns we were waging against that fierce enemy. I
never counselled violent or bloody measures, nor outrages
that could not be countenanced, but instead, subtle
strategems without sin. I am easy in my mind, dear niece.

You know very well that I have fought, that I worked like a black slave. Ah, when I used to come home at night and say: 'María, my girl, we're doing well, we're doing very well,' you were out of your mind with happiness and you kissed my hand a hundred times. You used to say I was the best man in the world. Why are you furious now, why are you doing violence to your fine character and gentle nature? Why are you quarreling with me? Why do you say you're angry, and imply that I'm a bumbling fool?"

"Because," said the woman, still angry, "you've suddenly turned coward."

"It's that everything is going against us, woman. That cursed engineer, the darling of the soldiers, is prepared to stop at nothing. The child loves him; the child . . . I'll say no more. It can't be, I tell you that it can't be."

"The soldiers! So you think, as Doña Perfecta does, that there's going to be a war, and that half the nation will have to rise up against the other half to throw Don Pepe out of here . . . The señora is out of her mind, and you're not far behind her."

"I think as she does. In view of Rey's intimacy with the soldiers, the personal equation is much more serious . . . But, alas, my dear niece, although two days ago I had hopes that our brave men would kick the soldiers out, I've lost confidence in everything since I've seen the turn things have taken; since I've seen that most of them were taken by surprise before they could strike a blow, and that Caballuco is in hiding, and it's all coming to naught. Good intentions still lack the material strength to crush the ministers and emissaries of wrong . . . Alas, niece, resignation, resignation."

Then Don Inocencio, employing the form of expression most characteristic of his niece, sighed loudly two or three times. Contrary to what might have been expected,

María kept a profound silence. Outwardly, at least, there was no anger in her, nor any of the superficial sentimentality she ordinarily displayed; there was nothing but a deep and modest suffering. When the good uncle had concluded his peroration, two tears slowly rolled down the niece's rosy cheeks, followed by some half-suppressed sobs, until little by little, like a storm-tossed sea that roars and swells, the surge of sorrow in María Remedios mounted and burst into violent weeping.

XXVII

A CANON'S TORMENT

"Resignation, resignation," said Don Inocencio again.

"Resignation, resignation!" she repeated, drying her tears. "Since my beloved son is to remain forever a beggar, so be it. Lawsuits are falling off; soon the day will come when it will be nothing at all to be a lawyer. What's the use of having talent? What's the use of so much studying and beating out his brains? Ah, we're poor. The day will come, Don Inocencio, when my poor son will not have a pillow on which to lay his head."

"Woman!"

"Man! . . . If I'm wrong, tell me what sort of legacy you're planning to leave him when you close your eyes? Four pennies, six old books, poverty, and that's all . . . You wait and see the times that are coming . . . bad times, Uncle! My poor son who's ruining his health with study, won't be able to work . . . his head swims now when he

reads a book; he's nauseated and his head aches now
whenever he studies at night . . . He'll have to beg for
a paltry job; I'll have to take in sewing, and who knows
but that we'll have to live on charity."

"Woman!"

"I know what I'm talking about . . . We'll have a fine
time," went on the excellent lady, accentuating the whin-
ing sing-song in which she spoke. "Dear God! What will
become of us? Ah, only a mother's heart can feel such
things . . . Only a mother can undergo such pain for the
well-being of a son. How could you understand? No,
it's one thing to have children and to endure the bitter
pangs we suffer, and something else again to sing *gori,
gori*[59] in the Cathedral and teach Latin in the *Instituto*
. . . What has my son got out of being your nephew and
making such excellent marks, and being the pride and
joy of Orbajosa . . . ? He'll starve to death, for we know
now how much a law practice pays; or else he'll have
to go licking some Deputy's boots for a post in Havana,
where he'll die of yellow fever . . ."

"But, woman! . . ."

"All right, I won't worry. I'll keep still. I won't bother
you any more. I'm very troublesome, very weepy, very
full of sighs, I don't suffer in silence, because I'm a
loving mother and I'm looking out for the welfare of my
dear son. Yes, sir, I'll die without a word and stifle my
sorrow. I'll swallow my tears so as not to annoy the fine
canon . . . But my beloved son will understand, and he
won't cover his ears as you're doing right now . . . Poor
Jacinto knows I'd let myself be killed for him, and that
I'd buy his happiness at the cost of my life. My poor,
darling little boy! To be so good, and to have to spend
his life condemned to poverty, never getting ahead—and

---

[59] A mocking expression for the lugubrious chant of the priest
at funeral services.

don't you get on your high horse, my fine uncle . . . For all the airs we put on, you'll always be the son of Uncle Tinieblas, the sexton of San Bernardo . . . and I'll never be anything but the daughter of Ildefonso Tinieblas, your brother, the tinker, and my son will always be the grandson of the Tinieblas . . . We'll always be children of darkness and obscurity, and we shall never emerge from obscurity nor have a piece of earth to call our own, nor shear our own sheep, nor milk a goat of our own. I'll never be able to sink my arms up to the elbows in a sack of wheat threshed and winnowed on our own threshing floors . . . all because of your lack of spirit, your folly, and your cream-puff heart . . .

"But—but, woman!"

The canon's voice went higher each time he repeated this phrase, and he rocked his head from side to side, his hands over his ears, with a dolorous expression of desperation. The shrill refrain of María Remedios grew constantly sharper, piercing the brain of the unhappy and now stupefied clergyman like an arrow. But suddenly the woman's face changed. Her plaintive sobs were replaced by a hard, defiant voice. Her face turned pale; her lips trembled. She clenched her fists, and some locks of dishevelled hair fell over her forehead. The heat of the anger burning within her dried her eyes completely. She rose from her chair and screamed, not like a woman, but like a harpy.

"I'm getting out of here. I'm going away with my son! We'll go to Madrid. I don't want my boy to rot in this miserable town. I'm tired of seeing my Jacinto forever a nobody, under the protection of your cassock. Do you hear me, Reverend Uncle? My son and I are getting out! You'll never see us again, never again!"

Don Inocencio had clasped his hands together and he was receiving the furious tongue-lashing of his niece with the consternation of a prisoner whom the presence of the hangman is stripping of all hope.

"For God's sake, Remedios," he murmured in a stricken voice, "for the sake of the Blessed Virgin . . ."

Those crises and dreadful outbursts from his meek niece were as devastating as they were rare. As many as five or six years would pass without Don Inocencio being forced to witness Remedios change into a Fury.

"I'm a mother! . . . I'm a mother! . . . And since no one else is going to look out for my son, I will, I will myself," roared the transformed lioness.

"For the sake of the Blessed Virgin, don't let your passions get the better of you . . . You're committing a sin . . . Let's say an Our Father and a Hail Mary, and see if this won't pass away from you."

As he spoke, the Confessor was trembling and sweating. Poor chicken in the talons of a vulture! The transformed woman gave him the final, mortal squeeze with these words: "You're a good-for-nothing. You're a coward . . . My son and I will leave this house forever, forever. I'll find a job for my son; I'll find him something that will pay, do you understand? Just as I'm ready to clean the streets with my tongue if I have to in order to help him earn his bread, I'll move heaven and earth to find a good job for my son, so he can rise, so he can be rich, so he can be somebody, and a gentleman, and a property-owner, and be called 'Sir,' and a nobleman, and everything else there is to be, everything, everything!"

"God help me!" cried Don Inocencio, letting himself fall into his armchair and bowing his head to his chest.

There was a pause during which nothing could be heard but the panting of the enraged woman.

"Woman," said Don Inocencio at last, "you've taken ten years off my life, you've made my blood run cold, you've driven me crazy . . . God give me the calm I need to bear

with you! Patience, patience, Lord, is all I ask. As for
you, niece, do me the favor to cry and sob, to sniff and
sigh for the next ten years, for your awful habit of snivel-
ing which makes me so angry is better than these mad
rages of yours. If I didn't know you were a good woman
at heart! . . . Come, look how you're behaving, after
having confessed and received Holy Communion this
morning."

"Yes, because of you! Because of you!"

"Because I advise resignation in that business about
Rosario and Jacinto?"

"Because when everything was going well, you turned
back and let Señor Rey take Rosarito."

"And how can I prevent it? The señora is right when
she says you have a mind like a brick. Do you want me
to rush out of here, sword in hand, and in the twinkling
of an eye make mincemeat of the soldiers, and then go
up to Rey and say to him, 'Either you leave the girl alone
or I'll cut your throat?' "

"No. But when I advised the señora to give her nephew
a good scare, you were against it, instead of advising her
the same as I did."

"You're crazy with that nonsense about a good scare."

"Because 'A dog that's dead can't go out of its head.' "

"I can't advise what you call a good scare which may
turn out to be something terrible."

"Yes, of course, I'm a killer. Isn't that so, Uncle?"

"You know that rough games are villain's games. Besides, do you think that man will scare easily? What
about his friends?"

"He goes out alone at night."

"How do you know?"

"I know all about it. He doesn't make a move I don't
know about. The Widow Cusco keeps me informed about
everything."

"Stop, don't drive me crazy. And just who is going to give him this good scare? . . . Let's hear about it."

"Caballuco."

"Do you mean to say he's willing?"

"No. But he will be if you tell him to."

"Stop it, woman. Let me alone. I can't order such an outrage. A scare! And just what is that? Have you talked to him about it already?"

"Yes, sir. But he paid no attention to me. Or rather, he refused to do it. There are only two people in Orbajosa who can make up his mind for him with a word: you and Doña Perfecta."

"Well, let the señora tell him to do it, if she wishes. I will never advise the use of violent and brutal means. Do you know that when Caballuco and some of his ilk were discussing the armed uprising, they couldn't get one word out of me to incite them to bloodshed? No, not that . . . If Doña Perfecta wants to do it . . ."

"She doesn't want to either. I spent two hours talking to her this afternoon, and she says she will speak out in favor of war and will help by all means, but that she will not order any man to stab another in the back. She'd be right to oppose me if it were a question of something serious . . . but I don't want any injuries. All I want is a good scare."

"Well, if Doña Perfecta doesn't venture to order good scares administered to the engineer, I don't either. Do you understand? My conscience comes before anything else."

"Very well," replied the niece. "Tell Caballuco to go with me tonight . . . Don't tell him more than that."

"Are you going out late?"

"I'm going out, yes, sir. Why? Didn't I go out last night, too?"

"Last night? I didn't know it. If I had known it, I'd have been angry. Yes, señora."

"Don't say anything to Caballuco except this: 'Dear Ramos, I'd be much obliged if you'd escort my niece on a certain errand she has to do tonight, and if you'll defend her in case she might be in danger.'"

"Yes, that I can do. Let him escort you . . . let him defend you. Ah, you rogue! You're trying to deceive me and make me an accomplice in some mischief."

"Why, to be sure," said María Remedios ironically, "between Ramos and me there's going to be plenty of throats cut tonight."

"Don't joke. I tell you again I will not advise Ramos to do anything that bears even a trace of wrongdoing. It seems to me that he's here . . ."

A noise was heard at the street door. Then the voice of Caballuco, speaking to the servant, and soon afterward the hero of Orbajosa entered the room.

"The news, let's hear the news, Señor Ramos," said the priest. "Come, you ought to give us some hope in exchange for your supper and our hospitality . . . What's going on in Villahorrenda?"

"Something," replied the bravo, seating himself and showing signs of fatigue. "You'll soon see if we're worth our salt."

Like all those people who are important or try to make themselves appear so, Caballuco showed a great reserve.

"Tonight, my friend, you may if you wish take with you the money I was given for . . ."

"It's about time . . . But if the soldiers get a whiff of it, they won't let me pass," said Ramos, laughing stupidly.

"Be still, man . . . We know you go back and forth as often as you want to. The soldiers turn a blind eye on you . . . and if they made any trouble, a couple of dollars would fix it, eh? Come, I see you're pretty well armed

. . . All you need is an eight-pounder. Pistols, eh? And a knife, too."

"In case of emergency," said Caballuco, drawing the weapon out of his belt and displaying its murderous edge.

"For the Lord's sake!" cried María Remedios, closing her eyes and turning away her face in fright. "Put that thing away. The sight of it horrifies me."

"If you don't mind," said Ramos, closing his weapon. "Let's have supper."

María Remedios quickly made everything ready, lest the hero grow impatient.

"Listen to me, Señor Ramos," said Don Inocencio to his guest as they sat down to supper. "Have you much to do tonight?"

"I've got a lot to do," answered the bravo. "This is the last night I'll be coming to Orbajosa, the very last. I have to gather up some boys who are still here, and we're going to see about getting out the saltpeter and sulphur which are in the Cirujeda house."

"The reason I asked," added the priest kindly as he heaped his friend's plate, "is because my niece wants you to escort her for a minute. She has to run some sort of errand and it's a little late for her to go out alone."

"To Doña Perfecta's house?" asked Ramos. "I was there a minute ago. I didn't want to stop."

"How is the señora?"

"Kind of scared. I took off the six boys she had in the house tonight."

"Why, don't you think they're needed there, man?" said Remedios anxiously.

"They're needed worse in Villahorrenda. Brave people can manage inside four walls, isn't that so, Reverend Canon?"

"Señor Ramos, that house ought never to be left unguarded," said the Confessor.

"With the servants, they've more than enough. Do you think, Señor Don Inocencio, that the brigadier is going to bother attacking people's houses?"

"Yes, but you know very well that that devilish engineer . . ."

"There are plenty of brooms in that house to take care of him," declared Cristóbal jovially. "In the end there won't be any choice but to let them get married . . . ! After all that's happened . . ."

"Cristóbal," cried Remedios, with sudden anger. "I doubt that you understand much about people getting married."

"I say so because just a minute ago, tonight, I saw the señora and the girl having a kind of reconciliation. Doña Perfecta was kissing Rosarito over and over again, and it was all sweet words and petting."

"Reconciliation! With all that stuff about arms, you've gone off your head . . . But, anyhow, are you going to go with me or not?"

"She doesn't want to go to the señora's house," said the priest, "but to the Widow Cusco's inn. She was saying she didn't dare go out alone; she's afraid she'd be insulted . . ."

"By whom?"

"You know very well. By that engineer, that fiendish engineer. Last night my niece saw him there and gave him a piece of her mind, and that's why she isn't easy tonight. That young man is spiteful and insolent."

"I don't know if I can go," said Caballuco. "Since I'm in hiding now, I can't challenge Don José Piddler. If I weren't as I am, with my face half-hidden, half-showing, I'd already have broken his back for him a dozen times over. But what happens if I jump him? I'll be discovered, the soldiers will jump me, and good-bye Caballuco. As for stabbing him in the back, that's something I wouldn't do. It isn't in my nature, and the señora wouldn't allow it, anyway. Cristóbal Ramos is no good for drubbings in the dark."

"But, man, are we mad? . . . What are you talking about?" said the priest with unmistakable signs of aston-ishment. "It never crossed my mind to advise you to mal-treat that gentleman. I'd rather cut out my tongue than counsel such villainy. It's true that evil men will perish; but it is God who must fix the moment, not I. There's no question of a beating, either. I'd sooner receive ten dozen blows myself than recommend to a Christian the administration of such medicine. I say to you only one thing," he added, looking at the bravo over his spectacles, "and that is that since my niece is going there, and since it's probable, very probable—isn't it, Remedios?—that she may have to say a few words to that man, all I ask you is to stand by in case she's insulted . . ."

"I've got a lot to do tonight," replied Caballuco dryly and laconically.

"You hear him, Remedios. Leave your errand until to-morrow."

"That I certainly can't do. I'll go alone."

"No, don't go, niece. Let's hear no more about the matter. Señor Ramos can't escort you. Just imagine if you were insulted by that brutal fellow . . ."

"Insulted, a lady insulted by that—" cried Caballuco. "It couldn't be."

"If you weren't so busy . . . I'd be easy in my mind."

"I'm busy," said the Centaur getting up from the table. "But if you insist . . ."

There was a pause. The priest had closed his eyes and was meditating.

"I do insist, Señor Ramos," he said, finally.

"Then there's nothing more to be said. We'll go, Doña María."

"Now, dear niece," said Don Inocencio, half-serious, half-jovial, "since we've finished our supper, bring me the bowl."

He turned on his niece a penetrating stare, and suiting the action to the words, he said: "I wash my hands."[60]

XXVIII

FROM PEPE REY TO

DON JUAN REY

Orbajosa, April 12.

Dear Father: Forgive me if I disobey you for the first time by not leaving here and giving up my plans. Your advice and request befit a good and honorable father. My stubbornness befits a foolish son. But a strange thing is happening to me. Stubbornness and honor have become so conjoined and commingled in my mind that the idea of desisting and yielding would shame me. I've changed a lot. I never used to experience these rages which consume me. Formerly, I used to laugh at any violent deed, at the exaggerations of impetuous men as well as the stupid acts of wrongdoers. Now nothing of that sort surprises me, for I constantly find within myself a certain capacity for wrongdoing. I can talk to you as I would speak alone to God and my conscience. I can say to you

---

[60] The reference is to Pilate who, when he handed Christ over to his accusers, "took water and washed his hands . . . saying 'I am innocent of the blood of this just person.'" (Matthew, xxvii, 24).

that I'm a wretch, for a man who lacks the moral strength
to rule himself, to subdue his passions and submit his
life to the hard rule of conscience is a wretch. I have
lacked the Christian fortitude which sustains the spirit
of a wronged man against the offenses he suffers and the
enemies who inflict them. I have yielded to the weakness
of giving myself over to a mad rage, descending to the
level of my detractors, returning them blow for blow,
and trying to confound them by methods learned in their
own unworthy school. How sorry I am that you weren't
at my side to turn me from this path! Now it is too late.
Passions brook no delay. They are impatient; driven by
a burning moral thirst, they roar for their prey. I have
succumbed. I cannot forget what you've so often said to
me: that anger can be the worst of the seven deadly
sins, for by suddenly transforming our character, it breeds
all the other sins and lends them its own hellish fire.

But it was not anger alone that brought me to such a
state. It was also a strong, warm-hearted emotion: the
deep and ardent love I feel for my cousin. That is the
only extenuating circumstance. If not love, pity alone
would have impelled me to challenge the fury and intrigues of your terrible sister. For poor Rosario, torn between an irresistible affection and her mother, is today
one of the most unfortunate creatures on the face of the
earth. Doesn't the love she has for me, which equals mine
for her, give me the right to open the doors of her house
as best I may, and to take her away from there, using the
law insofar as the law reaches, and then using force beyond the point where the law protects me? I think your
rigorous moral scruples would not reply affirmatively to
this proposition; but I have ceased to be a reasonable,
pure being, faithfully obeying a conscience as exact as a
scientific formula. I'm no longer that man to whom a vir-
tually perfect upbringing gave an amazing control over

his emotions. Today I'm a man like any other. With one step I've entered upon the common terrain of the unjust and the wicked. Prepare yourself to hear of any kind of barbarity as the work of my hands. I shall take care to inform you of such deeds as I commit them.

But not even the confession of my faults will relieve me of the responsibility for the grave things which have occurred and will occur, nor will that responsibility, however much I may argue, fall entirely upon your sister. Doña Perfecta's responsibility is immense, certainly. How great is my own? Ah, dear father! Don't believe anything you hear about me; only what I tell you myself. If they say that I have committed some deliberate villainy, tell them it's a lie. It's difficult, very difficult, for me to judge myself in my present disturbed state. But I venture to assure you that I haven't deliberately caused scandal. You know how far passion can carry one, if its dreadful and pervasive growth is favored by circumstances.

What most embitters my life is having used untruth, deception, and dissimulation. I, who used to be truth itself! I'm no longer myself at all . . . But is this the greatest wickedness of which the soul is capable? Am I now at the beginning or the end? I don't know. Unless Rosario, with her own lovely hand, takes me out of this hell which is my conscience, I hope you'll come and rescue me. My cousin is an angel; she's suffering on my account; and she's taught me many things I never knew before.

Don't be surprised at the incoherence of what I'm writing. Various emotions are surging through me. At times I'm filled with ideas truly worthy of my immortal soul; but at other times I slip back into a state of miserable dejection, and I think of the weak and wretched men whose baseness you've pictured to me in vivid colors in order to teach me to abhor them. As I am today, I'm equally disposed toward good and evil. May God have pity on me. I understand what prayer is; it is a grave and reflective entreaty, so personal that one does not approach it in formulas learned by rote; an expansion of the soul which ventures to spread its wings in a search for its origins. It is the opposite of remorse, which is a contraction of the soul, which wraps and hides itself in the foolish hope that no one will see it. You have taught me wonderful things; but now I'm out in the field, as we engineers say; I'm studying the terrain, and as I do so my knowledge broadens and hardens . . . I'm wondering if perhaps I am not so bad as I myself believe. Could that be true?

I must finish this letter at once. I have to send it by some soldiers who are going toward the Villahorrenda station, for I cannot trust the mail among these people.

April 14.

Dear Father: You would be amused if I could make you understand how the minds of the people in this town work. You must know by now that almost this entire region has risen up in arms. It was a foregone conclusion, and if the politicians imagine it will all be over in a couple of days, they're wrong. The Orbajosans have in their very spirit this hostility toward us and the Government, and it forms a part of them like a religious faith. Confining myself to the matter of my aunt, I'll tell you a strange thing: the poor lady, who preserves feudalism in the very marrow of her bones, has taken it into her head that I'm going to storm her house in order to steal her daughter from her, as the barons of the Middle Ages used to assault an enemy castle to consummate some such outrage. Don't laugh. It's true. Such are the notions of these people. Needless to say, she takes me for a monster, for some kind of heretic Moorish king, and the officers here with whom I've struck up a friendship are no better in her eyes. Among Doña Perfecta's friends, it's completely accepted that the soldiers and I form a diabolical coalition with the object of despoiling Orbajosa of its treasures, its faith, and its girls. I know for a fact that your sister firmly believes I'm going to take her house by storm, and I don't doubt that there's some sort of barricade behind the door.

But it couldn't be otherwise. Here the most antiquated ideas concerning society, religion, the State, and property are generally accepted. The religious fanaticism which impels them to use force against the Government in the defense of a faith which no one has attacked and which they themselves don't actually possess, revives feudal feelings in their souls; and since they would settle their disputes by brute force and by fire and bloodshed, slaughtering anyone who doesn't think as they do, they believe that no one in the wide world would use other methods.

Far from intending to make quixotic forays on the house of this lady, I've managed to have her spared certain of the annoyances which other citizens have not been spared. Owing to my friendship with the brigadier, they haven't required her to present a list of all her manservants who have gone off with the rebels, as she was ordered to do. And if they searched the house, it was only for form's sake, and if they disarmed the six men they found there, she afterward replaced them with the same number, and nothing has been done about it. You can see from this what my hostility to the señora amounts to.

It's true that I have the support of the military leaders. But I am using it simply in order not to be insulted or maltreated by these implacable people. My chances of success consist in the fact that the authorities recently installed by the military commander are all my friends. I draw moral strength from them, and thus intimidate the enemy. I don't know whether or not I shall find myself in a position where I'll commit some violent deed. But don't worry, for the idea of my storming and seizing the house is a ridiculous feudal notion of your sister's. Chance has placed me in an advantageous position. The anger, the passion, which burns inside me is driving me to take advantage of it. I don't know quite how far I shall go.

April 17.

Your letter has brought me great comfort. Yes; I can attain my object by using only the resources of the law, which are wholly adequate. I've consulted the local authorities and they all confirm what you've suggested. I am glad. Since I've planted in my cousin's mind the idea of disobedience, let it be at least within the framework of social law. I shall do as you tell me. That is, I shall give up the somewhat dubious help of Pinzón. I shall break the terrifying solidarity I've established with the military. I shall stop priding myself on their power. I shall put an end to adventures, and at the opportune moment I shall proceed with calm, prudence, and all possible kindness. It's better this way. My coalition with the army, half serious, half in jest, was formed with the object of protecting myself from the brutality of the Orbajosans and the servants and relatives of my aunt. Apart from that, I've always rejected what we shall call *armed intervention*.

My friend who was on my side has had to leave the house; but I'm not completely out of communication with my cousin. The poor little girl is showing heroic courage in the midst of her troubles, and she'll obey me blindly.

Don't worry about my personal safety. For my part, I'm afraid of nothing and I'm very calm.

April 20.

I can't write more than a few lines today. I have a

great deal to do. Everything will be over in a few days. Don't write me to this town again. You'll soon have the pleasure of embracing your son,

Pepe

XXIX

FROM PEPE REY TO
ROSARITO POLENTINOS

Give Estebanillo the key to the garden and tell him to watch out for the dog. The boy is on my side body and soul. Don't be afraid of anything. I'll be very sorry if you can't come down, as you did the other night. Do everything you can to come. I'll be there after midnight. I'll tell you what I've decided, and what you must do. Keep calm, my child, for I've given up all my rash and forceful measures. I'll tell you all about it. It's a long story and must be told in person. I can picture your fear and dismay to think I'll be so near you. But it's been a week since we've seen each other. I've sworn that this separation must soon come to an end, and it will. My heart tells me that I shall see you, and I will—I swear it.

XXX

STALKING THE GAME

A woman and man entered the Widow Cusco's inn past ten o'clock, and left there after the clock had struck half past eleven.

"Now, Señora Doña María," said the man, "I'll take you home, because I've got things to do."

"Wait a minute, Ramos, for the love of God," she replied. "Why don't we go to the Club to see if he comes out? You heard it . . . This afternoon he was talking to Estebanillo, the gardener's boy."

"Is it Don José you're looking for?" demanded the Centaur in a very bad humor. "What does it matter to us? The courtship of Doña Rosario went as it was bound to go, and now the señora has no choice except to let them get married. That's my opinion."

"You're a fool," said Remedios angrily.

"Señora, I'm leaving."

"What's that? Are you going to leave me alone in the middle of the street, you rude man?"

"Unless you go to your house quickly, yes, señora."

"So that's it . . . you'll leave me alone, exposed to any insult . . . Listen, Ramos. Don José will leave the Club as usual. I want to find out whether he goes back to his house or keeps on. It's a notion, just a notion."

"All I know is that I've got things to do, and it'll soon be striking twelve."

"Be still," said Remedios. "Let's hide ourselves around the corner . . . A man is coming down Tripería Alta Street. It's he."

"It's Don José . . . I know him by his way of walking."

They concealed themselves and the man passed by.

"Let's follow him," said María Remedios excitedly. "Let's follow him a short way, Ramos."

"Señora . . ."

"Just far enough to see if he goes into his house."

"Only for a minute, Doña Remedios. Then I'm leaving."

They walked on, keeping about thirty paces behind the man they were watching. The Confessor's niece stopped finally, and said: "He isn't going into his house."

"He must be going to the brigadier's house."

"The brigadier lives up that way, and Don Pepe is going down the street, toward the señora's house."

"The señora's!" exclaimed Caballuco, walking more rapidly.

But they were mistaken. The man who was being spied upon passed in front of the Polentinos house and kept on going.

"You see now; he's not going there."

"Cristóbal, let's follow him," said Remedios convulsively clutching the Centaur's hand. "I have a hunch."

"We'll soon find out, for it's the end of the town."

"Let's not go so fast . . . He might see us . . . What I was thinking, Señor Ramos, is that he's going through the walled-up door to the garden."

"Señora, you've lost your mind!"

"Come on, and we'll see."

The night was dark and the watchers could not see precisely where Señor de Rey had entered; but they heard the squeak of rusty hinges and the fact that they could not see the young man down the whole length of the wall convinced them that he had indeed gone inside the garden. Caballuco looked at his companion with stupefaction. He seemed stunned.

"What are you thinking? . . . Do you still doubt me?"

"What should I do?" asked the bravo, filled with confusion. "Shall we frighten him away? . . . I don't know what to expect of the señora. I say this because I went to see her tonight and it seemed to me that mother and daughter were reconciled."

"Don't be stupid . . . Why don't you go in?"

"I remember now that the armed servants aren't here, because I ordered them to leave last night."

"And this blockhead still wonders what ought to be done! Ramos, don't be a coward. Go into the garden."

"How can I if he's locked the little door?"

"Jump over the wall . . . What a fool! Oh, if only I were a man!"

"All right, I'll go over . . . There are some loose bricks here where the children climb to steal fruit."

"Get over quickly. I'm going to knock at the front door to wake up the señora if she happens to be asleep."

The Centaur climbed up, not without difficulty. For a brief moment he straddled the wall and then disappeared at once into the black thicket of the trees. María Remedios ran swiftly toward Condestable Street, and seizing the knocker on the front door, she knocked . . . she knocked three times, with all her heart and soul in it.

XXXI

DOÑA PERFECTA

Observe the calm with which Doña Perfecta is concentrating upon her writing. Enter her room, without considering the lateness of the hour, and you will surprise her hard at work with her mind divided between her thoughts and the long, painstaking letters she is writing with a steady pen and careful hand. The light from the lamp falls full on her face, bust, and hands, while the lamp shade leaves the rest of her body and most of the room in pleasant shadow. She looks like a luminous figure evoked by the imagination in the midst of the vague darkness of fear.

Strangely enough, up to now we have omitted one very important statement about her. Doña Perfecta was handsome, or to be more exact, she was still handsome, her face retaining traces of great beauty. Life in the country, a complete lack of vanity, her simplicity of attire, her dislike of fashion, her scorn for the vanities of the court, were all reasons why her innate beauty failed to shine, or that it shone so little. The intensely yellowish tone of her face also detracted from her appearance, indicating as it did a bilious constitution.

Her eyes were black and full, her nose delicate and slender, her forehead broad and smooth. Any observer would have considered hers a finished example of the human face. But in her features there was a certain expression of hardness and pride which caused a feeling of aversion. Just as some people, although ugly, attract, Doña Perfecta repelled. Her glance, even when accompanied by affable words, drew an impassable line of uneasy respect between her and strangers. But for members of her household, that is to say, her dependents, friends, and associates, she possessed a definite attraction. She was supreme in the art of domination, and no one could equal her in her skill at speaking the language best suited to her hearer.

Her bilious nature and her constant dealings with devout persons and objects which excited her imagination without purpose or result, all had prematurely aged her, and although she was young, she did not appear so. It might be said of her that through her habits and manner

of life she had grown a shell, an insensitive, stony cover-
ing which enclosed her within herself like the snail in its
portable house. Doña Perfecta seldom emerged from her
shell.

Her irreproachable conduct and outward benevolence,
which we remarked in her from the first moment of her
appearance in our narrative, were the basis of her great
prestige in Orbajosa. Moreover, she kept up relations with
some important ladies in Madrid and it was by this means
that she had brought about the dismissal of her nephew
from his post. Now, as we have already said, we find her
seated in front of her desk, the only confidant of her
plans and the repository of her numerous accounts with
the villagers as well as of her moral accounts with God
and Society. There she used to write the quarterly letters
which her brother received; there she composed the notes
to the judge and notary which embroiled Pepe Rey in
lawsuits; there she spun the plot through which he lost
the confidence of the Government; there she held long
conferences with Don Inocencio. To become acquainted
with the settings of other acts whose effects we have seen,
we should have to follow her to the bishop's palace and
the houses of her various friends.

We cannot know how Doña Perfecta might have been
if she had loved. Hating, she possessed the fiery vehemence of a guardian angel of hatred and discord among
men. This is the effect of religious fervor on a character
which is hard and without native goodness when it draws
its lifeblood from narrow dogmas which serve ecclesiastical interests only, instead of nourishing itself on its conscience and the truth revealed in principles as simple as
they are beautiful. Only the pure in heart can afford
fanaticism. Indeed, even then it brings forth no good. But
souls that are born without the angelic purity which cre-
ates a preparatory Limbo on earth, must take great care

not to grow overexcited with what they see on the re-
tables, in the choirs, in the locutories, and the sacristies,
unless they have first erected in their own consciences an
altar, a pulpit, and a confessional.

The lady occasionally rose from her desk and went to
the next room where her daughter was. She had ordered
Rosarito to go to sleep; but the girl, already over the
precipice of disobedience, was awake.

"Why don't you go to sleep?" asked her mother. "I
don't intend to go to bed at all tonight. You know that
Caballuco has taken away the men we had here. Something may happen, and I'm keeping watch . . . If I didn't
keep watch, what would happen to you and me?"

"What time is it?" asked the girl.

"It will soon be midnight . . . You are probably not
afraid, but I am."

Rosarito trembled. Everything about her indicated the
deepest dismay. Her eyes would turn to heaven as if she
wanted to pray. Then she would look at her mother,
showing the utmost terror.

"What's the matter with you?"

"Did you say it was midnight?"

"Yes."

"Well . . . But is it already midnight?"

Rosario tried to speak. She shook her head on which
the weight of the world seemed to rest.

"Something is wrong with you . . . something is the
matter with you," said the mother, fixing her penetrating
eyes on the girl.

"Yes . . . I'd like to say," stammered the daughter. "I
mean . . . Oh, it's nothing, nothing. I'll go to sleep."

"Rosario, Rosario. Your mother can read your heart like
a book," said Doña Perfecta sternly. "You're upset. I've
already told you I'd forgive you if you would repent, if
you'll be a good and well-behaved girl . . ."

"Why, am I not good? Ah, Mother, Mother, I think I'll die."

Rosario burst into anguished and heartbroken weeping.

"Why those tears?" said her mother, embracing her. "If they're tears of repentance, bless them."

"I don't repent, I can't repent," cried the girl in a burst of fury which made her sublime.

She raised her head and a sudden, inspired energy showed on her face. Her hair was falling over her shoulders. A more beautiful example of an angel on the point of rebellion could not be imagined.

"But are you going mad, or what is this?" cried Doña Perfecta, putting both hands on the girl's shoulders.

"I'm going away, I'm going away!" exclaimed Rosario in a frenzy.

She sprang out of bed.

"Rosario, Rosario . . . My child . . . Dear God! What is it?"

"Ah, Mother," the girl went on, embracing the woman. "Tie me up."

"Indeed, you deserve it . . . What foolishness is this?"

"Tie me up . . . I'm going away. I'm going away with him."

Doña Perfecta felt a rush of heat rising from her heart to her lips. She contained herself, and answered her daughter only with her black eyes, blacker than the night.

"Mother, I abhor everything that is not he," cried Rosario. "Listen to my confession, for I want to confess it to everyone, and first of all to you."

"You'll kill me. You are killing me."

"I want to confess it so that you'll forgive me . . . This weight, this weight crushing me won't let me live."

"The weight of sin! . . . Add God's curse to it and then try to walk with that burden on your back, you wretched girl . . . I'm the only one who can take it off you."

"Not you, no, not you," screamed Rosario in despair. "But listen to me. I want to confess everything, everything . . . Then drive me out of this house where I was born."

"Drive you out!"

"Then I'll go myself."

"You will not. I'll teach you the duties of a daughter, which you have forgotten."

"Then I'll run away. He'll take me away with him."

"Has he told you to do that, has he advised you to, has he ordered you to?" asked the mother, hurling the words like bolts of lightning at her daughter.

"He advises me to . . . We've decided to be married. We must, Mother, dear Mother. I'll always love you . . . I know I should love you . . . May I be dragged to perdition if I don't love you."

She wrung her hands, and falling on her knees, kissed her mother's feet.

"Rosario, Rosario!" exclaimed Doña Perfecta in a terrible voice. "Get up."

There was a short pause.

"Has that man written to you?"

"Yes."

"Has he been back to see you since that night?"

"Yes."

"And you . . . !"

"I wrote to him, too. Oh, señora! Why do you look at me like that! You're not my mother!"

"I wish I weren't. Enjoy the harm you're doing me. You're killing me, you're truly killing me," screamed the señora in indescribable agitation. "You say that man . . ."

"He's my husband . . . I will be his, under the protection of the law . . . You're not a woman . . . Why do you look at me like that? You make me tremble. Mother, Mother, don't condemn me."

"You've already condemned yourself. That's enough. If you obey me, I'll forgive you . . . Answer me: when did you get a letter from that man?"

"Today!"

"Such treachery! Such shamelessness!" cried the mother, roaring rather than speaking. "Did you intend to see each other?"

"Yes."

"When?"

"Tonight."

"Where?"

"Here, here. I'm confessing it all to you. I know it's wrong. But you, who are my mother, can get me out of this hell. Give your consent . . . Say one word, only one."

Rosario followed her mother on her knees. At that moment they heard three knocks, three crashes, three detonations. It was María Remedios pounding on the door, beating with the knocker. The house shuddered in a tremor of fear. Mother and daughter stood like statues.

A servant went down to open the door, and María Remedios quickly entered Doña Perfecta's room. She was not like a woman but like a basilisk wrapped in a shawl. Her face, scarlet with anxiety, seemed to send out fire.

"He's here, he's here!" she cried as she entered. "He's got into the garden through that walled-up little door . . ."

She was panting with every syllable.

"Now I understand," said Doña Perfecta in a kind of bellow.

Rosario fell fainting to the floor.

"Let's go down," cried Doña Perfecta, paying no heed to her daughter's swoon.

The two women glided down the stairway like two serpents. The maidservants and the manservant were on the veranda, not knowing what to do. Doña Perfecta passed through the dining room into the garden, followed by María Remedios.

"Luckily Ca . . . Ca . . . Caballuco is here," said the clergyman's niece.

"Where?"

"In the garden, too . . . He jumped over the wall!"

Doña Perfecta scanned the darkness, her eyes filled with rage. Anger gave them the singular power of a cat's eyes.

"I see a shape there," she said. "He's going toward the oleanders."

"It's him," screamed Remedios. "But there goes Ramos . . . Ramos!"

They could distinguish perfectly the colossal figure of the Centaur.

"Toward the oleanders! Ramos, toward the oleanders!"

Doña Perfecta took a few steps forward. Her harsh voice which rang in a terrible tone, fired the words:

"Cristóbal, Cristóbal! . . . Kill him!"

A shot was heard. Then another.

XXXII

FROM DON CAYETANO POLENTINOS TO A FRIEND IN MADRID

Orbajosa, April 21.

Dear Friend: Please send me without delay the edition of 1562 which you say you found among the books from

the estate of Corchuelo. I'll pay any price for that volume.
I've been searching for it a long time in vain, and I shall
consider myself the luckiest of mortals when I own it.
You should look on the colophon for a helmet with an
emblem above the word *Treatise,* and the X in the date
MDLXII should have its serif backward. If, in fact, these
signs appear on the volume, send me a telegram, for I'm
very anxious . . . although now I remember that, owing
to these inopportune and annoying disturbances, the tele-
graph system is not working. I'll expect a reply by return
mail.

Soon, my friend, I shall go to Madrid for the purpose
of publishing this long-awaited work on the *Genealogy
of Orbajosa.* I thank you for your kind words, but I can't
accept that part of it which is flattery. My work does not,
indeed, deserve the superlatives you lavish upon it. This
work that I erect to the greatness of my beloved locality
is a labor of patience and study, a rude monument, but
big and solid. Poor and ugly though it is in execution, it
contains something noble in the idea which generated it,
which is solely to turn the eyes of this unbelieving and
arrogant generation toward the marvelous deeds and tem-
pered virtues of our forebears. Would that the studious
youth of our country might take the step I urge on them
with all my strength! Oh, that the abominable studies and
intellectual habits introduced by philosophical license
and wrong-headed doctrines might sink into eternal oblivion! Oh, that our savants would devote themselves
exclusively to the contemplation of those glorious epochs
in order that our modern age, imbued with the substance
and the fructifying wisdom of those times, might forswear
this mad desire for worldly things and this absurd mania
for appropriating foreign ideas, so at odds with our splendid national way of life. I'm very much afraid that my
wishes will not be granted, and that the contemplation

of past perfections will remain limited to the narrow circle where it is now, amidst the turbulence of demented youth which goes chasing after vain Utopias and barbarous novelties. What hope is there, my friend? I fear that within a short time our poor Spain will be so disfigured that she won't know herself even if she looks into the shining mirror of her unblemished history.

I do not want to conclude this letter without passing on to you a very unpleasant piece of news: the shocking death of an estimable young man, very well known in Madrid, the construction engineer, Don José de Rey, my sister-in-law's nephew. This sad event occurred last night in the garden of our house, and I have not yet formed an exact opinion regarding the causes which led the unfortunate young man to this horrible and sinful act. According to what Doña Perfecta told me this morning on my return from Mundogrande, Pepe Rey, at some time around midnight, entered the garden of this house, and shot himself in the right temple, dying almost instantly. Imagine the consternation and alarm this produced in such a peaceful and honorable house! Poor Perfecta was so overcome that she gave us a scare; but she is better now, and this afternoon we've succeeded in getting her to take some broth. We are using every means to console her, and as she is a good Christian, she knows how to bear the worst misfortunes with edifying resignation.

Here, between the two of us, my friend, I shall tell you that to take this terrible decision to end his life, young Rey must have been greatly influenced by a hopeless passion, or perhaps by remorse for his conduct and the bitter hypochondria into which his mind had fallen. I had a high regard for him. I believe he was not lacking in excellent qualities. But he was held in such low esteem here that I never once heard anyone speak well of him. According to gossip, he made a display of extravagant ideas and opinions; he scoffed at religion; he entered the church smoking and with his hat on; he respected nothing, and in his eyes there was no purity, no virtue, no soul, no ideal, no faith in the world; nothing but surveying instruments, T-squares, rulers, machines, levels, pickaxes, and spades. Can you believe it? In honor of the truth, I must say he always concealed such ideas in his conversations with me, doubtless through fear of being demolished by the cannonade of my arguments; but a thousand tales of heresies and shocking improprieties are openly circulated about him.

Dear friend, I must close now for I hear gunfire. Since fighting fails to rouse my enthusiasm, nor am I a fighter, my pulse grows a bit weak. I shall keep you informed on how this war goes. Your affectionate friend, etc. etc.

April 22.

My cherished friend: Today there's been a bloody skirmish near Orbajosa. The big rebel group organized in Villahorrenda was attacked by the soldiers with great fury. There were heavy losses on both sides. Finally the brave guerrillas scattered; but their morale is good, and you may hear of great feats. Cristóbal Caballuco, the son of that outstanding Caballuco whom you knew in the last war, commanded the rebels despite a wound, received no one knows how or when, in the arm. He is the present chief, a man of great talent for leadership, and honorable and simple besides. As in the end there must be some sort of friendly truce, I presume that Caballuco will become a general in the Spanish Army, an arrangement that would be of mutual benefit.

I deplore this war which is taking on alarming proportions; but I recognize that our brave peasants are not responsible for it, for they have been provoked to bloody battle by the audacity of the Government, by the demoralization of its sacrilegious delegates, by the systematic fury with which the representatives of the State attack what is most venerated by the conscience of the people—religious faith and pure Hispanicism—which have luckily been preserved in places not yet infected by the devastating pestilence. When an attempt is made to despoil a people of its soul in order to implant another soul; to despoil it of its birthright, let us say, by altering its feelings, its customs, its ideas, it is natural that the people should defend itself like a man on a solitary road when assailed by vicious thieves. Let the spirit and the sound body of my work on the *Genealogy* be brought into the sphere of the Government (forgive my immodesty) and then there will be no more wars.

A most disagreeable matter arose here today. The priest, a friend of mine, refused to bury the unhappy Rey in consecrated ground. I intervened in the case, appealing to the Bishop to lift such a heavy anathema, but was able to accomplish nothing. We finally buried the young man's body in a grave dug at Mundogrande, where my patient explorations have uncovered the wealth of archaeology you already know about. It was a very sad occasion for me and I cannot rid myself of the painful impression it made upon me. Don Juan Tafetán and I were the only ones who accompanied the funeral cortège. Strangely enough, those girls called the Troyas went later and prayed a long time over the rustic tomb of the mathematician. Although this seemed a ridiculous excess of solicitude, I was touched.

Regarding the death of Rey, there is a rumor going about the town that he was murdered. It is not known by whom. The story is that he himself said so, for he lived about an hour and a half. I repeat this version without either refuting it or supporting it. Perfecta doesn't

want anyone to talk about the matter and she gets very
upset every time I mention it.

One misfortune had barely occurred when our poor
little girl suffered another which has saddened us all very
much. My friend, we now have another victim of the
baleful old illness which is congenital in our family. Poor
Rosario, who, thanks to our care, was progressing nicely,
has now lost her mind. Her incoherent words, her acute
dementia, her mortal pallor all remind me of my mother
and sister. This case is the most serious that I have witnessed in my family, for it is not a question of manias
but of true madness. It is sad, most sad, that among so
many I am the only one who has succeeded in escaping
and in keeping my judgment sound, entirely free from
that dreadful illness.

I have not been able to convey your regards to Don
Inocencio because the poor man has suddenly fallen ill,
and he won't see anyone, nor allow his closest friends to
see him. But I am sure that he would return your regards,
and I don't doubt that he will soon set to work on the
translation of the various Latin epigrams you suggested
to him . . . I hear shots again. They say there will be a
skirmish this afternoon. The soldiers have marched out.

Barcelona, June 1.

I have just arrived here after leaving my niece Rosario
in San Baudilio de Llobregat. The director of the establishment has assured me that she is an incurable case.
She will be given the best of care in that large, pleasant
insane asylum. My dear friend, if I should some day fall
a victim, take me to San Baudilio, too. On my return
home I hope to find proofs of the *Genealogy*. I am thinking of adding six pages, for it would be a great omission
not to publish my reasons for maintaining that Mateo
Díaz Coronel, author of the *Metrical Encomium* is de-

scended from the Guevaras on the maternal side, and not from the Burguillos, as the author of the *Floresta amena* erroneously states.

I am writing this letter principally to give you a warning. I've heard several people here speak of the death of Pepe Rey, recounting it as it did indeed occur. I revealed this secret to you when we saw each other in Madrid, telling you what I learned some time after the event. I am very much surprised that, as I had said nothing to anyone but you, they are telling it here in all its details, explaining how he entered the garden, how he fired his revolver at Caballuco when he saw the latter about to attack him with a knife, how Ramos then fired with such excellent aim that he dropped him in his tracks . . . In short, my dear friend, if you have inadvertently talked about this to anyone, I must remind you that it is a family secret, and to a person as prudent and discreet as you, that is enough.

Good news, good news! I read in a little paper that Caballuco has defeated Brigadier Batalla.

Orbajosa, December 12.

I have some painful news for you. We no longer have the Father Confessor, not exactly because he has passed on to a better life, but because the poor man has been so downcast, so melancholy, so taciturn since April that you wouldn't know him. There isn't even a trace left of that Attic wit, that choice and classical joviality which used to make him so lovable. He shuns people, he sets himself up in his house, he won't receive anyone, he scarcely takes any food, and he has broken off all relations with the world. If you were to see him, you wouldn't recognize him, for he has become nothing but skin and bones. The strangest thing is that he has quarreled with his niece and lives alone, entirely alone, in a hut in the suburb of Baidejos. They say now that he is going to give up his chair in the Cathedral choir and go to Rome. Ah, Orbajosa is losing a great man in losing its eminent Latin scholar. I think many years will pass before we have another like him. Our glorious Spain is finished, it is annihilated, it is dying.

Orbajosa, December 23.

The young man whom I recommended to you in a letter brought by his own hand, is the nephew of our beloved Father Confessor—a lawyer with some ability as a writer. Having been carefully tutored by his uncle, he has a judicious mind. How painful it would be if he were to become corrupted in that sinkhole of false philosophy and unbelief! He is honest, a hard worker, and a good Catholic, for which reasons I believe he will give a good account of himself in an office like yours . . . Perhaps his little ambitions (for he has them, too) may carry him into the political arena, and I believe the cause of order and tradition would not suffer thereby, since the youth of today is perverted and captained by the radicals. His mother is accompanying him. She is a plain woman without any social graces, but with an excellent heart and a fervent piety. In her, mother love takes the somewhat unusual form of worldly ambition, and she says her son will one day be a Minister. It may very well be so.

Perfecta sends you her regards. I don't know precisely what is wrong with her; but she is causing us all some anxiety. She has lost her appetite to an alarming degree, and either I know nothing about illnesses, or she is coming down with jaundice. This house has been very gloomy since Rosario went away, for she brightened it with her smile and her angelic goodness. It is as though there were a black cloud over us. Poor Perfecta often speaks of this cloud, which grows constantly blacker, while each day she turns yellower. The poor mother finds some consolation for her sorrow in religion and in the exercise of her faith, which she practices with ever increasing dutifulness and edification. She spends almost the entire day in church, and pours out her great fortune in splendid functions, in novenas and brilliant expositions of the sacrament. Thanks to her, the faith has regained its former splendor in Orbajosa. This is one consolation in the midst of the decadence and dissolution of our native land . . .

The proofs will go off tomorrow . . . I shall add two more pages, for I have discovered another illustrious Orbajosan, Bernardo Amador de Soto, who was footman to the Duke of Osuna, and who served him during the viceregency in Naples. There are even indications that he had nothing, absolutely nothing, to do with the plot against Venice.

XXXIII

This story is ended. For the moment, it is all we can say concerning people who appear to be good and are not.

WORLD CLASSICS IN TRANSLATION

New modern translations of foreign language classics introduced by interpretations of authors, works, literary and historical backgrounds. Everyone who reads for pleasure and relaxation should augment his library of the world's best by these charming yet inexpensive books.

Classic Tales from Spanish America	COLFORD (Editor)
Classic Tales from Modern Spain	COLFORD (Editor)
Doña Perfecta	GALDÓS
José	PALACIO VALDES
La Gaviota (The Sea Gull)	CABALLERO
Life is a Dream	CALDERÓN
Pepita Jiménez	VALERA
Six Exemplary Novels	CERVANTES
The Life of Lazarillo de Tormes	
The Maiden's Consent	MORATÍN
The Mayor of Zalamea	CALDERÓN
The Three-Cornered Hat	ALARCON

BARRON'S EDUCATIONAL SERIES
Woodbury, New York